Prophecy's End

by Harlowe Frost

ISBN eBook: 978-1-959981-29-9
ISBN paperback: 978-1-959981-30-5
ISBN hard back: 978-1-959981-31-2

Editor: Weslee Imrisek
Editor: Fiona Foster
Developmental Editor: Angela Grimes
Cover Art: Getcovers.com
Formatting: Huckleberry Rahr

Books In the Kam Strega Series

Series 1: Child of Three Halves Saga

Book 1: Glass Witchling

Book 2: Child of Three Halves

Book 3: Prophecy's End

Series 2: Lucere Amon Saga

Book 1: Demon's Intrigue

Book 2: Hope of Angels and Demons

Book 3: Angel's Dream

Content Warning:

- This is a high spice book.

- There are male/female, female/female, as well as, male/male open-door scenes.

- There is bed play with toys.

- Because there are vampires, there will be mentions of blood.

- There is dubious consent and non-consent in this book.

Chapter 1

Casey stood in a sea of kids' toys, holding the small cherub of a girl. Her blond curls framed her round face, and her blue eyes were wide as she stared back at the stranger who held her. The girl's mouth looked to be a perfect bow under the button of a nose. As her eyes grew larger with a fear Casey could smell on her, the girl's lower lip stuck out and began to quiver.

"It'll be okay ... Kam. I'll figure this out."

Casey held the girl tighter as Skyler and her mother fled the room. Annoyance and fear tightened Casey's muscles. The girl's body tensed as her tiny fist was stuffed into her mouth, and her wide blue eyes shot towards the back of her retreating mother. With a sigh, Casey tried to relax as she dashed after the pair, attempting not to trip on any of the detritus on the floor.

They'd only made it as far as the kitchen where Hildegard and Casey's grandfather expected departing handshakes from Skyler and her mother. Skyler and her mom kept darting looks over their shoulders and slumped when they saw Casey approach.

Skyler's mother's face scrunched up in disgust when she saw her, and her chin lifted so she could look down on her despite her shorter stature.

Kam pulled her hand out of her mouth with an audible slurping sound. "Mama!" Both her arms swung towards Skyler, who only shook her head and backed up towards the door.

"It'll be okay, dove, your father will explain everything to you." She smelled scared as her gaze shifted between Kam and Casey. There was also an underlying love and sorrow, but the overlying emotion was fear.

Holding tightly to the child, who squirmed wildly enough to land on her head if she'd gotten free, Casey tried to calm her beating heart. "She's mine? I'm her ..." Her mind spun, *father? Oh, gods!* "I'm her ... other parent?"

Skyler's eyes narrowed and the scent of fear shifted to disgust. "Yes, idiot. You're Kam's father. You are the *only* guy, or whatever, I've ever been with, so it wasn't hard to piece things together."

Casey's heart was going to pound out of her chest. Her confusion and scattered thoughts homed in on Skyler, and Casey realized she was livid. All her confusion had morphed to burning hot anger. "Then, why, Skyler, in three years, haven't you contacted me once?" Red colored her vision as she tried to keep her voice level so as not to scare the kid. "Why haven't you told me about her? For goodness sakes, I could've helped raise her."

Eyes narrowing, Skyler stepped forward, pointing a finger at Casey. Casey thought if Skyler could, she'd manifest fire from her eyes. "I never thought I'd have a chance to have a kid of my own. Kam was supposed to be mine. I knew ... I *knew!*" she practically yelled the last two words, apparently not worrying about scaring the three-year-old, "if you *ever* found out about her you'd try to take her from me." Skyler's eyes grew wild, and she was practically spitting. "Kam was supposed to be mine ... but then ... why do you have to ruin everything?"

Her mom came up behind her, placing an arm across her shoulders. She spoke low and soothing, trying to deescalate the situation. "Not now, Sky, love. Let's just leave. It isn't worth it. *She* isn't worth it. We'll figure something else out."

The two gave Casey scathing looks that defined, 'if looks could kill,' then they both stomped towards the door. Hand on the knob, Skyler turned. "Don't call me, got it? When Kam asks, just make something up. I love her ... I really do ... I just ... just lie. There's a letter in the suitcase. It explains why it has to be this way." Skyler gave Kam a final look full of love and fear, then she closed her eyes, turned, and left. Her mom retreated without a backward gaze.

There was a stillness in the room. Casey watched the door, half-expecting it to open and the pair to come back saying, "Joking!" But that wasn't going to happen. The only reality was the weight of the squirming child she held, sniffling back tears.

Slowly, she shifted her focus to the other witches in the room. Both Grandpa and Hildegard watched her as she tried to contain the three-year-old in her arms—her daughter.

She wasn't sure what was on her face, but Grandpa started to laugh. "Oh, honey child, this isn't the end of the world. We'll figure it out. They said the child's name is Kam?"

Nodding, she dropped her gaze to her daughter. "Hi, Kam."

The girl stared back. Her large eyes got bigger. "Where Mama go?"

Casey hugged the girl tighter to her side. "Your mama had to go for a bit. Can we play a game?"

She seemed hopeful. "Play?"

Kneeling on the ground, Casey placed the girl on her feet. "What do you like to play? Or are you hungry?

Hildegard cleared her throat. "Fräulein Strega, there is much to determine with this child, and I need to tidy up the barn. I believe it is time for you and Parker to head home. You can play with or feed the child there. There's a bag in the back room with some of her things."

Standing, Casey grabbed Kam's hand. "Hildegard ... did you know? Did you know about Kam? That I was her ... her father?"

The coven leader's face, normally hard as stone, softened a bit. "No, child. Skyler has kept away, and she and her mother hid the pregnancy. They showed up with Kam and said they'd explain everything after testing. All I knew was Kam was hers, nothing more. Please have more faith in me."

With a quick nod, Casey shut her eyes and let out the breath she'd been holding. "Yes, ma'am. I'm sorry, I'm just ... I don't know what I am."

She turned towards the back room, but her grandpa stopped her. "I'll grab the bag; you head out to the car."

Nodding, she started to walk, but the girl didn't move. Her scent of her fear filled the room. She was surrounded by adults she didn't know; it really wasn't a surprise she didn't want to leave.

Casey knelt again, realizing she'd done this all wrong. "Kam, I know you don't know me, but I'm ... well, I'm your second mother. You can call me mom, or Casey. But I'm one of your parents. I know you've never met me, but I'm really happy to finally meet you."

Kam scrunched up her face. "You're Casey?" Casey nodded. "But Mama said you were my daddy."

Casey rubbed her eyes. "Well, that's fine too. You can call me Daddy, if you'd like. Either way you look at it, I'm one of your parents. You've been living with Sky ... um ... your mama, but now I get you ... which will be fun ... and ... um ... exciting." She tried to make the last word sound upbeat. "We'll have lots of fun together."

The girl bit her lower lip, then nodded. She lifted her arms to be picked up, and Casey stood to oblige her.

From behind, Hildegard chuckled. "She was the spitting image of you when she bit her lip. Anyone questions who her parent is just needs to watch her!"

Hitching the girl up, Casey headed for the door. Grandpa arrived at the same time, holding two bags. When they got to the car, there was a kids' car seat sitting next to the back wheel, an additional suitcase, and Riley, who leaned against the car with an amused smile on her face.

Grandpa looked at her. "Your drive home will be tight."

It took some finagling, but they managed to get the seat into the back of the Chameleon, Casey's VW-Bug. Kam's bags fit around her and in the storage area of the car. Once everything was secured, they succeeded in finding a place for the three adults. Riley sat in the back and immediately started a conversation with Kam. The two of them seemed to hit it off, which was weird.

The drive between Hildegard's farm and Grandpa's home was short. When they got there, Riley started running bags up to the room the two of them shared.

Gramps watched as Riley ran. "There's a small mattress in the attic."

Riley's voice floated down the stairs behind her. "I'll find it, you just get the food ready. I got the room."

Casey carried Kam into the living room. Before she could step away, Riley ran down with a box of old toys she'd found in the attic. Kam began digging through the box. Riley returned to the upstairs while Grandpa moved to the kitchen.

Watching Kam grab out an old Raggedy Anne and Raggedy Andy that Casey used to sleep with made Casey smile. Then, digging deep into the box,

Kam found a view-master with five white disks. She started stuffing the round cardboard circles into the red viewer, checking out what each film box had to offer. Throwing the toy to the side, she found a Mr. Potato Head, which miraculously still had some of its original pieces. Casey couldn't believe Grandpa had kept these old toys of hers.

Casey stood in the archway between the living room and kitchen, enjoying the scene of her daughter playing and her grandpa cooking. The sound of gravel crunching in the driveway alerted her that someone was driving up the path to the house. Not sure who would be coming out to visit, she navigated over to check out the window. Her parents' car pulled up and parked next to the Chameleon. "Grandpa! Did you know Mom and Dad were coming for a visit?"

His voice floated from the kitchen. "No, dear, but I'm not surprised. They missed your graduation because of a business trip of your father's. They're very proud of you. I may have mentioned you'd be here this weekend."

Her heart began pounding again. "But, Grandpa ... Kam." She headed over to pick the girl up. Kam grasped the Raggedy Anne, hugging it in the same position she held Kam. If her parents were here, she wasn't going to hide her daughter. She wasn't embarrassed, she just had no idea how to explain her life to people who had no idea about any of it.

Though witches and vampires were out in the world, most didn't reveal their natures to norms. Casey's parents were both norms. She wasn't sure how her witch powers had skipped a generation. The fact that she was both a witch *and* a vampire would be an even harder pill for them to swallow.

Isn't it enough that I just found out I have a child? Couldn't this meeting with my parents be put off for a week or two, or a year or two? Gah! I am not prepared for this!

She heard footsteps approaching the front door, as Grandpa joined her. He put a hand on her lower back. "It will be fine, honey child. We'll figure this out, just like we do everything else." As always, his words calmed her.

While Casey tried to control her breathing, Grandpa opened the door. "Stan! Dottie! I didn't know you'd actually make it up to visit this weekend."

Casey wasn't trying to hide from her parents, but she stood just behind the door, still out of sight. Her body was tense with her nerves, jaw clenched, and hands fisted. She wanted to get herself calm before her parents saw her.

Mom's voice came from the other side of the door. "We don't need a formal invitation, Dad. You said Casey would be here, and we haven't seen her in ages! I was bummed to've missed her graduation! Now, let us in so we can see our daughter."

Stepping out from behind the door, Casey saw her parents. They really hadn't changed. Casey took after her mom, except her mom had dark brown hair. Her dad was tall with short blond hair and blue eyes. He was fit. They both wore jeans and button-down shirts. Her dad a white one, her mom in light pink. Seeing them, Casey's nerves spiked.

Mom's brows furrowed. "Who is that child, Case? She looks so much like you, especially with your bleached hair. Oh, I do love your natural brown hair better. Why do you do that to yourself?"

A small squeak escaped her before Kam disappeared, and Casey was left holding air.

Chapter 2

There was a thump and a, "What the!" from upstairs as Mom screamed "witch," and Dad blanched.

Casey slowly backed up, ready to bolt, as Grandpa's hand snapped out, clasping her arm. His voice came out low as he faced his daughter. "Now, Dottie, you *are* talking to your daughter, my granddaughter. You have two choices: come in and be civil or leave." There was steel in his words.

Mom began to shake. "But, Dad, that kid just disappeared. That's magic. Is Casey a witch?"

Spinning on his heel, Grandpa harrumphed. "Fool! Choose: stay or leave." And he returned to the kitchen to continue his cooking.

Casey backed up slowly, observing her parents until she reached the kitchen, then she sat on one of the stools at the counter. She watched as her parents whispered back and forth. If she tried, she could've listened in, but at this point she didn't want to. If they said words that damned her, she didn't want to hear them, it would be too much. They could come in or leave. That would be enough to let her know their decision.

She heard a pounding on the stairs and Riley, fully punked, but now wearing a Ramone's shirt, came down holding Kam. Casey could feel her parents' fear grow. "Hey, Case, did you learn how to mist another being or can your kid do vampire tricks?"

Casey rubbed her forehead and groaned. *Can this get any worse?*

From the doorway, Mom emitted another high-pitched shriek. "Vampire!"

Casey's hands flew to cover her ears as Grandpa started to swear. His lumbering footsteps retreated to the door. "My neighbors are pretty far away, but that was loud enough that they could probably hear you. This is getting ridiculous, Dottie. As ludicrous as your prejudices are, make a decision and make it now. I'm shutting this door, and this may be you being shut out of your daughter's life, your granddaughter's life, and my life." Matching action to words, he began to shut the door. Dad immediately slipped inside.

With a sound of disgust, Mom followed him in.

Riley carried Kam into the living room and sat with her, playing with the assortment of toys. Casey's parents followed Grandpa into the kitchen, sitting at the small table in the corner as he continued to prepare dinner—pasta with meatballs, and garlic bread, heavy on the garlic.

Mom spat out, "So, what are you?" She stared back and forth between Casey and Grandpa, stealing quick glances into the living room at Riley and Kam.

Dad placed a hand on his wife's arm. "Parker, this is hard on all of us. How long have you known about Casey?"

Grandpa's eyes narrowed as he considered Dad. "That she was a witch and could do magic? Since she was six."

Dad nodded. "Is that the real reason she took time off before college? Did she need to train for the coven?"

Casey gaped at her dad. "How do you know all of this?"

His mouth quirked up on one side. "My mom, your grandma. She died before you were born. I never told anyone because it was never accepted even when it should've been. Her coven was strong. When I didn't show any signs of magic, I moved away. It was too hard being so close but not having the gift. She told me to watch my children. She said magic didn't usually skip a generation, but when it did, the next generation had the power of both."

Grandpa started to chuckle as Casey rubbed her forehead. Dad watched and nodded. He faced her grandpa. "You're a witch then?" After he got his confirmation, he laughed too. "So, Casey has the double power from both sides. I bet that's been fun."

Getting up, Casey gave Dad a hug. "Oh, yeah, tons of fun." Then she returned to sit at the stool where she could be part of this discussion while paying attention to Riley and Kam in the living room as well. The two were getting along famously.

Mom sat ramrod straight, taking everything in. "So, you're telling me my father and daughter are witches. My husband wishes he was a witch. And no one, no one at all, thought to tell me any of this? Did Mother know?"

Grandpa shook his head. "No, she was brought up in a family that was close-minded about witches and vampires. I loved her with all my heart and never had it in me to tell her. Sometimes I wish I'd been honest with the woman I loved. I think if she'd lived long enough to know about Casey, she would've opened up her world for your daughter, thrown out her hate for love."

Mom's face scrunched up. "I've heard the word vampire a few times. Which is it? Witch or vampire? You can't be both, can you? They're both—"

"Dottie!" Dad's voice whipped out, stopping her from saying anything hurtful. "You do not want to continue whatever it is you were about to say. We have established that all your living family are witches. The word vampire *has* been bandied about. Again, we are speaking of our *only* daughter. I, for one, am not going to lose her."

Searching the faces of her parents, then gazing at her grandpa, Casey squeezed her hands together. "During my freshman year in college there was a … misunderstanding. I was attacked. Yes, Mom, a person *can* be both. Because of that … misfortunate event, I am both: witch *and* vampire."

Leaning back, Dad's eyes narrowed. "Are you a coven witch?"

She huffed out a laugh. "Yeah. After I was turned into a vampire, the coven moved up my testing. They wanted to be sure I could master both sides of my new life."

He smiled. "And you passed. Are you as strong as my mom predicted?"

Grandpa snorted. "She's the strongest mind witch any of us has ever seen. She's also pretty good at conjuration. Her fire and ice could use practice, but I believe she'll get there. Her walking stick topper is a dragon."

Her dad shouldn't have known what that meant. Only coven witches who had passed all their tests should have known, but judging by the widening of his eyes, he had some idea that the animals at least represented strength. He placed his hands on the table and gazed at her. "I'm proud of you, Case. Not only did you pass your classes, you dealt with all of this ... and had a kid?"

Groaning, she rubbed her forehead. "Kam, my daughter, is a longer story yet. She *is* your granddaughter."

Mom's gaze went to the living room where the duo played. "And she's a witch?"

Grandpa shook his head. "We don't know ..."

"But she disappeared, Dad!" Mom interrupted.

"Dottie, would you listen?" Grandpa was losing his temper, something that rarely happened. "Witch traits don't usual present until a child is between six and eight. Casey presenting at six was young. Kam is only three, and just turned three. If she *is* a witch, she probably won't show any powers for three to five years. What you saw was a vampire power."

Mom gaped.

Before she could say anything else, Kam's voice rang out from the living room. "I wan' my daddy! Daddy! Daddy! I wan' my daddy!"

Mom looked around the room. "Where is the father? Did you get in trouble? You said the child is what? Three ... so, four years ago? Right when college started? Did you take any of college seriously, Casey, or did you go in right away to have fun? And weren't you into girls?"

Dad's face hardened as Mom continued to speak. "Again, I don't want this to be the last time we see our daughter. Maybe we shouldn't jump to conclusions."

"Daddy!" Kam shrieked.

Casey rotated in her stool and locked eyes with Riley, who just shrugged. With a sigh, she hopped off the stool and headed into the living room as Kam ran and leapt into her arms. "Daddy!"

Chapter 3

Grandpa called for dinner before any more conversation could be had, and, with the instinct of a cat, Kam crawled onto Mom's lap. Mom froze for a second, but then her parent instincts took over, and she grabbed the girl's plate and helped her with her food.

Casey savored the garlic mixed with cheese melted on the bread, Grandpa's specialty. Casey watched as Mom began to relax as the magic of grandkids and food worked on her. Then, biting her lip, she asked Dad, "Why didn't you ever tell me? I always thought you and Mom were both anti-witches. It would've been nice, when I was growing up, to know that one of my parents understood what I was going through."

A sadness came over Dad. "I know, sweetheart. Your mom and I had been married a few years before the discussion came up. Ironically, in most day-to-day conversation, it doesn't. I hadn't realized she was so against the paranormal ... but I loved her," he smiled warmly at his wife, "love her. I decided it wasn't a fight worth fighting unless you were born a witch. I hadn't predicted Parker hiding you from us."

She took a bite of her pasta and savored its goodness. "Do you still keep in contact with the coven your family was a part of?"

He shook his head. "No, it's been too long. I wish I could get you in contact with them, but hiding is one of those things witches do well."

Casey thought about that while watching Kam wiggle on Mom's lap. Mom had lost her cold, hard demeanor as she laughed at the challenge of feeding a three-year-old. The two of them were getting covered in the pasta, but Kam's smile lit up the room. Riley sat across from them, ready and willing to help if it was needed.

Once Mom got Kam distracted with the bread, her focus shifted to Casey. "Did you grow up thinking your father and I didn't love you?" There was pain in her voice.

Casey closed her eyes and shut her mouth. She let her chin hit her chest for a minute of thought. This was such a hot wire of a question for them both. Once she had her thoughts in order, she took a breath and spoke. "No, Mom, it wasn't that." She looked up. "I knew you loved me, I just worried that you'd also hate me, or disapprove of me. I knew that if you kicked me out, Grandpa would take me in, but I didn't want you to have to make that choice, so I hid."

Mom's eyes began to mist. "From the age of six? You kept the secret from such a young age?"

Making fists, Casey nodded. "Yeah, I was scared. I liked my life, and I loved you both. What would happen to me if my parents stopped loving me? I saw the stories on the news. There were kids on the street, kicked out because their parents disapproved of them being witches. They didn't know where to go because the covens are so secretive. There have been witch hunters that use teens 'kicked out' to find them, so many of these witches end up in the system. To me, it was more important to keep my secret and my family than to share and tempt fate."

Nodding, her mom hugged Kam. "I'm sorry for how I was acting when we arrived. It's all very new to me, but I'll learn. I like having a granddaughter and hope to have many more."

Casey felt herself blanch as she sat back in the chair. "Um ... probably not anytime soon. Kam is a bit of an anomaly. Enjoy her for now."

Dinner wrapped up, and her parents decided to head home. They didn't live close, but they didn't live that far away either.

The day had been long, and they'd gotten Kam to fall asleep. Casey, Riley, and Grandpa sat in the kitchen having tea.

Riley gazed at the mess of the living room. "You know, we made it back here from that farm, but with our bags, I don't think we'll all fit into your car."

With a sigh, Casey nodded. "I was thinking of calling Rowan. He'd freak if he knew we had more than two people in my car."

Grandpa laughed. "There's a bus. It leaves at seven in the morning. It takes two hours."

Scrunching up her nose, Casey considered. "Okay, how about this. I'll take the bus with Kam. Riley, you drive back with all our stuff. We'll meet at witch house. I know I technically have a few more days at Cambia House, but I'm thinking so many switches will be hard on Kam."

Riley nodded. "I'll drive home and get our stuff packed. I can figure out what you need. Witch stuff and work clothes should be enough?"

Thinking it over, Casey nodded. A bit nervous about what Riley would pick out for her, she was nevertheless happy they had a plan. Once they'd figured that out, Casey made a call to Rowan to warn him. Riley would need to invade his area for some of her stuff. Her guess was he'd have it packed and ready to go by the time she showed up.

At least I'll be presentable most days if Rowan selects my clothing.

The next morning, Grandpa drove Casey and Kam to the bus station. They boarded and found a couple of seats near the back. It was a nice bus with individual seats, each padded with an ugly blue and red fabric. Casey let Kam take the window seat and she took the aisle.

Kam had brought her Raggedy Annie doll and immediately curled up on the seat and fell asleep. The air conditioning on the bus was high, and Casey wished she'd warn more than a black flare skirt that barely went to her knees and a Madonna t-shirt. She'd worn a sports coat as well, but she'd taken it off to cover Kam like a blanket.

I really need to figure out this parenting gig. Traveling with a kid means being ready for more than just sitting on a bus!

As she waited for the bus's departure, she took out a book to read. By five minutes after seven, every seat in the bus was full and it was about to take off. The doors were closed, but one more person tried to pay to get on.

The driver opened the door. "Sorry, sir, all the seats are full."

The person sighed loudly enough to be heard. "My ... wife ... is on this bus, with my ... um ... daughter. I don't feel comfortable with them traveling alone. I'm sure I can share a seat with one of them, sir."

Putting a bookmark in her book, Casey's eyes narrowed. *It can't be ... why is he here?* The two of them had just acknowledged the bond they'd been feeling over the years, a yearning she thought only she'd been feeling. It started with sharing some blood and ended with sharing much more.

Over the years, Rowan had carefully not been intimate with members of his vampire family. He worried about traitors and secrets getting out. Casey felt a bit sad that he'd lived such a solitary life, separate and alone. But he'd opened up to her, revealing truths and details that she cherished. They finally gave in to the yearning they both felt.

Once they became physical, he'd let his desires for her be known not only to her, but to the rest of the house—his vampires. After that, she had to decide what that meant to her, and to them. They were still navigating what their relationship was. She needed blood, and that led to desire and passion, but she knew she loved him, and he loved her.

The driver sounded tired, and it was his first drive of the day. "Listen, sir. I'll take your money. If no one is willing to share their seats with you, you're off the bus and out your cash. No refunds, got it?"

She could hear the smile in his voice. "Deal."

Still in disbelief, Casey sat stunned as Rowan entered the bus. His lean body in jeans and a Queen shirt had everyone on the bus looking up to see where he'd stop. The red in his hair was more obvious than normal in the lighting of the bus as he slowly made his way down between the seats. When he finally got to Casey, his gaze landed on Kam, curled up and asleep, and he smiled.

She tilted her head back, quirking a half-smile up at him. Leaning down for a quick kiss, he pulled back and said, "I can't imagine waking her up. How about *you* sit on my lap instead."

His words were innocent, but she didn't trust him, even as she stood to let him sit under her. She'd grabbed the back of the seat in front of her for stability, and when she sat, her skirt billowed out. Too late, she realized very little fabric sat between her and him. Glancing into his face, she saw he realized it too.

Twisting to face the window, she tried to fix her skirt, but he grabbed her hand, whispering in her ear, "Don't you dare." Mischief danced in his eyes.

They were on an express bus which meant there were three stops before theirs. The first two were right away. After that, they had over an hour before the bus would stop again. Based on previous rides on this bus, when Casey was in high school, many people would fall asleep, listen to their Walkman, or just read during that hour. Reading had been her plan, that was, until Rowan had shown up, eyes full of mischief.

She leaned into his hard chest, enjoying his minty scent. At the start of the hour leg of the journey, Casey could hear small snores coming from Kam.

Watching the trees fly by, she asked, "What are you doing here?"

His outside hand sat on her hip, securing her on his lap as she bounced with the uneven road. "I wanted to meet your daughter, and thought you'd like company ... and I missed you. I knew you'd go straight to the witches. I left a bag for Riley then came to meet you."

After she graduated from college, Hildegard explained she'd been spending too much time with the vampires. She needed to split her time evenly between the witches and vampires. Both homes had a room for her. Rowan, being the head of his family of vampires, couldn't spend half a month living away from the vampire house, so even though their relationship was new, they'd been spending quite a bit of time apart. She missed him too and knew she'd miss living with him, sharing his bed.

She sat with her back to the aisle, facing the window. Rowan's hand had been under the skirt, playing with her panties for most of the ride. He'd mostly behaved, tracing the seam and stroking her lower belly. Suddenly, she heard a slight tear and felt a yank, and her jaw dropped. "Did you just—"

His free hand slid up her back and twined in her hair. He pulled her in close and kissed her deeply. When he released the kiss, he held their lips together. "Let's play a game, my love. First rule, no sounds. We don't want to wake up the kid ... Kam? Second Rule, no discussion of what we're doing. We don't want anyone else knowing our game. Third Rule ..." Casey sat waiting for the third rule as his thumb, currently under her skirt, probed private areas. Then she heard a zipper.

He lifted her slightly, adjusted her, and then she felt him slowly entering her. She slammed both hands over her mouth to stop the groan from being heard by the people sitting near them.

Bringing her close again, he said, "That's right ... keep it quiet, Miss Strega."

The motion of the bus did enough to move her up and down on him. He kept a hand between them, playing with her clit. His free hand, holding her hip, moved higher to trace the side of her breast. The fact that they could be caught had her mind tripping over itself. They were so public, more so then when they'd played at the restaurant.

Every second, she thought she would scream from exposure, from the heat building, from his hands on her. Her breathing was getting rough, and she realized she was making small sounds.

She leaned closer to him, and he kissed her neck. He kissed it again. And then he bit her. Her world exploded. Every muscle contracted. She wanted to scream but couldn't. She wanted to pant, to squirm, to bite him back ... but she didn't want the bus to know what they were doing, or what they were.

A moan escaped her as he pushed her over the edge, a spasming of muscles she couldn't hide. He took two more pulls on her neck, elongating the pleasure, as fireworks exploded behind her eyes. Her head fell back, and her body trembled as she bit back the scream that threatened to give their game away. He licked her neck closed, and she pushed into him, wanting more. Barely able to get any breath, she collapsed on his chest, vision blurry with her orgasm.

Sliding his hand out from under her skirt, he wrapped his arms around her. After a few minutes, she finally caught her breath. Licking her lips, she pushed back from him enough to give him a kiss. "How are we going to get you off the bus without a scandal?"

He bit her bottom lip, pulling back for a longer kiss. "Let me worry about that. We have some time."

"And what *is* it about you and being in public?" Her mouth was right by his ear, and she hoped she spoke low enough for no one else to hear her.

His deep chuckle made muscles low in her gut tighten. "It's more of the surprise than the public."

She was about to ask another question when she heard the rustle of cloth beside her.

"Daddy, I haffa go pee."

Chapter 4

Riley picked Casey and Kam up from the bus stop and drove them over to witch house. Rowan misted back to Cambia House. Riley planned on staying with Casey during her time with the witches. It would be good to have someone around who understood the blood needs of a vampire. Two of the witches, Damion and Tilly, had agreed to donate blood, but having someone who knew the drill was nice.

They parked out front, and Casey and Riley each took one of Kam's hands as they approached the house. Kam gaped at all the trees and plants. "This looks like mama's house. Are there swings in the back?"

Biting her lip, Casey thought about all the things she'd have to change to adapt her life to living with a toddler. "No, but maybe we can figure something out. There's a park close by."

When they got to the door, Zen opened up. He was tall and lean, with short blond hair and blue eyes. He had a disapproving air to him, but that was normal. His mouth tightened and eyes narrowed as he took in the three of them. "I didn't know you were bringing a family, Casey. I thought you were coming alone."

Her face hardened as she stared at him. "Didn't Hildegard call you? She said she would."

Standing in the doorway, hands braced on both sides of the frame as if he wouldn't let her in, his head tilted, considering them. "She may have mentioned something."

With a huff of frustration, Casey backed up a step. "We can do one of three things. I can leave. I'll call Hildegard from Cambia House and leave it to you to explain why you refused us entry. I can enter your mind and figure out why you're being an

...." She looked down at the tiny girl whose hand she held. "Jerk, why you're being a jerk. Or you can just let us in. I'd rather explain what has happened once."

Stepping back, he waved his hand eloquently to allow entrance. "I was just making small talk, not blocking passage, Casey." He said her name as if his actions were obvious.

Rolling her eyes, she walked towards the kitchen, where she heard other voices. She found the rest of the local witches sitting around the large oak table. She got Riley and Kam situated before she sat. The others served up tea and juice before joining them. It took a few rounds of tea, but soon everyone knew what had happened and why Casey was there with two extras. They weren't happy about Riley, but they saw the advantage of an extra blood donor.

Sadie, a petite woman with frizzy brown hair who appeared to love to wear flowing dresses, returned to the table with the third pot of tea. "The biggest issue I see is we have set aside a small room for you, but now you are three people."

Casey bit her lip. "Is there a slightly bigger room, one I could share with Kam? Riley could take the room I was originally assigned."

Kam banged her hands on the table. "Kam gets her own room. I'm a big girl now. Mama said so!"

They all paused and stared at the girl who smiled at the attention. They'd given her paper and crayons, and she'd been drawing, but now she smiled back at all the adults who were gaping at her.

Steepling her hands in front of her face, Sadie shifted her attention from the girl back to Casey. "If Kam can be in a room alone, and you two don't mind sharing, there is one more room ready. It has a king-size bed and is across the hall from your room—well, the one that *was* your room. I guess it's Kam's room now. We thought you could use it for ... you know. But if you and Riley could share it ... platonically, then we can figure out a better solution later."

Riley's mouth twitched. "I believe we can manage ... sleeping ... on a king-size bed. It was good of you to understand her needs, though."

Leaning back, Casey sipped her tea. "I need to check in with Cambia House, and we need to unpack. Thanks for being so understanding."

Tilly put down her tea. "I'll be in the garden if Kam wants to hang out with me while you are getting yourself situated."

Casey and Riley headed out to grab the bags while Kam ran off shouting, "Finding Tiwy!" And she was gone.

Casey and Riley grabbed the bags from the car and saw Tilly with Kam. Tilly waved. "I have her. You two go rest. I know you've had a long day. We'll be fine."

Once upstairs, Casey called Sydney on the rotary phone in her room. *Gods above, a rotary phone, how old was this place?* "Cambia House."

"Hi, Sydney. I just wanted to officially say I'm at witch house for two weeks and get an update."

Sydney laughed. "I heard you were heading out. Things are good. No updates from Micha or Cyran. We'll keep you updated, even though you've switched sides for a few weeks."

"Sydney!" Casey yelled, appalled.

Sydney chuckled again. "Kidding. Go, relax. We'll talk later."

Casey hung up and sighed. Nothing from the two vampires out searching for Jude. The fact that Jude, the vampire who'd kidnapped her, had gotten away, still irked her. They had two of the best from their security team out searching for him. If he hadn't been found yet, he had solidly gone to ground.

Casey found the small room. Riley was unpacking Kam's stuff. She was almost done, so Casey went off to shower off the bus ride, leaving Riley to finish the job. After her shower, she found a clean skirt and a tank top to wear.

Despite what Skyler said, Riley couldn't find a letter with her reasoning for not being able to raise the girl. The two searched the bags, looking through all the clothes, pockets, and even patted down the lining. There was no note. Casey decided if a reason didn't present itself, besides the girl being able to mist, she'd call Skyler, or have Hildegard call her, in a few days. She wanted to make sure she knew everything that she needed to know about her daughter.

Once in the room she'd be sharing with Riley, Casey collapsed on the bed. Riley joined her and locked the door. "When was the last time you had blood?"

Lifting up onto her elbows to stare at Riley, she thought. "Umm. A few days ago? Worse, Rowan took some of mine on the bus." Feeling tired, she flopped back down.

Riley's brow went up. Then Casey felt her panties being removed from under her skirt. Pushing back up, she eyed the punk vixen. "What do my under garments have to do with blood?" She tried to sound serious, but feared she just sounded tired.

"Scoot up on the bed." Riley's voice brooked no argument. Casey moved to the center of the bed. Kneeling between her legs, Riley yanked the skirt off in one motion, tossing it on the floor, then, dropping, placed her chin just below Casey bellybutton. "So, you want me to stop?"

Looking into the black eyes of the woman between her legs made her heat with need all over again. Casey began to squirm, and she bit her lip, shaking her head 'no.'

Riley slipped her hands up Casey's shirt, her cool hands lightly playing up Casey's stomach. "Tell me you want me to continue, Casey. That I should have fun before you take my blood." Her voice was low and as she spoke, she lowered her mouth closer and closer towards her clit.

Without thought, Casey bucked up in need. Her body sang out for Riley. Riley's tongue lashed out, licking up her most sensitive area. "No more until you tell me, love."

Casey's head fell back, and she gulped in air before she managed to say, "Gods above, woman, don't stop. Yes, please, continue. Do what you will, I'm your playground, and then I'll take your blood." She knew they were the wrong words, but it was the best she could do with that mouth ... there. She groaned with need.

Riley's mouth suctioned onto her clit and two fingers plunged into her. She sucked and scraped teeth, probing her fingers in and out. Lightning scorched her from the inside in waves. Heat built up. Riley pulled away for a minute. "Play with your breasts, babe, I want to hear you come with me between your legs. But not too loud. I don't want any of the witches barging in."

She slid her hands up to her own nipples. The extra sensations were the last bit she needed to bring her over. Using one hand to cover her mouth, she let loose a yell she'd been holding since the bus as she crashed over. Her hand was removed, and a neck was there. Her teeth descended, and she started to drink the sweet metallic elixir of life.

Riley's warm body fitted atop hers, and she wrapped her arms and a leg around the sexy woman, reveling in the feel of the body pressing into her.

At first, the blood filled her body with strength and vitality, then each pump gave her a punch of need and desire. After a few sips, she flipped the dark vixen over, licking the wound shut, then let her tongue travel down Riley's curvy body.

It was her turn to play.

Chapter 5

Casey woke from sleep with a moan. A tongue slipped into her mouth, a hand grasped her breast, and a finger began playing with her ... eyes snapping open, she returned the kiss, angling her hips to grant better access.

Moving away, Riley knelt beside her. "You up, sleepy head?"

Using deep breaths to slow her heart, Casey focused on the dark eyes floating above her. "What?"

The devilish eyes danced with amusement. "Are you awake?"

Rubbing her face, she shifted onto her back. "Maybe. Was all that your idea of a wake-up alarm?"

The bed dipped then bounced up as Riley got out of bed. "Yep, we need to get ready for the day. If you don't like my methods, wake up first and be *my* alarm. You won't hear *me* complaining. Anyway, you and the witches are going to start doing stuff. I thought I'd take the scamp off, visit some parks, get her ice cream, maybe bring her to the obstacle course at Cambia House. She misted Casey; she needs to be trained."

She sat and stared. "Gods above, you're right. Are you okay watching her today?"

Riley pulled on a black tank top. She already had on black panties. "Of course, the girl likes me. We'll have a grand time."

Casey crawled to the edge of the bed and began pawing through her clothes, finding items to wear for the day. *Rowan didn't do half bad packing for me.* She settled on stone washed jeans and a pale-yellow button-down shirt with ruffles lining the buttons.

Once dressed, she crossed the room to find Kam in her pajamas playing with tiny plastic bears in different colors. Each belly had a different picture on it. There were also jeweled-toned horses. "Morning, Kam. Let's get you dressed and then get food."

Bright eyes gazed at her. "But, Daddy, I'm playing!" She looked down at her toys. "Will mama be at breakfast?"

The girl's hope hit Casey like a punch in the gut. She bit her lip and squatted down. "Not today, dear. I know you're playing, but darling, it's time to eat."

"Daddy, is the reason mama didn't want me anymore because I bit her?" Kam ducked her head and dropped her toys.

A sword of premonition slid down Casey's back as she stared at her daughter. She shivered and fell to her butt. Pulling the girl on her lap, Casey gave her a hug. "Why did you bite your mama?"

Her tiny face scrunched up, and she tucked it into Casey's chest. Casey rubbed Kam's back. They sat there for a few minutes. *The poor girl is terrified. She thinks I'll send her away too.* "You know, love, you can tell me anything, and I won't get mad. I sometimes need to bite people, too."

Kam suddenly pulled back and gaped at Casey, mouth dropping open. Her tongue ran over her own teeth. "My mouth felt funny. Then mommy smelled like ... yummy. I bit her arm ... it was an accident, but ..." She hid her face again, and Casey felt a wet spot on her shirt.

It felt like Casey's heart was breaking. *What would it be like if her daughter was born a vampire, with all its needs? Would she have its desires too? Is this what the missing note talked about? No wonder Skyler freaked out.* "Did the blood taste good, sweetheart?"

The girl froze. "No, no, no, no, no. Mama yelled at me. Good girls don't do that. She said I shouldn't even talk about it." Her eyes got wide, and her hands flew up and slapped over her mouth.

Riley opened the door. "You two coming?" She saw the two of them together on the floor and she backed up. "Oh! Sorry, I'll go."

Casey closed her eyes and hoped she was making the right decision. She felt like the rug was being pulled out from under her ... all the rules were changing.

"Wait." Casey waved her in. "Sit with us for a second. I want to test a theory, if you're okay with it."

With a tilt to her head, Riley shut the door, sat down at an angle to them, and raised her brows. "You know I'm okay with anything. Test away, my friend."

Casey held out her hand. "Thanks. Can I have your hand?" Riley placed her hand in Casey's. Placing Riley's thumb in her mouth, Casey let her teeth descend and slowly broke the skin. Both Riley and Kam watch, mesmerized. Then Casey shut her lips around the digit and sucked. She didn't get much of Riley's blood, but the tiny bit, as always, tasted of ambrosia. Even more satisfying than the first cup of coffee in the morning.

Kam sat frozen, watching. Casey removed Riley's thumb. There was a bit of blood on the finger, and she moved it to Kam's mouth. The girl pressed her lips together for a second, then, as if unable to control herself, her tongue lashed out, licking the blood. A shiver went through her, and she grabbed Kam's hand and began to suck the small cut clean.

Eyes wide and mouth gaping open, Riley stared between the child and her mother. "Casey, how did you know?"

Casey shook her head. "Long story. We'll discuss it later. Let's stick with the plan and figure this out later. We need to talk with Rowan."

Kam was done with the thumb and looked happy, smiling at both adults. Then her face fell. "Am I in trouble?"

Riley's gaze narrowed. "Just don't put any fingers in your mouth without my or your ... um, Daddy's permission. I may add people to the list. And for goodness sake, don't put your fingers in other people's mouths."

Kam stared between Casey and Kam, then nodded solemnly. Then she giggled, "Put my fingers in other people's mouths, that would be silly, Riley!"

They stood and rummaged for clothing for the girl. She wore jean shorts and a t-shirt sporting her favorite cartoon character. Once she was dressed, they headed down for breakfast.

After breakfast, Riley left with Kam. The five witches that remained were enough to form a minor circle. A full coven needed thirteen, but a minor circle only required five.

With Jude out on the loose, it was important they figure out how they worked together. They needed to determine the type of spells they could do and practice them.

Jude had escaped his punishment after kidnapping Casey twice. He had Kailey, the traitor who had been a blood donor in Cambia House for years, pretended to be everyone's friend, but who really had been a spy for Jude the entire time. The two were out there working to undermine the coalitions Rowan had been helping to set up all over the world.

Being an emotion vampire, he fed off what humans felt. He wanted vampires to be held separate and above witches and humans, to feed off their fear they felt that a vampire would eat them at any moment. The information that vampires were civil and safe went against everything he wanted.

Though the witches had been living in town for the better part of four years, Casey had been busy learning what it meant to be a vampire as well as trying to be a college student. The five of them hadn't spent any time working together.

After Kam and Riley left, the others stayed at the kitchen table for a few more minutes. When they finally decided to start work, Sadie collected the dishes while Zen washed. Damion had a book with runic symbols across the front. "I'd like to start with fixing the wards on the house. That's something we're all good at and will allow us to figure out how we work together."

Tilly, sitting next to him at the table, nodded. "That works. I'd also like to do a blanket spell to see if we can find any witches in town. We tried the spell a few weeks ago with Casey, but that didn't work very well. It would be good to see if we've missed anyone."

Zen gazed at her over his shoulder, flat and disapproving. Then he went back to washing dishes.

Sadie shrugged. "We don't have many resources if we find anyone, but it isn't the worst idea. It will also give us to ways to blend our magics." She faced Casey. "Anything you want us to work on?"

She bit her lip. "There is one spell. I've done some research on it, and I think we can work it on a five-person circle. I'd like to figure out a binding spell so that if we go up against Jude, we can place it on him in battle."

Zen whipped around, while the other three nodded in thought. He snarled. "You want us to take a full coven spell, adapt it down to our small circle, then create a one-time talisman so that we can cast the spell on the fly in battle?" His voice held more derision than Casey thought possible for one person.

She smiled sweetly and lifted a single eyebrow. "What, too much for you? Have I hurt your brain?"

He snorted and turned back to his cleaning.

They'd constructed a gazebo in the backyard so they could do their circle work outdoors, but the sun would be blocked. Too much sun gave Casey's vampire side a headache. There was also an open patio for bigger spells that needed the open sky or moon, but for smaller spells, the gazebo was nice.

Tilly requested to lead the ward spell. They sat in a rough circle, lit white candles, and created a physical circle with stones. They sat cross legged, hands palm up on their knees, eyes closed, and waited to be called into a magic mindscape that Tilly created. They could do things on the real plane, but a mindscape allowed for more flexibility.

It took a few minutes, but Casey found herself in a field of light blue grass, a light purple sky, and trees with orange leaves. Small animals ran and flew about, and when Casey knelt, one bounced over for a pet. The others took in the mindscape, rubbing their eyes at the bright colors.

Tilly skipped to the center of the field. "Okay, let's do this!" They all joined her and began chanting. This type of spell was so common in the witching homes that it almost felt like a child's rhyme they all could spit out at a moment's notice. A miniature of the house appeared in the center of their circle. As they continued, a bubble appeared around the house. The more they worked, the thicker it got. When they finished, the house was barely visible through the barrier protecting it.

Once done, Tilly's smile took over her face, and her eyes danced. "Do we want to add in a specific expel for Jude and Kailey?"

Hearing Kailey's name, her old friend, and remembering her traitorous nature, still hurt. Having her spend years building a friendship only to stab everyone in the back, was almost unbelievable.

Sadie nodded, looking contemplative. "Do you know how to do that?"

Tilly bounced on her heels. "I do. I did some research. Hold my hands."

The basic ward spell may have been child's play, but adding specific persons into the spell was advanced. That must have been why Tilly wanted to lead the spell today; she'd done some extra homework.

With a snap of her fingers, sheets of paper appeared in front of each witch. "Okay, gang, read over your chants. The parts are simple, but we need to get each part right. Since we're figuring each other out, I lined us up how I figure our magic will work. With this type of spell, if I guessed wrong, it shouldn't matter."

Casey read over her part. She wasn't placed as strongest, that was given over to Zen. Tilly took the spot of lead. Cutting her eyes to Zen, Casey saw his smirk.

Whatever! Your magic is strong—it's part of the reason you're one of five in this house—but so is mine, buster.

Everyone joined together again. They each did their parts, chanting when and where their turn demanded. Tilly led the group in the more challenging magic. The power built. Once it was at a vibrating peek, Tilly let out a push, and the images of Jude and Kailey appeared on the dome within huge red circles with slashes across them. The universal image for 'nope.'

One more push, and they were all in the backyard again. Tilly grinned widely. "That was great! Do we want to do more today?"

Rubbing her hands on her pants, Casey gazed at them. "I was wondering if I could be trained more on fire and ice magic."

Tilly smiled. "I can teach you ice magic. I'm tired after the warding, but while you're here I'll be happy to teach you. As for fire, the best there is would be Zen."

Casey knew that, but was happy with good, not the best. She met Zen's gaze, and he slowly smiled. "I could give you a couple of hours now. I know your first day on your job starts at noon."

The others left, leaving just the two of them to literally play with fire. Between the magic and their personalities, Casey hoped there would be a house left by the time they were done.

Chapter 6

Casey sat in the gazebo alone with Zen. He sat cross-legged staring, at her with narrowed eyes. "I know you think your magic is top-notch, Casey, but this is an area you need to practice. You may have skills in the mind, but just remember, you can't do everything."

She bit her cheek, remembering his guest lectures from when she was younger. Those hadn't been fun then either. His holier-than-thou personality meant he always looked down on everyone. Having a personal lesson now wasn't starting off any better. *I wonder if he respects anyone.* Once she knew she had her emotions—and face—under control, she gave a curt nod. "That's why I'm here, Zen, to learn. If I thought I knew everything, I wouldn't have asked for lessons."

With a small half-smile, he tilted his head down. "Very good. We have the candles from earlier. There are only a half-dozen, not enough for a full skill drill, but we'll see what you can do. We'll start with you lighting whichever candle I point to. You'll light it for a count of five, then put it out."

His eyes pierced her. She knew he was waiting for her to complain that the game was juvenile. If he wanted her to jump through hoops to get to the lessons she wanted, then she'd jump through hoops. She plastered a smile on her face she feared looked manic and waited for the game to start.

"Before we start, I want to remind you, fire comes from several places. Some use emotion, but when you use emotion, it's harder to control. Everything has cells, and the cellular respiration releases heat. This means, everything has fire caught within its heart, fighting to get out. If you can harness that heat, you can master this skill."

Has Zen always been this poetic? His lessons back in the day never involved fire fighting its way out of inanimate objects. She licked lips and nodded. "I think I'm ready."

Zen's face fell, and she smelled disappointment on him. "You need to know yourself. Either you're ready or you're not."

Casey smiled wide, then fought to keep a solemn expression. "Ready, I am." She wondered if her Star Wars reference was lost on him ... probably, he was too stiff to be interested in movies.

Zen set up the six candles from their earlier working between them in a small hexagonal pattern. His hand lifted slowly, then his finger snapped out as he pointed to a candle.

Lighting a candle was easy. Almost without thinking, Casey lit the candle. She counted to five and pulled the fire out of the wick.

His face blank, he gave her a single nod. "That's how the game is played. I'll point, you light the candle for five seconds, then extinguish the flame."

He didn't ask her if she was ready this time. He pointed to a different candle. Again, Casey lit it. Just as she got to five in her countdown, he pointed to another candle, she pulled the fire from the first one at the same time she lit the new one. Four, five, and he pointed again.

All her focus centered on his finger and the candles. After the fifth candle, he started pointing to the next candle before her count of five was done. She now had a different count for two different candles, three different candles, two different candles. The game continued for several minutes as candles flickered to life then extinguished. She had a fleeting thought that if the flames were different colors, this would be very pretty.

"Casey, you aren't focusing! You're messing up your timing." He dropped his hands to stare daggers at her. "Fire is dangerous, and if you can't keep your focus, you'll harm yourself or someone else around you. This isn't a joke." His voice whipped at her like a cat-o-nine-tails, practically drawing blood.

She closed her eyes for a moment. If she snapped back, her lesson would be over, and in the end, she wanted to learn more. Opening her eyes, she asked, "Can you tell me how I messed up?"

His mouth tightened. "You should know, and if you'd been paying attention, you would."

She took a deep breath to calm her nerves. "I obviously missed something." She dug her nails into the heel of her palm. "Will you tell me what happened?" Two candles still burned between them.

Zen shook his head, and the scent of disgust wafted up from him. "You should be able to keep track of all six of these candles. The game is usually played with a dozen. You should've put out this one before this one."

Her brows lowered. "Are you sure?"

"Yes, Casey. Just because you are a mind witch, doesn't mean your memory is perfect."

"I'll review the exercise later, learn from it." She'd spoken low, musing over her mistake. It wasn't one she'd normally have made.

He leaned back. "What do you mean by that exactly?"

Casey lifted her knees, hugging them to her chest. "In my glass bubble. I'll go rewatch the lesson later, see everything that happened. Try to learn from my mistake."

"I've never heard the glass bubble being used that way. I've heard it being used as a place to study, hold books, practice, but not for reviewing memories." His voice was slow, doubtful.

"Do you want me to show you?" Casey tried to remember when she started doing it. She'd been doing it since she was young, trying to remember a lesson from Hildegard and Grandpa. She was at her parents' and suddenly it was like she could see the lesson on a TV. *Grandpa seemed confused, but I was so young, I thought it was because he hadn't taught me first. It's odd that it's not something all witches know about.*

He slowly extended his hand. Casey reached out and clasped his hand and the two of them slid into her glass bubble. She gazed around and tried to see it as he would see it. In the center was the magic door that had appeared when she'd officially became a coven witch three years prior. The runes glowed around the edges. *I wonder if they do that when I'm not around.* She could only open it when Lucas came here with her. There was a long wood table that sat to the side with the prophecy book open in the center. A small bookcase with books that Lucas had collected for when they studied together stood next to it. Lining a third of the bubble were massive bookcases filled with what felt like endless books. The majority of the area was an open space for her to set up and practice spells.

Off to the side, across from the study table, was a small room, what she thought of as the control center of the sphere. She used this area to review memories, secure memories she didn't want anyone to know about—her hidden memories—and when she was under attack, protect herself.

Zen spun in place taking everything in. "It's massive. Is it because you're a mental witch that you have so much more in here than other witches?"

"I don't think so. I think it's all just what we need and create. But that's not why we're here. We can discuss mental magic and glass bubbles theory another time. I'm sure I can help you expand yours and adapt it to be more like mine, if that's really what you want, but for now, let me show you what we're here for. Come on." She led him to the command room and showed him how she'd created something similar to a TV with a VCR. She put the latest memories VHS in the machine and hit play. The two of them watched the lesson, and she saw where she messed up the candles, mixing up the order in which she'd pulled the fire from them.

Damn it! I hoped he was wrong! I'll have to be more engaged in my lessons with him.

A grunt of disappointment left her involuntarily. She'd been convinced she hadn't made the mistake. "When I'm alone, I can immerse myself into this memory, bring up how I was feeling and try to recreate the mood, figure out why I made the mistake. It lessens the chance of a repeat in the future."

His mouth gaped open, and he stared back and forth between her and the TV. "Can anyone learn how to do this?"

She shrugged. "I believe so."

"No wonder Hildegard wants to get you on the teaching roster. Who taught you how to do all of this? Parker?"

Casey laughed. "I taught him, if you must know. No, I just played around in here a lot as a kid. I wanted to figure out all of the glass bubble's secrets. The more I played, the more books appeared. Some books seemed to be modeled after what I was doing, as if the magic learned from me. Some seemed to appear after I'd done something, as if the magic decided I'd passed some benchmark and was ready to learn more. Sometimes I think the books were created to summarize the actions I took, a kind of journal. I also found a stash of books that I may have incorporated into my mental library when I was young from boxes I found in Grandpa's attic. It all helped. Anyway, can we get back to the lesson?"

"At some point, can you share any of those books with me? I'd be curious to learn some of what you know."

Casey led him to the bookcase, found a couple of beginner books on what they'd been discussing, and replicated them. She handed them to him.

He nodded and in a second, they were both sitting in the gazebo, the candles in a circle between them. Zen stared at her for a few moments. "We'll play the game again at our next lesson. Let's move on. Can you make a flame float?"

Zen matched action to words, and a ball of fire floated in front of his face. He had it fly around the backyard in a specific pattern, then just as quickly as it had appeared, it was gone.

Taking in a big gulp of air, Casey felt for the heat around her. Playing with candles had always been easy. This was something completely different. Imagining a third hand, she gathered the heat and a flame igniting on the hand in front of her.

She jerked in surprise when the ball appeared. But instead of floating it slowly sank.

"Keep it steady!" Zen snapped at her. If she thought sharing her insight into mental magic would bridge a friendship between them, she was wrong.

Her body began to tremble. "I'm trying ... I ... I can't get it to stop dropping."

It still hung in the air, but its descent was constant.

With a disgusted snarl, Zen asked, "What's going through your head right now? Anything beyond, 'please stay up'?"

Anger blossomed in her chest. "Yes!" she snapped at him, and the descent halted. "I'm imagining a third hand holding the fire up, but it isn't staying up. It's what we were taught."

"Do not yell at me, Miss Strega. I am doing you a favor here. Do *not* presume the favor has to continue."

She slammed her jaw shut, grinding her teeth together. *How could I forget the first rule?* After she got her anger under control and the fireball started to sink again, she ground out, "Will you help me figure this out? Obviously, the hand trick isn't working."

"You're focused only on the fire; magic is a tapestry of everything around you. The hand isn't supposed to be literal, Casey, there are more elements in the world."

She gaped at him, trying to suss out the meaning of his words. A tapestry? Elements? The fire kept falling, and if it hit the gazebo, the wood would catch fire. She trembled, trying to control the fall, but outside of anger, nothing worked ... though she thought she could find anger easily enough.

He snapped his fingers, and the ball disappeared. She tilted forward, almost falling on the six candles. He glared at her. "We're done for today. We can continue this lesson when you're in a more respectful mood. Until then, enjoy your first day at your new job."

He got up and disappeared into the house, leaving her with the candles. She debated scrambling his brains but decided, in the end, he was needed for the small coven circles.

Chapter 7

Casey drove up to the address she was given over the phone. It was a yellow house with white trim in a nice-looking neighborhood. The windows had curtains, and the lawn was mowed. There was a garbage can up against the garage. The house looked like every other house on the block.

She parked in front of the friendly home, got out of her car, and double checked the address. Then she walked to the corner to make sure she was on the right street before returning to walk up the flower-lined path to the porch. There was a swinging bench seat on one side of the porch and a small table with three chairs on the other. Next to the door was a small plaque that read: *Sand Hill Girls' Home*. It was the right place. She rang the bell.

An older lady answered the door. Her graying brown hair was pulled up in a severe bun, she had on thick glasses, and she wore a sweater vest and slacks. Casey guessed she was somewhere in her sixties. She scrutinized Casey from head to toe. "Are you the new girl for room seven, or the new help?"

Casey's brow rose. "I'm Casey Strega, ma'am. I'm here to help."

She snorted, turned on her heel, and headed into the living room. "Shut the door behind you, Casey Strega. We'll see if you're here to help, or one of many using my front door as a revolving door: here for a day, then gone."

Her words were sharp, and Casey wondered how many people didn't last in this job. She shut the door and ran to follow the spry woman who had made it to the kitchen. It was huge, with a table large enough to seat ten. There were girls sitting around it with books. Others were in the kitchen cleaning.

"Casey Strega, this is Sand Hill Girls' Home. These girls were arrested for one reason or another. They were put here on their way to recovery. They have a strict schedule, and you'll be here to help them during the afternoon three days a week. You'll be doing individual and group counseling, amongst other things. I've been running the group sessions for years, but I've decided having a few hours off would be nice. Today, we'll both be there so you can see how things are run."

She walked out the back side of the kitchen, disappearing. Casey looked at the group of girls who were all staring at her. A girl with short curly brown hair seemed competent. "Am I supposed to follow her?"

The girl shrugged and went back to washing the dishes. Unsure of what else to do, Casey followed, hoping to catch up to the nameless old woman.

The back of the kitchen led to the back yard, stairwells that led up and down, and a hallway. Casey chose the hallway. She ended up back in the living room. She found the old coot in a rocking chair, glasses low on her nose, reading a book. She had a cat sleeping on her lap. The pair looked as if they'd been there for hours.

Spying Casey over her readers, the woman laughed. "About time you figured it out. This floor is the living room, den, kitchen, and through there is the dining room. Upstairs are bedrooms for the six girls in residence. I have the master bedroom, which is also on this floor, but it is off limits to everyone but me." The woman handed Casey a piece of paper. "Here is the daily schedule. We don't deviate from that. The girls have chores; the list is on the wall in the dining room. They know to do what is expected of them, or they lose what few privileges they have."

Casey took the paper and read. Lunch was normally from noon to twelve forty-five. Then a half-hour of clean up. One-thirty to two-thirty was group session, though time allowed for an extra thirty minutes if needed. The girls were then given some alone-time to decompress. At three-thirty, Casey was given time to start one-on-one sessions. She could have time for two a day. Then there was dinner, cleanup, chores, reading time, and lights out.

Sitting in one of the chairs, Casey turned to the woman. "So, do I get to learn your name?"

The woman smiled and said, "I like you Casey Strega. My name's Cindy Tollard, but you can call me Cindy. The girls call me Mrs. T. They like to compare me to Mr. T."

Casey snorted out a laugh, thinking Mr. T didn't have anything on this woman. "Well, Cindy, you can call me Casey. I don't know that I've ever heard my last name said so many times."

The woman patted her hand. "Get used to it. We try to teach respect around here, and the girls will be expected to call you Miss Strega. You'll adapt. It may take a bit, but we all get used to it ... eventually."

As she finished off her introduction, the girls began piling in, filling up the two couches and the remaining chairs. Once everyone was settled, Cindy started the session. "Okay, girls, I would like you all to introduce yourselves to Miss Strega. State your name, and your biggest struggle living in this house. If you want to tell her why you're here, that's up to you. She will have access to your files, since she was hired by the police department in conjunction with the Department of Health Services, but whether or not she looks at them is another matter."

A brown-skinned girl, with light eyes and a slight build went first. She sat in one of the chairs alone. "I'll start. My name is Blake. My biggest struggle is all the things we do outside. The sun makes me itchy. I'm also really tired, like, all of the time. I've been here a week, and I'm not sure what's wrong with me. I was arrested for beating up a guy downtown, but, I didn't do it. I shouldn't be here." She slumped in the seat.

The room erupted as all the girls proclaimed their innocence. Gently reaching out, Casey touched Blake's mind and was unsurprised to find she was telling the truth, there was more to her story. "Nice to meet you, Blake. Would you be okay being one of my first interviews? I have a few questions I'd like to ask you."

Blake shrugged, then hugged her knees into her chest, looking miserable.

The next girl sat on the couch. She had long, straight blond hair, and gray eyes. "Yo. My name's Tammy. I've been here a few months. I hate that we have to do all the cooking and cleaning and, like, no TV. It really sucks. I just want to watch 21 Jump Street, is that so much to ask? And, like, I totally didn't do it either." She turned to smile at the person next to her. "I'm innocent."

The girl next to Tammy with long brown wavy hair and brown eyes, shoulder-butted her. "Right, sister, neither did I. Innocent as the day is long. Yo, I'm Veronica. I don't mind the cooking, it's kind of fun, but the cleaning suuucks." She made the one syllable word into two.

On the other couch were two girls. One with short curly brown hair, the other with spiky blond hair. They both had blue eyes. The blond smiled shyly. "I'm Delilah. I love the gardens. When we have free time, it's where I like to go."

Tammy snorted. "Yo, Delilah, we're supposed to say what we don't like, not what we like. Probably because Mrs. T. thought we wouldn't have anything to say if we had to list what we liked."

Delilah shrugged. "I don't like all the attitudes and fighting or the lack of television."

The brown-haired girl smiled. "Hi," she waved. "I'm Phillipa. I also like the gardens." She glared at Tammy before she could say anything to interrupt. "I don't like the food, or the lack of privacy." Phillipa gazed directly into Casey's eyes. "I never have a chance to meditate or spend time in my mind bubble for study ... it's frustrating." Phillipa's gaze bored into Casey, willing her to understand her meaning. Casey wasn't out about being a witch, not really, but apparently this girl knew, and was asking for help.

Tammy threw her hands in the air. "The hell you talking about, Phillipa? Mind bubble. You're such a freak! Both of you spending time out in that garden, the sun's fried your brain good and gone."

Casey just nodded at the girl. "I bet that's hard. I'll see what I can do to help."

The girl sat back on the couch. "Thanks."

The final girl, wearing all black, with black hair, buzzed on the sides, and eyes so dark they may as well be black, gazed up at Casey from her seat. "I'm Betsy. It's not worth hating anything here. I'm just passing through."

After that, Cindy began the session in earnest. Each of the girls had time to discuss obstacles, and things they were working on. Cindy gave them a challenge to focus on for the day and asked them about their weekly goal. They had a book with their goals written down. Some were simple. Tammy's goals were about not interrupting and not putting others down. Some were intricate. Betsy was asked to be more involved with the others in the house.

The goal of the house was to transform the girls into productive members of society. Help them grow from the crimes they'd committed and learn how to integrate back into society.

During their free time, Casey watched what they did. Some went and hid in their rooms, a few stayed in the living room and read or journaled, and two went outside to the gardens. Cindy headed to her room to be alone and to relax with her cat.

Casey followed the two who went out to the gardens. She had twenty minutes before her first one-on-one session with Blake. Just outside the back door there was a dirt path, and she followed it. As she walked, she marveled at the gardens on each side of her. There were vegetables, newly planted but already peaking up through the soil, vibrant, and full of life. On the other side, spring flowers were in heavy bloom, their scents perfuming the air. Bordering the gardens and the property were a tall fence and mature trees and bushes. The purple flowers on the lilac trees called to Casey, but she'd have to spend time with them another day. She had a goal in mind and cataloging the plants would have to wait.

When she found the two girls, she cleared her throat. "Hi, Delilah, Phillipa. I hope you don't mind me interrupting. I like gardens too, and thought I'd come see what you're growing. If you don't want me out here, just tell me, and I'll leave."

Delilah smiled. "No, you're fine. This is the one place we can be alone. None of the others follow us. We only get a few minutes each day, and it's lovely out here. Will you help us practice?"

Casey sat on the bench between the path and the garden. "How old are you two?"

Delilah continued pulling weeds. "I'm sixteen, and Phillipa's fifteen."

Wringing her hands, she considered them. "I want you two to be explicit in what you're asking of me."

Delilah scrunched up her face. "I saw in one of the newspapers that you helped some vampires who'd been poisoned with silver. Only a witch can do that. I recognized you as soon as you walked into the kitchen ... you're a witch ... a coven witch, right? I don't know much, but I know that much. So, can you help us?"

"You can't test for close to ten years, if not more. I know it's exciting, but what are you so worried about?"

Phillipa wiped her hands on her jeans. "We don't know any witches. We don't have a coven. She may have read about you, but I was at the restaurant when you pulled the silver from that vampire, then you disappeared ... that's how I knew what you were. When I saw you walk in today, I had to reach out to you. We were at school when things started happening. We've tried to hide, but we don't know what we're doing. A store said we stole something, but I touched it and it started to burn. I freaked out and ran ... I just ... I'm sorry." She ducked her head and went back to pulling weeds.

Lifting her clasped hands to her mouth, Casey stared at the two girls. "Don't apologize to me, hon. I'll see what I can do for you two. Do your parents know?" They both shook their heads. "Okay, I'll look into it. For now, give me your hands."

They each took one of her hands. She pulled them into her own mental glass bubble. Once there, they both gasped. Eyes wide, they stood frozen for a moment before turning in place then tentatively taking a step and moving around.

Once Casey knew they were going to be okay, she said, "Okay, let me look." It took a few seconds, but she found a magic primer book on her bookcase. She hadn't seen or used the book in over fifteen years. She wondered if the magic of her sphere helped put the book where it needed to be. A quick spell duplicated it for each of the girls, and she handed them out. Then, she projected the directions on how to move the books directly to their own mind bubbles. "Got it?"

It took them a second to shift their focus from their surroundings to the book she was handing them. Once they did, they nodded, and, slowly, one by one, first the books disappeared and then they did. She opened her eyes, and after a few seconds, they both did as well. "That should get you two started. It isn't ideal, but it's better than nothing."

Phillipa's hands were shaking. "I knew you were a witch ... but I didn't, you know, I guessed. That was ... that was amazing. Your bubble, it was ... I can't believe what I just saw. Can I do that one day?"

After Zen's reaction, Casey no longer knew what other witches could do with their glass bubbles. She didn't want to overpromise. She shrugged. "I'll be honest, that's my strength. I don't know. But you'll have a magical strength, too. Now, I have to go in and speak with Blake. Good luck, you two."

She retraced her steps, again appreciating what Cindy had created, and found Blake waiting for her in the living room. There was a small den that Casey hadn't seen in her initial tour of the house. It was a private room that she could use for her interviews. She and Blake stepped in. She sat behind the desk, and Blake took the chair opposite. Not liking the desk between them, she scooted the chair around, so they were sitting next to each other.

"Hi, Blake, I'm Casey. I know you're supposed to be formal with me, but for right now, I really need you to trust me. We need to figure out what happened to you a week ago."

Blake's brow furrowed. "What ... happened to me? Nothing happened to me. I'm fine."

Casey bit her lip. "No, you're not. And if you don't get this figured out, you'll become dangerous, and you *will* commit a crime."

Her eyes grew to the size of saucers, and she gaped at Casey. "You believe me that I didn't do anything wrong?"

Nodding, Casey placed a hand on the girl's forearm. "Actually, I do. I think you ended up in a really bad place, and need some hard truths, but I don't think you did anything wrong ... yet."

The girl paled. "What do you think I'll do?"

Casey rubbed her hand over her lower face, then quickly scraped her thumb over her sharpest tooth. The scent of blood overtook the room. "Ouch, my thumb, it's bleeding." *Maybe I need to work on my acting skills.*

Stiffening, Blake's focus lasered on Casey's bloody thumb, much the way Kam's had early that morning. Instead of putting it in her mouth, she held it out between them, letting the blood pool. Blake began to shake; her hand rose slowly until it cupped Casey's. She leaned in, mesmerized. Ignoring everything but Casey's thumb, Blake hand began to tremble. Then, in one sudden motion, the thumb was in Blake's mouth, and she sucked hard.

Casey could feel the girl's need as a slow trickle of blood slipped from her to Blake. More than what Kam took, but not nearly enough for a fledgling vampling.

After a minute, the girl moaned, then froze, pulling the hand away. She looked horrified. "What have I done? What did I do?"

Casey checked out her thumb, but it was already healed. "You need blood, Blake, and I can't provide it. You are a new vampire."

Her head shook fast. "No, I'm not."

Casey huffed out a laugh. "Denying it won't change the fact that that's exactly what you are. If you don't feed soon, you'll attack someone, and probably kill them. I could give you more blood, but my being a vampire as well, my blood won't help you. The other side of the coin, you'll feel lust for whomever you feed from." Casey wanted to growl. "I could tear out the eyes of whoever change someone as young as you."

The fear rolled off Blake. "What do I do?"

Checking her watch, she saw they had over forty minutes left. She reached out and found ... Lucas, he must've been close. Lucas felt her push, and a second later misted into the room. "Casey, dear, how may I be of assistance?"

She quickly explained what she'd figured out. He considered Blake. "Have you figured out who made her?"

Casey shook her head. "I figured we'd worry about that after we satiate her immediate needs. Blood first."

He sighed in agreement and misted away. It took only a moment and he returned with a human donor, a young woman wearing stone-washed jeans and a light-blue t-shirt. Her brown hair was tied back in a high ponytail.

"Blake, you need to take blood from the arm, it will settle your nerves."

All color drained from her face. "But I can't. That's awful! Blood?" Her body recoiled at the word. Watching her, Casey recognized her own initial reaction and felt bad for the girl. She'd reacted in almost the same way when she first learned she was a vampire and had to drink blood. Searching the room, she found a small trash can, fearing the worst.

Casey placed her hand on the girl's arm. "I know this sounds awful, but you have to trust me, trust us. Someone made you into a vampire, and if you don't do this now, the need for blood will force you to take it from someone. If you lose control, that taking won't be pretty."

"Or safe," Lucas added. His warm voice added a calmness to the room.

Blake's eyes darted between them, and, hands shaking, she nodded. "What do I need to do?"

The blood donor stepped forward and reached out her arm. Blake extended her hands, then paused with a yelp. "I have more teeth in my mouth!"

Casey couldn't help her chuckle. "You need them to break through her skin. Trust me, it won't hurt. When you're done, lick the wound, and it will go away. You have healing properties now."

The baby vampire slowly lifted the arm to her mouth and began to feed from the human's arm. They had to help her stop as well, being too young to know the signs to watch for. Lucas agreed to help with blood donors until they had Blake figured out.

"Let me know what you figure out, Casey. Call my house and leave a message. The more I know, the more I can assist you." He smiled warmly.

"Will do. And thank you for your quick help." She gave him a squeeze.

Once he left, Blake's eyes seemed to glow, and she smiled. Her face was pale, and she looked nauseas, but healthy. Casey remembered that feeling from the first time she'd had blood. It was both wonderful and horrible. "I haven't felt this good in weeks. Thanks! But I feel nauseous."

Grasping her hand, Casey's thumb rubbed soothingly. "The blood is yours now. I know mentally it's hard to figure out, but your body knows what to do with it. It'll get easier."

Blake nodded.

Sitting back, Casey smiled. "Are you up to me figuring out who made you?"

Chapter 8

Blake leaned back in her seat. "How will you figure out what happened to me? The police already asked me." Despite the blood she'd just received, her nervousness filled the room. Casey could see her jaw clench and feel the need thrum through her at someone figuring out how she'd ended up the way she was.

There was a long silence as Casey considered the question. The girl continued to sit, her dark skin pale with apprehension, eyes wide. Her fear wafted off her. "Are you scared I'm going to hurt you?"

She shook her head. "I don't know. How do vampires read minds? Will it hurt? Will you wipe the memories away? Once you have the memory, can you tell the police about it?" Casey wasn't sure if Blake blinked as she sat tight as a rope, but she finally took a breath. "I just don't know what to expect."

"I'm not going to cause you pain, Blake." Casey leaned back in her seat. "I won't be entering your mind as a vampire. Others here have figured this out, though I'm not really trying to advertise it. I'll be entering your mind as a witch. I can review a memory, see what happened, and retreat. In all honesty, you shouldn't feel a thing. Though I can tell the cops what I saw, it won't be able to help you. It's just my word, and as of yet, that won't be enough."

"So, why do this?"

"So that you know." Casey slid her hand into Blake's. "I can review this memory alone, or I can unlock it so that you know what happened."

Her eyes widened. "Yes! I want to know." Her body trembled and she leaned forward. "Please."

"I'd prefer to review it first, make sure there isn't anything traumatic."

"No. If I'm going to let you into my mind, I want to know what you find out too." Her resolve was absolute. As much as it frustrated Casey, she knew she'd feel the same way. With a final nod, Casey bit her lip and agreed. Having something taken away from her wouldn't make Casey happy. If someone had gone through and covered up one of Blake's memories, they were both about to learn who and why.

"Okay, let's do this." Casey squeezed Blake's hand and entered her mind. She saw a few boxes, similar to what she'd seen in her friend Ginger's mind a couple of weeks ago. There were clear boxes surrounding a red box, a blue box and a golden yellow box. The blue box would be the true memory that had been covered up by the golden yellow one. The red would be a command given to Blake.

This appeared to be the same manipulation Jude had done, but maybe it was the pattern of any emotion vampire. Though her gut clenched at the thought of Jude having a hand in this, she forced herself to calm down. *I won't make any assumptions. Watch what happened, find out the truth.*

Casey connected to Blake's consciousness. "Are you ready for this?" She felt Blake jerk in her hand as she spoke in her mind.

Blake's internal voice shook in response. "God above, this is the weirdest thing I've ever done, and I drank a stranger's blood today. Holy hell, what if that doner had a disease?"

With a snicker, Casey said, "Vampires don't need to worry about getting sick, not from blood. Now, I'm going to show you a memory. It will be like watching a show on TV. Once we're done, I'm going to release you and check out a few other memories. I know you want to be part of all of this, but please trust me."

Casey smelled her frustration, but before Blake could respond, she dipped them both into the blue box, her true memory.

'I shouldn't have volunteered to stay late. The kids wanted to hear the end of the story, but it's so dark, and I hate being out alone. It's only a mile and a half, but I just want to be home.'

A steady beat of steps behind me. My heart began to pound faster. Shooting a glance over my shoulder, I saw a plump man with dark-rimmed glasses, brown hair, and brown eyes, who stood just shorter than her. He wore brown slacks and a white button-down shirt. A tie was loosely hanging from around his neck, and he held a briefcase.

'Stop freaking out Blake, he looks like a businessman coming from downtown, just like you. Just focus and head home.'

Suddenly there was another man standing in front of me, I would've run into him if he hadn't put his hands out and steadied me. His piercing blue eyes stared into my soul. "You will not move, you will not make a sound, you will stand here and wait for me, my precious pawn."

Why can't I say no to him? "Yes sir."

Over the next few minutes, I stood there in terror. I couldn't yell out my fear. I couldn't run and hide. All I could do was watch as the beautiful man, with the jewel-like blue eyes moved to the man who had been following me and punch him in the throat.

The man tried to crawl away, but the enchanting devil leaned over and whispered into his ear, then I heard a snap. My body shook, but I couldn't turn away. Bile filled my mouth, but there wasn't anything I could do but cry.

The man smiled at me, then licked up my neck to my ear. A shiver ran through my body. "Go over *and punch the dead man, love, until I tell you to stop."*

Once he called me back, he bit my neck. My vision blurred and I sank to the sidewalk. Head pounding, his mouth moved to my ear. "You'll be a fun surprise for all those goody two-shoes. Once you start killing people, you'll either come home to me, or be killed. Either way, you'll be a lovely tool."

His wrist landed on my mouth, and blood filled me. His eyes drew me in again. "Drink until I tell you you're done, and then you'll forget it all. Don't worry dear, it will all be gone."

Casey pulled them out of the real memory. She didn't need to check out the red box, she knew what she'd find. As gently as she could, she cleared out the blocks, returning Blake's memories to her. She deserved to have her mind back.

She slid from Blake's mind and thanked the girl. Now all she had to do was figure out who she could tell that Blake hadn't killed Mayor Simmon's aide, she'd been framed by Jude. The bigger question became ... why?

Chapter 9

All the girls were in bed, or at least their bedrooms, as Casey made her way to her car at ten p.m. When she originally spoke with Officer Shade about the job, he'd mentioned ten-hour shifts. Cindy explained she really only wanted the help three days a week. That worked well, especially with Kam. The day had been long, and Casey felt like she hadn't seen her daughter at all.

She wanted to go home and give Kam a hug but knew her daughter would be asleep. *I haven't even had her for a week, and already I'm in love!*

She decided she'd stop by Cambia House before heading home to discuss with Sydney what she'd found out about Blake. There was also the call she'd promised to Lucas. While there, she also wanted to check in with Jen about training Kam. Her daughter was too young for regular training, but Jen was free for the rest of summer, and if she was already misting, Jen would be great at figuring out a way to make training fun ... a game.

At this time of night, the drive took no time, and Casey soon found herself standing in the foyer. Though it was late, vampires tended to be more active at night, and the house was buzzing with lights and voices. An animated group floated in from the front room. Casey headed that way. A few vampires played cards while others watched, cheering at different plays. Unfortunately, Sydney was one of the players. She felt bad for the fool playing against the house's security officer.

Searching the room, Casey saw Jen sitting at a side table reading a book. Giving the card game a final look, Casey made a beeline to her friend, flopping into the chair opposite her. "Hey, Jen. Why read in all this insanity?"

Holding up a hand, Jen continued to read until she got to a finishing point, and then, finding a scrap of paper to mark her place, she shut the book. "Hi, Case. Your daughter is adorable, and, holy hell, you have a daughter!"

A smile took over her face, and Casey leaned back in her seat. "It's crazy, right? Skyler just dropped Kam off, telling me she loved her but couldn't handle her anymore. She didn't say why, but I'm guessing it's because Kam needs blood ... or maybe it's the misting."

Jen's brow furrowed. "She really didn't give you anything?"

Sighing, Casey shrugged. "She said there was a letter in the suitcase, but when Riley unpacked, she didn't fine one."

"Would Skyler have lied?"

"I don't think so." Casey shifted in her seat. "But the important part is, we have her now, and she's here to stay. I'm not giving her up."

After saying the words, she realized just how much she meant them. The girl was her daughter, and no one would take her away from her. Casey stood and moved to the kitchen to grab a cup of tea. There was a tray of cookies on the counter, so she stacked a few on a plate, and took them back to the table. She and Jen each dug in, eating the oatmeal raisin cookies as the other side of the room cheered and jeered over the card game.

Once they'd eaten two cookies each, Casey leaned in. "Okay, now for the big ask." Jen mouth rolled in as she bit her lips and her eyes narrowed. "Kam can mist. She needs to learn how to control it and when it's appropriate to use that skill. I'm spending my mornings working with the witch circle and three days a week I'm at my new job ... I know this is a big request, but could you set up a schedule and work with her?"

Jen's eyes became saucers. "Me? But I'm not a vampire, Case."

"I know, but you're great with kids and finding ways to teach with games. You're the best person I can think of to do this."

Jen collapsed back, gaping at Casey. "Would I be doing this alone?"

Casey shook her head. "No, Riley will be bringing her around when I'm busy, so you'll have her. Kam seems to really like Riley."

"And I'll help, as will the other vampires of the house." Rowan's low voice came from behind her, reassuring them both. His hands landed on her shoulders, resting lightly. Casey turned and smiled wide. He leaned down to give her a quick kiss. "It's nice of you to come home for a visit, love." Her heart melted at his words, but Casey forced herself to stay focused on their conversation.

The scent of relief rolled off Jen as she smiled. "Okay, yeah. I can do it. I mean, I got you to pass your witch tests. I know how to train a Strega girl."

A loud cheer came from the group at the other end of the room and then the large crowd broke up. Watching, Casey jumped up. "I need to talk to Sydney." Turning back to Jen, she gave her friend a big hug. "Thanks, Jen. I really appreciate it. I don't know how much time I'll be able to spend here in the next couple of weeks, but I know you'll be great with Kam."

She headed across the room and approached Sydney. After her win, Sydney glowed with excitement. Casey tapped her arm, and the acting head of security spun to face her. While Cyran was out looking for Jude, Sydney was performing his duties. "Hi, Sydney. Kudos on your win. If you have a few minutes, I'd like to discuss something with you before I head back to witch house."

The vampire squinted and shook her head, as if switching her brain over from poker to the real world, then nodded. "Let's move to the study room to talk." She almost yelled to be heard over all the others in the room.

Sydney led the way down the hall. The room, one of Casey's favorites in Cambia House, had a huge oak table and a few paintings on the walls. It was a peaceful room and most of Casey's studying for her college degree had been done at that table. She went and sat in one of the wooden chairs. Sydney sat across from her, and Rowan, who had followed them in, sat at the head of the table.

Eyeing him, one of Casey's eyebrows almost hit her hair line. "Were you invited?"

His mouth quirked up in a smile. "I missed you ... and I assumed if you wanted the acting head of house security, it was a topic I'd be interested in as well."

She shrugged and gave him a tiny smile, then told them about Blake, what Jude had done to her, and to the mayor's aide. "I have a few worries. First of all, I don't think Blake should be in custody. She was attacked—a victim, not the attacker. I think Officer Shade should be contacted, but I'm not sure what can be done. The only evidence is in Blake's mind. Unless we can find a way to use my abilities as evidence, I'm not sure how I can help her."

Rowan nodded. "I'll talk with Lucas about this. Being such an old vampire, he has some sway, and he may also have some ideas. The evidence should show that the attack was done by a different size hand than this girl's. Sydney and I can take lead on this."

Relief flooding through her, Casey faced Sydney again. "I'm also worried about Jude's end-game. He doesn't like making vampires, drinking blood isn't his thing. So, if he's creating ignorant vamplings, he wouldn't have done this with just one person. How many vampires did he create? Why is he doing it? How long ago were they created? If he created several, they'll be hitting blood lust in the next week. And if we don't find these vamplings now, there will be real crimes ... deaths across the city."

Chapter 10

A warm heat built within Casey as sensations pulsed between her legs. A tight squeeze of her breast and then a tongue was in her mouth. Arching up, she kissed back, moaning into the sweet taste, rubbing against the fingers that were playing havoc on her body.

And then they were all gone. Falling back, she groaned. "I can't believe that's how you're choosing to wake me up." Her heart beat fast, and it took her a moment to get her breath back as her body trembled with need.

A soft laugh and the bed bounced, and then Riley was off and getting ready for the day. "If you can think of a better way to wake up, Case, get up before me. Now, you have a lot to do today, but I woke you early enough to spend some quality time with Kam this morning."

Casey sat up and watched as Riley got dressed. "I need to shower, and I arranged for Jen to set up a training schedule for her so that the three of you can help her figure out her misting."

Riley nodded. "Good, and I know you need to shower. Hop to it, time's a wasting, fang-girl."

After her shower, Casey found Riley sitting on the floor with Kam, the toddler's hair as wet as her own. Riley must have helped her to get cleaned up. They were playing a board game. When Casey walked in, her tiny replica threw herself at her, earning Casey a baby bear hug. She didn't realize how much she needed one until she got it. Kissing her daughter on each cheek, she set her down, lowering herself to join them.

Face glowing with happiness, Kam started to babble about the day before. "And then Riley took me to park and slide, and then to a house with so many people, and then ice cream, and then here, and then we had pizza."

Laughing, Casey watched as Riley took her turn in the game. "Breathe Kam, we have time, you don't need to get it all out in one breath! It sounds like you had a lovely time. From the top. What's your favorite thing to do at the park?"

Her face scrunched up. "Oh! That dumb girl! She hogged the swings, and then she wouldn't let me play with her and her sister and their dolls. Her mom was scared of Riley. They were just dumb." Kam swung her head to Riley. "Right Riley?"

Riley sighed. "We talked about your language. Everyone has a right to play with whomever they want to. It isn't our fault they lost out on playing with the coolest kid in town." She grabbed Kam up as she said the words, giving the young girl a tickle hug. Kam giggled, a lightness filling her.

Casey loved seeing them together, but a sadness filled that she was missing out on these activities, but she loved that Kam had Riley. "Okay cool kid, tell me, what's your favorite flavor of ice cream?"

Biting her tiny lip, her eyes squinted in concentration. "They're all good, but I love chocolate and marshmallow."

Riley chuckled. "Sounds like another vampire I know. Though, to be fair, she had to try just about every flavor at the shop before she settled on the one she wanted."

Casey's smile was so big it hurt. "Of course, she did, how else could she decide?"

Kam's face scrunched up. She looked very serious. "Daddy, will mama come today? I miss her."

A knife to her gut wouldn't have hurt as much. Kam looked so hopeful to see Skyler again, the parent who'd loved her and raised her, her whole life. And in an instant abandoned her.

She pulled Kam onto her lap for a quick hug and kissed the top of her damp head. "Not today love, she doesn't like to come to the big city." She placed her back down to continue playing her game.

"She doesn't? But there's ice cream here! With marshmallows. There weren't marshmallows in our ice cream back home." Kam's face was very serious when she said this.

Casey nodded in understanding. Marshmallows were important to ice cream after all. "I'll tell you what, when I know she's coming, you'll be the first person I tell. But I don't think it will be soon, sweetheart. She wants to give us some time together. Would that be okay with you?"

Her chin dipped and her eyes got wide. Casey saw the girl blink back tears, but she finally nodded. "While I'm getting to know you better, will Riley be around too? She's nice, I like her."

Casey smiled and Riley reached over to ruffle her hair. "Of course, pipsqueak. I'm here to watch you while your Daddy is busy. I'm not going anywhere. You're stuck with me and Daddy."

Kam gave a small smile and bounced. Then she paused. "And I won't get in trouble if I need ..." She didn't finish her sentence. She didn't know how to ask for blood.

"No. If you need blood, you can ask Riley if you can suck on her thumb. If it gets to be too much for her, we'll find someone else."

Riley's eyes narrowed. "But what are the rules?"

"Don't put anyone's finger but yours in my mouth and don't put my fingers in anyone else's mouth."

"Right you are, pipsqueak!"

After that, the two finished their game and cleaned up. Then the trio went down for breakfast, pancakes and sausage. Riley gathered Kam and a bag of snacks and toys and took off to Cambia House for kid care for the day.

For their circle work that day, the group decided to do some research on ways to bind a person, specifically a vampire, and if the work could be adapted down to a smaller circle. Though Zen had mocked her, the group saw the benefit of the research. They went to the library and began their studies. After an hour, Casey asked if Tilly could give her a beginning lesson on working with ice.

The two headed to the gazebo in the backyard. Tilly sat on the swinging bench and considered the question. "There is water all around us, finding that water and forming ice isn't hard. If you think of the process as performing several steps in a row, instead of on big push, it isn't bad ... kind of like how you brought the plates and cookies separately in your test a few years back."

Dropping her head into a hand, Casey groaned. "You knew, too?"

Chuckling, Tilly nodded. "Yeah, I could feel the two pushes in succession. It's probably because it's how I do a lot of my work as well. I'll try to do this without making too much of a mess, but I'll probably fail." She held out her hand. "First I call the water to me." Casey felt the push, and a sphere of water, about the size of a golf ball, appeared above Tilly's hand, then it disintegrated, splashing over her hand and onto the floor of the gazebo. She laughed. "See a mess. Now you try, just that."

Casey bit her lip considering. She played back everything she'd just seen and felt. Closing her eyes, she tried to envision the lines of magic Tilly'd used. She traced the lines that moved to and from her as she pushed out her magic to find the water. Holding out her hand, she opened her eyes and tried to imagine collecting it. Pushing out her magic, fireworks of water exploded a foot in front of her, drenching her.

Grumbling, she saw Tilly cover her mouth to stop the laughter, though her eyes were dancing with mirth.

It took a few minutes, but Tilly got herself under control. "Okay, that was really good."

With a raised eyebrow Casey objected. "Really good?"

Tilly nodded emphatically. "Yes, you called the water to you, that's a great first step. At least you didn't just sit there with your hand out. I mean, I assume the water didn't come from a cup in the kitchen you pre-setup, right?"

Shaking her head, Casey assured her tutor that wasn't the case. Though, thinking about it, that would've been brilliant.

Tilly smiled. "See, that's good then, you can call water, that's the hardest part. Every new water witch ends up wet ... trust me. So, next time, think about trapping the water in a shape. A sphere is easiest, though you can do any shape you want. But I'll show you the next step. Each witch is a bit different. When I freeze, I'm not really making water cold, I'm slowing the atoms inside the water down ... that's what I'm good at, slowing things down."

Casey's heart began to beat faster. "Wait, what? You aren't making things cold?"

Tilly's smile became wicked. "No, stand up and run in place."

Not sure where she was going, Casey followed along. Tilly's body stilled and suddenly the air around Casey became thick like a humid day in Florida. It didn't stop. The humidity got thicker and heavier. Then it was too much, and she stopped moving all together. She stared at the tiny witch and saw sweat pebbling across her brow.

With an exhalation of air, Tilly released her magic, and Casey slumped, nearly falling to the ground. Tilly smiled. "I only slowed the atoms in a small area around you, but you're big, and now I'm wiped. It's the same idea with the water. Slow the atoms in the water and the water freezes.

Sitting back down, Casey rubbed her hands together. "Can I enter your glass bubble and review what you just did to me?"

Tilly stopped moving, gaping at Casey. "Can you do that?"

Smiling, Casey shrugged. "Let's call it an exchange of skills. I'll show you mine if you show me yours."

Tilly laughed from her gut and nodded in agreement. To make things easier, Casey shifted to sit next to her on the bench, touching made the connection faster and less draining. Then she moved into Tilly's mind. Once inside she asked permission to enter the glass bubble one more time, and, upon receiving it, she was in. She could have slipped in without the permission but asking was more polite.

This bubble was smaller than Casey's and not as organized. Tilly had books stacked in a pile and a beanbag pillow for sitting on. There was a small area that could be used for practicing spells, but that was it. Casey hadn't been in many glass bubbles and wondered if she should offer to hold a class.

Taking Tilly's hand, she showed her how to make the glass bubble a bit larger. They were about to remodel, and they needed space. There was a tightening of the air and Casey's ears popped, and the sphere grew. Not a lot, but enough. The she projected the directions on creating an archive of memories and a projection screen for replaying them.

Gaping at her, Tilly asked, "Is this how you always knew everything? You could always watch and rewatch any class?"

Not feeling offended because the question was genuine, Casey just nodded. "It helped. I'm not sure why all witches don't know this. I can't be the only one who does it, can I?" Next, she helped Tilly create a library with a table. The idea of making the area have permanent useful space could be built upon.

As Tilly contemplated the restructuring of her glass bubble, Casey reviewed the memory of creating a ball of ice, and of slowing the atoms around her while she ran in place. The two actions were similar, but not identical. She rewatched parts of the memory, focusing on the actions and emotions the went along with the spell. She couldn't project herself into the memory as if it were hers, but she gleaned a lot from watching it a few times. Once she felt she had a grasp on what was going on, she got Tilly's attention, and removed herself from Tilly's mind.

Tilly stayed in her glass bubble a bit longer. Once out, her face was alight. "That was amazing. I had no idea the flexibility of our mental storage. I know we're out here for me to teach you, but Casey, thank you."

Nodding, Casey gave her friend a half hug, before holding out a hand and trying again. She focused on the water around them, especially the puddles they'd both created under the gazebo, the sphere she wanted to create, and slowing the atoms. Three pushes. Taking a breath and biting her lip Casey lined up her images, and pulsed, the water began to gather, as it did a second pulse, it shaped itself into a ball, and her third push of magic, slowing the atoms ... a ball of ice dropped into her hand.

She almost dropped the ball as she slumped. The newness of the magic drained her, and her arms began to shake. Licking her lips, she gazed up at Tilly and smiled. "I did it."

Tilly beamed back at her. "You did, I'm really proud of you, though if I look as dead as you, we both need to sleep for a week. I'm not sure how to ask this delicately, but do you need blood?"

Closing her eyes to take inventory, Casey realized that she did need blood. If she didn't take care of her base needs prior to returning to Sand Hill Girl's Home, it would be a disaster. Taking in a deep breath, she nodded. "Yes, I do, but you aren't any better off than I am. Since you've done as much work as me, and Riley is off with Kam, I guess it's time for Damion to step up."

Tilly snorted. "That sounded as much of a question as a statement. You two will be fine. Let's go find him and tell him the good news!" She popped up, grabbing Casey's hand, and pulling her up, the ball of ice clunking to the floor.

They found the other three still in the library where they'd left them. Though he'd blanched, Damion was ready to do as he'd promised. He unfolded his tall frame from the couch he was sitting on, and they headed for the stairs.

When they got to Casey's door, Damion placed a hand on her shoulder to stop her. "I think I'd be more comfortable in my room, if that'd be okay."

She shrugged and followed him. His room was large, with a tall bed covered in brown and green soft covered linins. The bed was made. He had a matching bed set with a dresser and side table, all in dark mahogany. The walls were painted a light off white and the curtains were a light beige. It was beautiful and well kept.

Turning to her, he looked nervous. "What do we do?"

She wanted to put him at ease but knew things would get awkward if he really wasn't prepared. "I'll drink your blood, from your arm probably. The sensation will be ... well, pleasurable, for both of us."

His eyes darkened and he licked his lips. "How pleasurable?"

Her shoulders slumped. "In most cases, it leads to something ... it isn't always sex, but that isn't unusual."

His hands fisted before his palms came together in front of his face, his chin resting on his thumbs. "This will be ... difficult. I've never been with a woman."

Her jaw dropped, then her mind caught up with his words. "Oh, you aren't a virgin, you just like guys ... I get it."

He nodded slowly, hands falling to his sides.

Smiling, she closed her eyes and focused on her inner self. Forcing a change, she didn't force often, she morphed her outward appearance from female to male. First a numbness took over, then tingling permeated her full body.

When it was done, he gasped. "I always forget you can do that. If it isn't too bold," his hand rose halfway to her then froze. "Are you really? Can I see your body?"

He was doe eyed in wonder, and she felt he was asking out of curiosity, not perversion. She stripped off her shirt and saw him hold his breath. Gulping in air he continued to stare in awe. "It's amazing. Your face is so much the same, but your body ... As a female I can appreciate your beauty, but as a male you're stunning, Casey."

She quirked a smile. "No falling in love, Damion." She raised an eyebrow. "I'm just after your blood."

He smiled back. "And you'll pay for it, trust me." His voice had dropped to a husky timber and a shiver ran down her spine.

Casey was no longer sure who was in control, he stared at her way too much like the cat who'd gotten into the milk.

The two sat on the bed, and he gave her his arm. To make the drinking easier, he'd slipped out off his shirt as well. Being a witch, his scent was like candy. Her teeth descended and she slowly bit, knowing the chemistry of her body would ensure he'd enjoy the experience as much as her. His blood was headier than human blood and the effect made Casey giddy.

It didn't take long for heat to run through her veins. And she knew when she started to burn, he'd feel it too. He leaned down and licked her neck, she dropped her head to the side as far as she could while still feeding and he bit and nibbled up to her ear, moaning as she drank. The sounds he made went right to her core, a zing tingling to her cock, which jerked. The motion momentarily distracting and pleasurable.

When she finally licked his arm closed, he whispered in her ear, "Strip naked and crawl up on the bed. Hands and knees."

His words, strong and demanding made her hard and needy. Slow, and with deliberate movements, she stripped off her clothes. She didn't mind doing what he demanded, but she liked pushing a bit. He watched as she slipped off the panties, not suited for her current body, and smiled. "You put together a lovely body. This won't be our only test run, I hope. You do know gay men love to play, right. And this gay man will want to try out several things with you in this form. You're fantastic."

Every word hit home and made her want to whimper. She wasn't sure why, but her body was reacting to his every word, touch, lick.

He climbed onto the bed behind her, leaning in, his warmth seeped into her legs. She could feel his cock pressing against her as he reached down and grasped her cock and pulled in a demanding pace. She jerked back into him as heat pulled in her belly. He rubbed against her as he played.

Something cool hit her from behind, and she realized he was using lube. Using a finger, he pushed into her ass, slowly. "This okay?"

Prickles of sensation blossomed throughout her body, new and different. "I ... I think so."

He leaned to kiss, then bit her ass. "I'll go slow." He used more lube to get a second finger into her. At first her body seemed to reject this idea, but slowly she relaxed, as new avenues of pleasure erupted within her. Finally, he entered her fully with his dick. She gasped, bracing her hands, head exploding as he slowly made his way in, making sure she was ready as he slowly pushed in, inch by inch.

Once he was in her to his hilt, his hand reached around again, pumping her cock until she cried out, firework from her core snaking throughout her body. Her arms collapsed and her head hit her forearms as she gasped for air.

Just when she thought she couldn't take more, he slowly began to pump in and out of her. Damion's motion started slow, but as her groans got louder, he moved faster. Her body got used to the sensation, and his pace quickened more, and he pounded into her. Shock waves overwhelmed her, and as her mind was about to short circuit, she yelled out, hearing Damion's voice sing out with her.

Chapter 11

Taking a second shower, Casey contemplated her morning. Kam would need blood, and she trusted Riley. It seemed that Damion was going to be a willing volunteer for her, with Tilly serving as backup. *Who knew!*

Being in a mostly committed relationship with Rowan, she didn't like the feelings and needs she had, but Rowan understood. As the water streamed down, she thought about what she could control and what she couldn't. She decided there was something she could give Rowan. His preferred bed play was when she was female, and he was male. She could restrict these times to when she was with him. It was close today, but Damion's preferences gave her hope.

Dressing in slacks and a blazer, she headed out to her job. She arrived just before noon. When she knocked, Veronica answered the door and led her to the dining room. Lunch was pasta and salad with a side of garlic toast. It didn't look bad, but it wasn't up to her grandpa's standards, *he* knew how to garlic his bread.

As she started to take a bite, all the eyes of the girls were on her, though Cindy smiled to herself and ignored the drama. Before she'd taken the third bite, Casey figured out what was going on, grasped her chest theatrically and gasped, slumping in her chair.

The six girls went preternaturally still. Tammy, who didn't know how to be still for long, or quiet, asked, "Did we kill her?"

Giving it another beat, Casey jerked up and yelled, "Boo!"

All the girls jumped in their seats, several yelping. Cindy, at the head of the table snickered, then smoothed her expression. "Girls, please, we are eating. Please show some decorum and respect."

Casey picked up the toast and took a bite. "This is good, but it needs more garlic. You really should roast the full head, then rub the soft cloves on the buttered toast to get the perfect amount. You want to make sure your breath is stinky for days if you use garlic in a dish."

Blake slowly picked up the toast, which she'd been avoiding. "Aren't you a vampire? We saw an article in the newspaper. It showed a picture of Rowan Cambia, head of one of the vampire houses, and you were in the picture with him. We all started thinking that maybe you were a vampire too."

Mouth twisting up in a half-smile, she gazed at each of them in turn. "So, you decided I was a vampire, and instead of asking me right away, like mature teens, you test me with a root vegetable you *thought* was poisonous to me. Your goal was, what? To hurt me? Kill me? Tell me your end-game here, girls. I'd really like to understand your full train of thought."

Tammy blew out a breath of air that ruffled her bangs. "Yeah, I don't know that we really thought that far ahead. We just knew vampires and garlic were a connection, so we put them together. That's about it."

After taking another bite, Casey put down the toast and took a sip of her water. "Well, if I can make a suggestion: next time, think things out. This was definitely not a well thought out plan."

Phillipa's head tilted. "You're not mad at us."

Casey shrugged. "I could smell the garlic, you used enough that someone would have to be dead to not notice it ... not that for proper garlic bread, more shouldn't have been used."

Betsy, dark and quiet, stared up at her. "Aren't vampires dead?"

Nodding and huffing out a laugh, Casey considered the question. "Technically not dead. They have a heartbeat, they breathe. What's your definition of alive? Now, you have to remember, most vampires are not out to the public, nor are most witches. Though, in theory, it's safe to be out, most humans are afraid of what they don't know. Testing a person to force them to tell you what they don't want to share is generally considered a big no-no. That said, since you went to all this drama, I'll tell you ... vampires can eat garlic. You'll have to figure out a different test in the future."

Delilah, not willing to give up her query, put down her fork. "How would *you* go about finding out if someone was a vampire, or a witch, or just human?"

Casey shrugged. "I guess it depends *why* I needed to know."

Dropping her gaze to her plate, she shrugged. "I'm just curious, I guess. No real reason. I've never met anyone not human, not really, and I have questions, that's all."

Taking a bite of the pasta, Casey thought about these girls and their lives. How hard it must be to always be given small pieces of information and never the ones they wanted. "If I was in a social situation and wanted to know if someone was other than human, and I felt secure in our friendship, I'd probably just ask them. It would be important for my friend to know that I wasn't anti-vampire or anti-witch, first."

Phillipa finished off her water. "Do you consider us friends? You've only known us for a day."

Smiling, Casey shrugged. "You are all nice kids. But I don't know much about you. What do you all feel about vampires and witches? That *was* one of my conditions."

Going around the table, each girl gave her opinion of witches and vampires. They all were neutral, except Veronica. "I totally think they're fine," she said with a sneer. "Vampires are like, whatever. And witches, they're cool. Whatever." She rolled her eyes at the end.

Tammy, her best friend sitting next to her, turned to face her. "What do you have against vampires and witches?"

Veronica just stared. "What? Nothing, they're fine ... I just—it's nothing."

Casey smiled tightly at the pair. "Well, this is the type of question you usually ask in a more intimate situation anyway. Lunch is almost finished, and once we're done, I look forward to a group session."

Tammy's face lit. "Whose secrets will we reveal next?"

Chapter 12

Thursday morning, Casey decided to head to Cambia house with Riley and Kam for early practice. It was her first day off from her job and she could spend the afternoon working with the witches at witch house. She hoped they could have breakfast with Rowan and Jen. It would be something new for both her and Kam, and then she could see the obstacle course Jen had set up for her rascal of a daughter.

On the car ride over, Kam asked about Skyler again. Though they'd discussed it, it was apparent

Kam missed her mom and struggled with the idea that Skyler wasn't around. Casey seethed at the woman who refused contact with her daughter. "This is our time, Kam. Your mom wants to make sure we have space to really get to know each other. She loves you a lot, you know that. I also promise that if I hear from her, you'll be at the top of my list of people I tell. Okay?" She bit her lip, eyes wide. Kam blinked a few times before she nodded. "Okay, Daddy. I just don't want you to forget."

The words tore at Casey's heart. "I won't, I promise."

Gods above, I know she's a vampire, but how could Skyler not want contact with such an amazing girl? It took everything in her to keep her anger and disgust at the other witch off her face.

Casey reached over and squeezed Kam's knee. "I'm really excited about having Daddy-daughter time and getting to know everything I can about you."

"Me, too, pipsqueak. You're the best thing that's happened this summer," Riley said.

Kam finally relaxed with a small smile.

They parked in front of Cambia House and Casey rotated to face Kam who sat in the back. *I need to tell her more.* Though they'd concluded their talk on the drive over, Casey'd been angry, and focused on the road. Now she could give her daughter all her attention. "Kam, love, your mother and I think it would be best for you to stay with me, you know that. It goes beyond my wanting to spend time with you because I love you to pieces, because I absolutely do." She smiled wide. Kam smiled back. "You and I both need blood and have the ability to mist. As parents, we both think getting you to learn how to control your abilities and your needs is really important. You can only do that by living with me. Does that make sense? Is that okay with you?"

She stared down at her hands and bit her lip. "Yeah Daddy, it's okay. I miss mama and grandma ... but if you think this is better ... I love you, too ... and Riley. I love my Riley."

Casey quickly shot a look at Riley and saw the tough vixen's eyes widen, before she opened her door and slipped out. She opened Kam's door and smiled down and the girl. "Right. We should get in and find out what's for breakfast, shouldn't we, squirt?"

Nodding, Kam sat patiently while Riley unbuckled her from the car. "Right," Kam agreed.

They sat and ate scrambled egg sandwiches while Kam got pancakes in the shape of a unicorn, wings and everything. Looking at the artsy plate of food, Casey took a sip of coffee. "Don't Pegasi have wings and unicorns have horns? Why does that pancake have both?"

Rowan laughed. "You don't know the origin story of vampires, do you? In all your years of training, you didn't get to that?"

Taking another bite of her sandwich, she considered the question. "Origin story, like, the story of the first vampire?"

His brows waggled. "Yep. The story is vague, but I know it involves a flying unicorn. There may be a talking dog as well, but it's been awhile."

Kam's eyes widened. "Can I hear the story?"

Rowan leaned down and kissed her sticky cheek. "Maybe later, my sweetest of girls."

Jen sat back. "What else is in this fable?"

Finishing his coffee, Rowan checked his watch. "Oh, it's no fable, and there is a lot in the story, *and* I don't have time to tell it. You should ask Lucas, he's the oldest of us all, and he knows the story better than any of us. He's so old, he was probably there!"

They all laughed at that. No one was that old.

Leaning over to steal a kiss, she asked, "You have to leave now? I feel like I never get to see you."

He sighed. "I'm afraid so. I have a meeting with the mayor. We're discussing this issue you discovered with Jude. Apparently, there are several potential new vamplings in custody, and two have already attacked inmates with whom they were locked up. One died, the other survived. That means we have one full-on emotion vampire; the other is just traumatized and in need of regular blood. The meeting is with all the vampire heads, even Velvet, since this affects her house directly. It should be grand!" His sarcasm wasn't lost on any of them.

The thought of meeting with Velvet gave Casey the chills. She didn't like that vampire. She rubbed her temples, then asked. "What about Blake, what's going to happen with her?"

He stood and kissed her forehead. "Lucas is taking her under his wing, so to speak. Until she becomes a full-on vampire and needs to be sent to Velvet, he'll be a better guide." He gave her cheek one more kiss. "See you at lunch."

Once they were done eating, they headed off to the gym. Casey saw that one end of the large room had been sectioned off into an obstacle course. She climbed the bleachers that were opened for spectators and studied the rat maze that had been set up. Jen had created a series of corridors and closed rooms, each a different color, most covered with decorative wallpaper. The rooms were each completely closed off. There were no windows, doors, or visible opening beyond the roofless top to the maze.

Jen had a vampire with her each day to help reconfigure the challenges. Today it was Jaxon, though technically, Casey was there, too. Beyond restructuring, the helper would put a plate with a cookie into one of the rooms. It was Kam's job to find the cookie as quickly as she could. If she found it in under three jumps, she was rewarded with a second cookie.

As they sat and watched, Jen started to write in her book. Casey snuck a peek, and saw it was a chart of each of the colors of the rooms and corridors, and numbers under them. Jen saw her looking. "I keep track of the order she searches. It helps in her training."

"Makes sense. You're looking for patterns, like you did with me."

Jen gave a curt nod. "So, does she have any witch skills yet?"

Casey stopped breathing. "Warn a girl next time, will ya! And no. Witch abilities don't present until closer to ten. I started at six, and that was considered insanely young. She's only three."

With a shake of her head, Casey went back to studying the maze. There were four corridors—white, black, gold, and silver—each with a geometric design on the wallpaper. Then there were five rooms. Blue with white clouds, purple with yellow flowers, green with tiny bears, pink with unicorns, and red with a huge dragon that, including its tail, wrapped around three walls. The clouds and dragon looked painted. Scoping out the rooms, Casey was impressed. "That dragon is spectacular."

Jen face broke out in a smile. "I know, right. The people in this house are so creative! Speaking of dragons, as long as it's just us, why doesn't Zoryda join us? Has Kam met her yet?"

Casey shook her head. "Learning about familiars is a rite of passage for a witch. It's part of coven testing. That's why I had no idea what was happening when Zoryda first woke up and started flying around. I can't introduce them, that would've been like Grandpa introducing me to his griffin. That's a big negative."

Jen's face screwed up as she thought about that, and then she nodded. "Right, yeah, sure. I get it. I guess you do keep her away from most people, now that I think about it. That's a shame, though. I bet Kam'd love watching the dragon fly around."

She returned to the training area, and Casey watched Kam run around the gym, stirring up the other vampires in the room. Meanwhile, Jen and Jaxon figured out what they were going to do to test the girl. Once they had the game plan down, Jen called Kam over.

Kam ran to Casey first. "Don't worry about me, Daddy, I'll be good. You watch and cheer, okay?"

The earnest sincerity of the girl warmed Casey to her toes.

Casey bit her lip to keep a straight face. "I understand." Kneeling, she hugged her daughter and kissed her on each cheek. "I'm very proud of you, kiddo." Then she stood and trudged back up to the top of the bleachers.

Kam ran over to Jen who gave her a high-five then said, "Ready-set-go!"

Kam misted to the red room, then purple, then the pink, green, and finally the blue room. The cookie was in the blue room. She ate it and misted to Jen.

Once Kam was out with Jen, Jaxon put the next cookie in the white corridor. Jen gave Kam the signal, and she went through the rooms in the same order, then the corridors: silver, gold, white, and she found her cookie.

As Kam ate her cookie, Casey made her way down the bleachers to join them. Jen smiled and explained, "She always approaches the rooms in the same order. We can get her more practice in control if we choose a room near the end, or a corridor. If you're wondering, she really likes the red dragon."

Casey couldn't blame her. "This is the third day of the same rooms and corridors?"

Jen nodded. "Yeah. We'll change things up this weekend. She has amazing control. We may expand the game to areas around the house, so we aren't just in here. Use the study room, your old room, things like that. The challenge, of course, is her power level. We use cookies to help, but she's taking blood every day."

Concern bubbling up, Casey watched her daughter. "Is she always feeding from Riley?"

Riley, who'd been holding up a wall by the door, approached at her name. "Nah. There are a few of us here who have been donating. She doesn't take much, but I'm still only going to go every third day with her. I'm guessing you won't be needing my services."

"No, the witches have that covered. If I need more, I'll stop in here."

They ran the course a couple more times, but Jen switched it up, telling Kam the order she wanted her to jump through the rooms, testing her memory and listening skills. When they were done, they all played a game of kickball.

Tired, they returned to the cafeteria for lunch: tater tot casserole and a salad.

Sitting and eating, Kam stuffed a huge bite into her mouth. Barely swallowing first, she turned to Casey. "Can we go to the fireworks tonight?"

Choking on a tater tot, Casey drank some water. Jen laughed. "It *is* the fourth of July, Case. The girl just wants some excitement and normalcy in her life. Things have gotten pretty dull around here."

Glaring, Casey finally cleared her airways. "Jen, you know never to say that, even in jest. A new job, all the idiocy surrounding Jude, my sweet daughter ... dull? You are inviting trouble in!" She threw her hands up in mock exasperation ... partial mock at least.

She laughed as Rowan placed his plate next to Kam, kissed her cheek, and sat next to the girl. "Hi, my sweetest girl in the world."

She preened under his attention. "Hi, Rowan." Her small voice was full of adoration.

He took a bite of his lunch. "It seems we've found all of Jude's ticking bombs."

Casey felt a weight fall from her shoulders. "What about Blake?" she asked once again. She felt like a dog with a bone, having asked that morning, but she was worried about the girl. "Will she be able to leave the group home? She's obviously innocent."

He shrugged. "That's a harder situation. There are legal issues that need to be cleared up. I've also met the parents and they weren't very supportive of their child before, and it doesn't look like her being a vampire will be any better. They appear to want to wash their hands of her." The underlying snarl in his voice told Casey his opinion of the situation. Unsupportive families were a sore spot for Rowan.

Casey gaped at him. "They're anti-vampire, even with their child having been attacked?"

He pursed his lips. "Lucas is working on them with Gwen. If they continue to be obstinate, Gwen will take her in and care for her."

Jen paused at the sound of her mom's name. They'd just reconnected and, though they were working on the relationship, it was still a bit rocky. "I think Gwen, my ... ah ... Mom ... would be good at helping this girl with her transition. I think she'd be kind and warm with someone who'd been transitioned against their wishes."

They heard the front door crash open and all the people in the room swiveled towards the commotion. Micah, a stout vampire with brown eyes and curly, dirty-blond hair hanging to his shoulders, ran into the cafeteria searching the faces at each table. When he found Rowan, he froze. "Come quick! Cyran is dead!"

Chapter 13

Casey gaped at Micha as he stood in the middle of the cafeteria, breathing hard after making his proclamation. His words stabbed into her heart. Something in her broke. A tear traced a path down her face as her insides went cold and her hands shook. The room began to waver like a watercolor painting and breathing became difficult.

The trembling traveled until it encompassed her whole body.

A pressure in her chest felt like a vise grip squeezing tight. Why hadn't she ever told him she loved him? She wasn't in love with him, but she loved him. He meant so much to her as a friend, a trainer, and once as a lover ... and now he was gone ... dead. He'd been her connection to so much in the last four years and if her heart hadn't belonged to Rowan ... it could've been his. Colors swirled and she slowly blinked, but nothing made sense.

Cold numbness tingled her fingers as the cacophony of sound crashed around her. She didn't know what to do.

A small body climbed into her lap, but she couldn't give Kam the attention she needed. She wrapped her arms around her daughter, but she couldn't feel the tenderness the girl deserved. Casey was breaking inside, piece by piece.

A sticky finger touched her cheek. "Why is Daddy crying?"

Am I crying? I don't feel the tears.

Riley's blurry form, all spiky black hair, entered her line of vision, as she continued to stare towards Micha. "Hey, baby girl. Why don't we go for a walk? We can go get some ice cream in town together. What do you think?"

The girl squirmed out of Casey's arms, sliding to the floor. "Ice cream?"

Then Rowan appeared. Time stopped having meaning, just the disappearance and appearance of different forms. He took her hands. "Let's go to my office and find out what happened." He pulled her up and engulfed her in a hug, warming some of the numb spots. Casey breathed in his scent, grounding herself in his spicy mint that was Rowan. She wrapped her arms around him as her tears fell harder.

After a few minutes of letting her cry, the two left the dining hall. They were joined by Micha, Sydney, and Jen. Rowan handed Casey a box of tissues, then turned to Micha. "Tell us what happened. Where is Cyran right now?"

Still looking shocked, Micha wet his lips, his eyes red from his own tears. "We found the central office of H.O.A.P."

Casey wanted to snarl at the name: Humans Only, Anti-Paranormal. A group of humans hell-bent on eliminating all non-humans from the planet. They wanted to kill the witches and vampires. At Jen and Casey's graduation, they'd poisoned some of the hors d'oeuvres with a compound that would only harm vampires. In the end, Casey learned that Jude was part of the group.

The idea of stirring up fear thrilled the emotion vampire and gave him a constant food source.

With a shake of her head, Casey continued to listen to Micha. "The group had patrols out and we were watching them. Cyran decided he wanted to find out what they were up to, so he got out, without weapons, to talk to a patrol pair." Casey wanted to bang her head on the wall. *Of course he did.* "He didn't want to engage them or seem threatening. The patrols tended to move in twos or threes. When he got to them, they handed him a flyer. I guess they thought he was a regular bloke to be recruited."

Micha dug in the inside pocket of his jacket and pulled out a piece of folded up paper. He handed it to Sydney. When she opened it, it advertised in large light blue letters: "H.O.A.P, bringing hope to the city, one human at a time." After sneering at it, she passed it on.

When the flyer got to Casey, she saw that there were words and pictures, showing a bright future full of humans. The pictures showed people hand in hand, running through a field. In a second one, they were buying groceries. The last had them sitting in a park eating sandwiches. All the people looked so happy and, apparently, they could only do these things without vampires or witches about. *Because witches and vampires don't shop, or go to the park, or eat.* Before she could rip the flyer up, she passed it to Jaxon.

Micha watched, making sure everyone had a chance to look the flyer over before continuing. "The window of the car was open, and I heard Cyran ask if the people knew Jude. They didn't know who he was talking about, so Cyran showed them the picture we had. They were like, 'oh, him, he's our leader, Indra.' When Cyran asked if they knew their leader was a vampire, they freaked, saying Cyran was lying to them, pointing their guns, telling him to take it back."

Rubbing his hands on his pants, Micha looked agitated. "The men, you know, they were idiots. They kept saying it wasn't possible because Jude had been out in the sun, or they'd seen him eat garlic. All these superficial reasons why he couldn't be a fucking vampire. Cyran asked if they'd seen the news with the updated information about vampires, then the men, the *idiots*, kept insisting the people on TV were lying or were actors. They were trying to fool the public to make the humans easier to take over."

Micha's hands shook as he spoke. His breathing got rough.

Jen asked, "Do you want some water or coffee or something else?" He nodded. Jen slipped out and returned with a steaming mug and a few cookies. Micha smiled and sipped the tea. Casey could smell that it was chamomile, a calming brew.

Once his heart rate had slowed down and his breathing had evened out, he continued. "When those idiots proved they wouldn't listen to reason, Cyran asked, what if he could show them proof that vampires could be out in the sun. They just laughed at him. They said it was impossible. So, Cyran showed them his fangs as they descended."

Casey winced, thinking, *Again, of course he did. Why would he think of his own safety when he had a point to prove ... his people to protect?* He would do anything to make this world safer, even try to convince people too limited to be reasoned with.

Micha made fists as he stared Rowen directly in the eyes. "I failed you, sir. I was supposed to be his back up, protect him. When they saw his teeth, they both raised their guns and shot in one motion. They didn't warn him or give him a chance, they just fucking shot. I leapt from the car and grabbed him, getting him into the back seat and driving here as fast as I could. But it's too late, he's dead."

Rowan's hands were steepled in front of his face. "Did they shoot him in the head?"

Micha jerked back as if slapped. "No, sir. They had a gun which I believe shot silver bullets. At least that's what Cyran choked out. His last word was silver. They shot him in the chest with that. The second gun, sir, it shot tranquilizer darts."

Before she knew what she was doing, Casey ran out the door towards the front of the house. Barreling through the front door, across the yard and out the gate, she almost ran into Rowan, who had misted to the car with Sydney. The two were pulling Cyran out of the car and onto the sidewalk.

Dropping to her knees, Casey scanned Cyran, found the bullet and several fragments of silver. With all the strength she had, she pulled it out. A huge chunk landed in her hand, larger than any she'd pulled out before. Someone grabbed it from her before it could affect her magic as she did a secondary scan. Nothing, she'd gotten it all.

Her head swam and started to pound. Pulling out that much silver hurt, but she didn't care. If there was any chance, any at all, she was going to push through.

She laid a hand on his chest, his heart still didn't beat. No pulse. Placing her cheek on his chest, she breathed in his scent. "Come on, Cyran, breathe."

Cyran continued to lie on the ground, not moving. Tears soaked his shirt and she whispered to him in quiet pleas to wake up. "I've removed the silver, it's time for you to wake up. We still need you. No more sleeping on the job."

Hands pulled her up to sitting, and Rowan engulfed her in a quick, fierce hug. Then she leaned back on her heels and watched, but Cyran's condition didn't change.

Rowan knelt next to his old friend, someone who'd known him almost his whole life. His face was haunted as he gazed at a man he'd known almost from his first days as a vampire. Hand trembling, he split open his thumb. He let a pool of blood form before he placed it in Cyran's mouth. They all waited ... nothing happened.

As they watched Cyran for any twinge of life, hoping for something, Casey heard Kam and Riley approach. Kam spoke with a continuous prattle with Riley's few interjections. Looking over to watch her daughter, she saw as Kam noticed them. She leapt up into the air to wave, then she tripped and fell onto the hard cement.

Stunned, Kam stared at her hurt hand for a moment before she ran over to Casey crying. "Daddy, Daddy, I hurt myself. I'm bleeding!"

Cyran's broken body lay on the ground between them. Not caring about an adult she had to crawl over, Kam climbed over the obstacle, like a vampire mountain to conquer. All her focus was on Casey. In her haste, her tiny fingers, with their cut from their fall, slid into Cyran's mouth.

Casey watched everything as if it were in slow motion. Her daughter crawling over Cyran, the bloody fingers entering his mouth, and his lips quivering after a few drops of blood dripped into his mouth.

Kam reached Casey and grabbed a quick but fierce hug, and then ran to Riley. "Riley, my fingers went into that man's mouth. I think they leaked."

Everyone in the group froze at her innocent words.

Riley directed Kam towards the house. "What did I tell you about putting your fingers in other people's mouths?"

"To not to."

"Let's go get you washed up, silly goose."

Kam's tiny voice floated to them over the wind. "Sorry, Riley."

Chapter 14

Casey sat on the roof of Cambia House with Kam, Riley, and Jen. They'd set up a blanket and pillows to watch the skies. The fireworks wouldn't start for a few hours, but the day was nice, and Casey needed the distraction. They had water and juice for Kam and were laughing at the stories Kam told about bears and winged horses. Casey was pretty sure they came from Saturday morning cartoons but wasn't positive. The girl had quite the imagination.

A few hours earlier, after Riley had taken Kam away, they'd checked Cyran over again, and found his heart had slowly started beating. Rowan had misted him to the medical suite in the basement. The others followed. It didn't take long for everyone to be shooed away by the medical staff. Cyran was healing, but they were all getting in the way.

Knowing she wasn't going to just up and leave, especially with Kam's desire to see the fireworks, Casey found a phone and called the witches. She explained what had happened and let them know she'd be staying with the vampires for the rest of the day. She'd head back with Kam and Riley after the fireworks. Tilly told her if it got late, to spend the night and return Friday. Casey didn't think that would be necessary.

One of the vampires had dug through the storage cabinets and found an old trunk of toys. Going through them, Kam had decided to bring up a set of jacks. The group of them sat in a circle tossing the metal pieces down, bouncing the ball, and picking the pieces up. When the challenge was one or even two jacks, it wasn't bad, but as they had to pick up more and more of the sharp twisted pieces, Kam's small hand was a hinderance. She giggled as she tried over and over.

The house chef, a short Mexican woman with dark hair and brown eyes, came up onto the roof. She gazed at the group and zeroed in on Casey. "You, girl, you haven't been working your shifts."

Casey gave Monica a wary glance. "I'm not even living here right now."

Monica gave her a piercing glare, pointedly looking her up and down. The message was clear.

Sighing, Casey shook her head. She grabbed the bouncy ball and took her turn. She bounced the ball, grabbed four jacks, and reached for the ball, but it hit the spike of a jack and went flying. Leaping up, Kam ran after it, snatching the ball before it flew off the roof.

With a snort, Monica placed a tray of crackers, cheese, and small pieces of meat on a tiny side table, brought up for the evening. She faced Jen. "Make sure the girl eats." She gazed at Casey and Kam. "Both of them." Spinning, Monica left.

Casey reached over to move the table to the center of the group, disrupting the game. They all dug in. Riley chuckled. "I don't know what you did to Chef Monica, but she's always angry at you."

Jen swallowed the small sandwich she'd made, nodding. "True, but do you notice, we always get better food when Case is around. It's like she's trying to prove something."

Riley stared off for a minute before smiling in agreement. "She's mad you're better in the kitchen, isn't she?"

Casey eyes widened. "Hush, someone will hear you. Never say those words ... like, ever. Don't even think them. We'll get swill and nothing else. And of course not." Casey searched the roof, trying to find a hidden spy. "Monica is the best chef in the house."

The three of them laughed.

Kam ran over and stuffed some cheese into her mouth then danced around humming. In her next grab, she had a cracker. Then it was cheese again. In her final grab, it was a piece of sausage. She flopped onto Casey's lap, staring up at the clouds as she licked her fingers clean of the last bits of grease.

"Daddy, do you see the person up there?"

Leaning back on her hands and tipping her head back, Casey gazed up at the clouds. It was a good night for fireworks, the clouds were sparse. Searching for the one that looked like a person, she only saw one that vaguely had the shape of a whale, and another that was morphing into a ... well, a blob.

She dropped her chin to her chest. She saw that both Jen and Riley had their heads back and were viewing the bright sky as well. "Do either of you see the person?"

They both shook their heads no.

Kam's voice got sharp. "Right there, in the sky!"

Casey squinted again, but nothing had the shape she could make out as a human. "I'm not seeing it, sweetie. Which cloud are you looking at?"

"Not in the clouds, Daddy, the flying person. Do you see the person who is flying?" Her hand flew up and she pointed at something. "Right there!" Her arm swung around as she continued to point at the supposed person in the sky.

Squinting up, Casey realized her daughter was pointing at a bird. Focusing more, she realized it was some sort of hawk. "Kam, dear, that's a hawk."

Her daughter's voice dropped to almost a growl. "It's more than that, it's a human too. Why can't you see it?"

Feeling foolish but wanting to figure out what her daughter was talking about, she decided to try out Tilly's trick. Pushing out her will, she focused on the air around the silly bird. She slowed the atoms around it. As she watched, its wings slowed, and it dipped. She had to adjust where she slowed the atoms to the new position as it fell. When the hawk got to the roof of the house, Casey thought she was going to collapse. Her vision narrowed, her body trembled, and her breathing was rough. A pounding began behind her eyes.

As the hawk got closer and closer, Kam vibrated with happiness. When it landed, she ran over and pointed at it. "Talk to me! Play with me! Who are you? Are you friendly?"

Worried about her daughter, Casey forced her body up, though she almost blacked out. Riley was suddenly at her side, helping her to stand. They both moved to where Kam stood over the hawk. It seemed to glare up at them, if that was possible.

The bird suddenly blurred, or was it her vision blurring? She was glad of Riley's arm around her; she wasn't sure she could stand on her own. She felt Jen come up on her other side. "Can birds glare? Is that animal going out of focus? What was in that drink?" Jen looked back and forth between her glass and the out of focus creature.

When the blurring around the bird stopped, a naked man stood in front of them. He was tall, over six and a half feet tall, if Casey were to guess, with dark bronze skin. He had dark brown hair that went past his shoulders and glowing green eyes. He was muscular with a narrow waist.

Casey heard gasps come from the other two women, but she was too tired to react. "Who are you?" Her voice sounded tired as she met his angry, piercing gaze.

"The name's Donovan, and the better question is, how did you know I was a werehawk?"

Chapter 15

Jen handed Donovan a blanket that had been hanging over one of the chairs in case it got cold later on. They all sat on the roof near the food. Kam skipped around, and Casey was glad for the glass railing that would keep her daughter from falling off the roof. The girl sang about flying in the air with the flying people and she flapped her arms.

Donovan sat, discreetly shooting Kam questioning looks, while he created a cheese and meat sandwich, which looked ridiculously small in his large hands. "My people have stayed hidden for years beyond memory. We have a sordid history that I won't get into now, but it's ugly. We have a prophecy that states we are to stay hidden from all people, witches and vampire included, and not reveal ourselves until the birth of the thrice born child. It is dangerous for me to be here, to be talking to you, for you to have recognized me. Very dangerous. You shouldn't have been able to recognize me. So, I ask again, how did you know what I was? And how did you bring me down?"

Jen's hand flew to her mouth in shock, and Riley's expression hardened. For her part, Casey tried to keep a neutral expression. "You have a prophecy?"

The large man nodded. "At our start ... it wasn't good ... we weren't good. Then we were banned, compelled into hiding ... many of my people died testing that rule. I don't want to be the next."

Leaning forward, Riley watched the man, riveted by his words. "By whom? Who had the power to secret away an entire group of people?"

The man shook his head. "That's not important right now. What is, is I shouldn't be here." He began to stand.

Casey's hand shot out. "Tell me your prophecy ... please."

With a grunt, the man considered her, then sat back down. "Fine, but then I'm leaving, unless you can answer my questions. My people have survived under a practical imprisonment for years, barely surviving ... if you can *call* it surviving. No one beyond our flock can know of our existence on penalty of death. These are the words that define our existence. *Your existence will again be revealed to the land when the thrice born child walks the earth.*" He gazed at each of the women he sat with, ignoring the child dancing and singing around him. "So, unless you can explain to me why you knew what I was, and how you brought me down, I have to leave. You don't know the punishment I face for breaking the rules. If I'm found out, I won't see another sunrise. He'll find me ... and that will be the end."

Wetting her lips, and shooting a furtive glace at her daughter, Casey lifted one side of her mouth in a small smile, then gave a tiny shrug. "Donovan, of the werehawks, I'd like to introduce you to my daughter, Kam, the thrice born child. She's not technically walking, and we aren't on the ground, but I think dancing on a building counts, don't you? She recognized you as a person, even as you flew in hawk form above us. And who will find you? Is there a family? A group? What organization has been hunting your kind down?"

Donovan froze, gaping at Casey, then he turned to Kam, eyes wide. "She's the prophesied child? Are you sure?"

Casey sighed. "Yeah, pretty sure. She recognized you flying in the sky, didn't she?"

They all turned to watch Kam dance and flap her arms, head thrown back to the sky as she looked up. She suddenly stopped, as if she knew they were staring at her. Slowly rotating until she faced Donovan, her face scrunched up. "Flying man, will your friends come down too?" Her head flopped back so that she gazed up to the sky. "They keep circling up there. Aren't they getting tired?"

"How can she know? Who is she? Why are you so certain?"

Shifting her focus to the werehawk, Casey saw his face lose all color. "I received a prophecy too. It had to do with bringing the child of three haves into the world. And, well, Kam is that child."

He finally wrenched his gaze to her. "How did you know that you would be the mother?"

She couldn't stop the laugh. "It's a long story, but the prophecy came to me. Would—"

The roof door opened, and Sydney came barreling out. "Casey, why is there a naked man on the roof?"

Donovan shifted to his feet, crouched, with his hands up. He looked ready to attack. In response, Sydney stopped and got into a fighting stance.

Jumping up to stand between them, her hands out, palms to each of them, Casey whipped her head back and forth. "Whoa, whoa, calm down, both of you. Donovan, this is a friend. Sydney, it's a long story."

Shaking his head, Donovan eyed Sydney wearily. "This was a mistake. Our lives are at stake, and we don't want to be eliminated. The thrice born child might be here, but ... I'm sorry, I have to go. Maybe ... I need to talk with the others. Do you know the trails, near the college?" Casey nodded. "Look-Out Point, tomorrow, one in the afternoon. Bring the child and the humans, but, please, no other vampires. We are hawks, and we can see. If you bring more than these two," he jerked his chin at Jen and Riley, "then we are gone, and you won't find us." Then he ran for the glass railing and leapt from the roof.

Running after him, Casey looked first towards the sidewalk and then up, but she didn't see him, or his hawk. Jen, Riley, and Kam had followed her, and as she backed up, she watched them search the skies for the werehawk. It didn't seem like they were having any more luck than she had. Turning, she returned to the food, and smoothed out the blanket before she sat.

Her head still pounded from the abuse of everything she'd done, and if she didn't slow down, she still may pass out.

Sydney joined her, along with the others. "Sorry for scaring him off. Who was he?" After filling her in, Sydney thought about it. "We should call in Lucas and talk to him. If anyone knows about werehawks, it's him. Gods above, who knew, a wereanimal! But that's not why I came up here. We need to focus on more immediate issues. I've been thinking. I want to put together a small group to infiltrate Jude's compound and see if we can get information. Maybe we could go in on Saturday morning."

Casey squeezed Kam, who'd settled on her lap. "Who were you planning on going with you?"

Sydney gazed at the group. "If Riley could watch Kam, I was hoping to pair you up with Jaxon, and I'm with Micha. I want one more group. I believe three teams would be best for this mission."

Jen cleared her throat. "Could I go? I know I'm not a vampire, but I'm fit."

Sydney tilted her head. "You'd need a strong partner. Who are you considering?"

Scrunching up her nose, Jen thought about it. Then it came to Casey. "Gwen. Why don't we ask her? She could probably help with knowing Jude's techniques as well. And she'd watch Jen's back better than anyone I know."

Jen tensed, then sighed. "Yeah, Mom, that'd work. I'm still getting used to her being a thing."

Sydney nodded. "You're onto something. I'll go and give her a call. We'll meet here on Saturday morning, eight-thirty." She stood and headed out.

Kam gazed up at Casey, eyes wide with concern. "But, Daddy, that's when my cartoons are on."

Chapter 16

As the fireworks lit the sky, Rowan slid in behind Casey, wrapping his legs and arms around her. She leaned back into his hard chest. Kam's squirmy body wiggled on Casey's lap. The explosions went off above, some big booms, others that looked like falling stars.

Between explosions, she filled him in on her encounter with the werehawk Donovan and her plans on meeting him on the hiking trails. He wasn't pleased that she'd only have Jen and Riley as backup, especially with Jude still out and about, but he was as curious as she about who and what they were.

Rowan kissed Casey behind her ear, and whispered, "I want to have dinner with you Friday night. It's been too long."

Rotating slightly, she rested her cheek against his chest. "Can it be a quiet dinner here? There's been so much excitement lately."

His arms tightened around her. "If that's what you want, that works for me."

She smiled up at him and added, "I figured out one of those fancy French pastries. Maybe I can make them for dessert."

He pulled back to look her in the eyes. "Which dessert?"

A smile split her face and she bit her lip. "You'll just have to wait and see."

His sound of pleasure made her melt. Letting down her guard, her body began to tremble. He kissed her neck and whispered, "You need blood. You pushed yourself too hard when you brought that bird down."

Huffing out a laugh, she relaxed, letting him support her. "I do. But what option do I have? I'm watching Kam right now and then I'm heading home."

He nibbled on her ear. "This is your home."

She sighed. "You know what I mean."

Kissing down her neck, he scraped his teeth at the junction of her neck and shoulder. "I've missed you. First you were off to your grandpa's, then with the witches." He raised his voice. "Jen, Riley. Can you watch Kam? I need to talk with Casey for a few minutes. She'll be ready to take Kam home after the fireworks."

Riley laughed. "How about the three of us head back home in the morning? Then Kam can have a sleepover with us here. She can bunk with me. I'll call witch house and confirm."

Kam squealed, jumped up, spun, and flopped on top of Riley. Then with huge eyes, and a pouty lip, she gave puppy dog eyes to Casey. "Please, Daddy, can I? Can I have a sleep over with Riley?"

Tired and unable to think of a reason to say no, she nodded. Casey was about to stand, when Rowan's arms tightened around her, and she found herself sitting on his bed. She sighed in contentment. "This is where I want to be ... but what about the blood?"

There was a knock on the door and Tonya, one of the house human donors came in. She ducked her head, wide-eyed and nervous. "Hey, I've never been up here." Her strawberry blond waves bounced around her shoulders as she swung her head to take everything in. Her pale blue eyes landed on the two of them sitting on the bed. "I was told I was needed. I assume it's Casey. I've never heard of you needing blood, sir." The last was said to Rowan in an awed voice.

Roman hummed in her ear before answering her. "Yes, Casey here is in need. I think you'll be enough, but if you aren't, I can top her off."

Closing the final few steps, Tonya made fists, excitement flowing off her, as she gazed at them. "Is this a situation where I'm *just* a donor, sir?"

Rowan kissed her neck and moved his lips to Casey's ear. "What do you think, love?"

His words shot right to her core, and she felt heat blossom even before anything had happened. Turing in his arms to look into his face, she saw the possibilities, and suddenly forgot how to breathe. "I'm good with her staying ... joining us."

He slid out from behind her and encouraged Tonya to sit on the side of the bed. "You two start.

I'll join in once Casey's stable." He leaned in and kissed Casey deeply, his tongue possessing her mouth for a moment before he backed up to a chair against the wall.

Casey faced Tonya and bit her bottom lip. Her need made her want to attack the other woman, but she was an old enough vampire to not be controlled by her blood lust. "Are you sure you want more than sharing blood?"

Tonya gave a tiny smile and nod. "Oh, yeah." Her gaze shifted between Casey and Rowan. "I'm sure."

The heat in Casey's gut vied with her need for blood. She grabbed the bottom of Tonya's shirt and slipped it off, letting her eyes drop to take in her lovely form. Tonya slowly stripped off her bra, shorts, and panties. Casey managed to get her own shirt off before pushing Tonya back on the bed in a fit of need. She straddled the donor, staying up on her elbows and knees above her.

She controlled herself enough to give Tonya a small kiss before she started to feed from her neck. Casey's need for blood was so acute, it took several pulls before the sensual feelings began to build in her. The blood flowing down to her belly, igniting a fire throughout her body, need and desire combining in a heady mix she was coming to crave. Beneath her, Tonya writhed, making whimpering sounds. Her hands lifted to rub Casey's breasts, increasing the pleasure the blood had begun.

Casey lowered one of her hands down the length of Tonya's body in slow swirls, enjoying the soft feel of her silky skin. She ended at the other woman's clit. The gentle circling of her finger had Tonya moaning. Casey relished it when Tonya arched her body up and the lusty sounds of groans replaced her whimpers.

"Yes ... gods, yes," flowed to Casey's ear as she applied a bit more pressure and moved her hand a bit faster.

The blood filled Casey, burning a trail of fire and need down her throat, pooling in her core, filling her body's needs. She took another pull, and her soul sang. She licked the tantalizing neck, stopping the blood. She groaned, and, breathing hard, she sucked on Tonya's ear.

Once the waves of blood pleasure had passed, Casey kissed down the body below her, slow and deliberate. Her first stop was at Tonya's breasts. She sucked on the nipple, dragging her teeth over the tip. Her hand continued to play at the juncture of her legs. Tonya quivered below her, yelling out words of encouragement. Casey continued exploring downward with her tongue. When she got to where her hand had been playing, she was about to lick when she felt her skirt lift and her panties being torn off.

Kneeling over Tonya, she lowered her mouth to her as Rowan used his fingers to determine if she was ready, then slowly enter her, his cock thick and hot. She had to pause as she realized how deeply he penetrated her in this position. When he slowly pulled out, her eyes rolled back with the sensation. She bit her lip on a moan as her body screamed with desire, and he began his assault to her body, pounding in and out.

As Rowan continued from behind, Casey licked and sucked, mimicking Rowan's motions with her fingers in Tonya, in and out. She heard Tonya's gasp in response, another layer of heat growing with the need.

The cacophony of sounds and feeling almost became too much, and Casey muffled her own cries as she focused on Tonya's pleasure and bringing her to completion. Rowan leaned over and began to play with her clit. It was too much, she exploded, screaming her orgasm as stars erupted in her vision.

Casey experienced a second set of fireworks for the night. She heard and felt Rowan's release with her. She collapsed on top of Tonya. Scooting over so that she was next to the blood donor, Rowan curled in behind her, the three cuddled on the large bed.

Rowan's arm encircled her waist. "I'm glad you will stay the night, love."

Tonya rolled to her side. "I can't believe I was part of that. I'm heading back down to my room, but any time you want a third, I'm totally in ... unless it's before ten am." She rolled out of the bed, slipped on her shirt, and grabbed the rest of her clothes before heading out.

Rolling Casey onto her back, Rowan captured her mouth in a possessive kiss. Then he lay on his back. She cuddled into the crook of his arm, feeling at peace for the first time in over a week. Rowan pulled the covers up, and as she felt finally at home, sleep overtook her.

Chapter 17

Casey, Riley, and Kam walked into witch house at seven-thirty the next morning, early enough to have breakfast with the group. Heading into the kitchen, Kam ran to the table and found her crayons and paper. Riley joined her after securing a large mug of coffee.

Zen worked alone in the kitchen, making breakfast for everyone. "Want help?"

One regal brow rose. "Do you know how to do anything in the kitchen, or are you a wreck in here as you are in many other areas of your life?"

Tilly, who had come in from the other room, leaned against the archway. "Well, we know she can make a mean cookie. She's never given us store-bought in any of her conjurations."

Rotating on his heel, Zen looked down his nose at both of them. "We aren't having cookies for breakfast, girls, it's a meal."

Pursing out her lips and placing her hands on her hips, Tilly took a step into the kitchen. "And what do *you* think the proper breakfast is?"

With a sigh, Zen shrugged. "Honestly, a soft-boiled egg with beans and toast, but I know how well *that* would go over here. So, barring that, I'm making a scrambled egg and sausage sandwiches on crumpets."

Casey bit her lip and held out her hand, focusing. As she figured out his perfect breakfast, she said, "We eat English muffins here, not crumpets ... we aren't in England. Which is ironic, I know." The plate appeared in her hand with the egg in a tiny holder, beans, and toast, browned with melting butter. "Here, enjoy your breakfast. I'll finish the sandwiches for everyone else."

With a flat stare of disapproval, he took the plate and sat at the table. "Where did you get the egg holder?"

Taking stock of where everything was, she continued making the breakfast sandwiches. "They're in the lower cupboard, next to the dishwasher." The eggs were almost done, the sausage was sizzling, and the English muffins were in the oven. Running to the fridge, she found cheese, then grabbed a platter from an upper cupboard.

Zen made a weird noise from the table. Worried he may be choking, she shot him a look over her shoulder as she grabbed an oven mitt and the muffins from the oven. Zen gaped at the egg. "This is all perfect. How did you do this?" He sounded more aggravated than appreciative.

Riley snorted. "Above everything else, Casey is a kitchen witch, you fool!"

The oven door flopped open, and she placed the muffin tray on a trivet to cool. She spun and grabbed a bowl and dumped the eggs in to scramble then removed the sausage from the heat. After seasoning the eggs, she quickly heated them, then she moved the muffins to the platter, added the cheese on one side, and the sausage and egg on the other. Perfect!

She placed the platter on the long table and brought a stack of plates over. The rest of the house residents drifted in, and everyone dug in. The last thing she added was a carafe of coffee, a pitcher of orange juice, glasses, and mugs before sliding in next to Kam and digging in herself.

As Casey grabbed her second sandwich, Ginger walked into the kitchen. "Hi! I'm here for my weekly mind-control clean-up and protection."

Standing, Casey dropped her breakfast on the plate, and went over to give her friend a hug. "Ginge, I'm so glad to see you. I forgot you were coming today."

Ginger pulled back and let her hands fall away. Her face fell, and she just stared at Casey. Face hard and looking sad for several seconds, Casey knew she'd messed up. A knot of uncertainty built in her gut. Finally, Ginger crossed her arms over her chest like armor, and took a large breath. "You forgot about me? Again? Really? Am I not important enough compared to the world of witches and vampires?" There was a small hitch in her words.

Casey threw up her hands like a shield and frantically shook her head. "No, no, no, it's nothing like that. Gods Ginger, please believe me. This week has just been insane. You have to understand."

Her mouth forming a line of disappointment, Ginger's eyes narrowed. "Every week seems to be insane around you, lately. What's it this week? Werewolves?"

Every muscle in Casey's body froze, and her eyes began to get bigger, but before anyone in the room could say anything, Ginger's face broke into a huge smile. "Just kidding." She looped her arm in one of Casey's and turned to the kitchen. "Can you tell me about your week? Anything top-secret?"

Ginger's joke felt like whiplash. Casey tried to slow her heart as she dragged Ginger to the table to finish her breakfast. She started with introducing Kam to her friend. Ginger smiled down at the child. "You are the cutest girl I've ever seen!"

Kam preened before going back to her coloring.

Casey went on to tell her about her new job, Jude, and finally ended with the werehawks. The last she had to tell to both Ginger and the witches since just about everyone in the room needed to know.

Long before she'd finished her rundown on the week, Kam and Riley had left to check out new bikes. Riley hadn't ridden since she was a child, and Kam said solemnly that she could teach her. Riley said they'd return to Cambia House afterwards. They'd be back around noon to head over to the trails for the meeting at one.

Ginger leaned back and sipped her coffee. "So ... not werewolves, got it. But there really are werecreatures in the world? I can't believe it. And holy hell, you weren't kidding, that is one hell of a week. You have a kid! That is insane, my friend. There is so much to think about in what you've told me. I can't believe you're a parent, and to that sweet little girl. She really is the cutest. But Jude, what are you going to do about that jerk? When can we take him out?"

Damion placed his mug down on the table. "That's the big question, isn't it? If we can bind his powers with just the five of us, then he'll be all but human."

Ginger's brow furrowed. "Why not just gather a full coven? And human? Sounds fantastic!"

Leaning on his elbows, Damion smiled. "Smart. If the coven was close, that's what we'd do. Our goal, if we can accomplish it, is to create a talisman that can hold the spell, but with such a complicated binding, the spell will only hold in an object for twenty-four hours. At least, that's our guess. In a working as complicated as this, the people who create the spell need to practice as a group. We can't keep calling the same people down here, and a random thirteen may not be successful. So, if we can figure something out with the five of us, that would be ideal."

Gazing down at her hands, Ginger played with one of her rings. "Would it be easier if you didn't have to worry about me?"

The chorus of 'no's around the room convinced her. What Jude had done to her mind over the course of three years disgusted all of them. Everyone in that room wanted Ginger to have both her brain back and the knowledge that her mind was protected. The others offered to clean up the breakfast mess while Casey and Ginger headed into the front room to work on her mind.

They spent an hour clearing out Jude's compulsions then stopped. They didn't want to do too much. Once done, Ginger left with hugs, and Sadie lead them all to the gazebo in the back. She'd spent the previous two days doing research and had done some spell-writing, hoping one of the spells would work. "Okay, everyone, here's the first one. Each of you has a series of words, actions, and symbology you have to do precisely. Once we're done, we'll have the binding talisman. Lucas has informed me that he has a vampire that is being punished that we can test the binding out on."

Casey and Tilly both stiffened, but Tilly got the words out first. "Wait, what did this vampire do? We're not a justice system for the vampires. Not to mention, this spell won't be a minor working, it will block all vampiric magic. What could this vampire have done to deserve being our test subject?"

Nodding, Sadie started handing out the papers. "No, we aren't, however this is an exchange. They are giving us a way to test our spell, and they are getting a reprieve. Not even a long one because our next spell to work out is the reversal spell. You know that, Tilly; we aren't monsters."

Tuning out the conversation, Casey read the steps she had to take. The point of this morning's exercise was to do a walkthrough of the steps. She saw she had to set the white candles at the four cardinal directions and the four intermediate directions, eight pillars, and light them. With an eight-candle working, eight-point calling—four cardinal and four intermediates—this was high magic. She'd only ever read about that. Once everyone was sitting, she would walk counterclockwise thrice, and clockwise four times, ending with a locking counterclockwise rotation with a chant. Eight rotations to lock them in. She was locking the circle—not just setting it, locking it. If felt as though a knife ran down her back, cool tendrils icing down her arms, and she shivered.

Something big brewed around her.

Biting her lip, she continued to read the spell. After locking the circle, she moved to the center of the group, becoming the eye, where she would stand, feet planted, arms crossed, but palms together as the others circled her and chanted before they sat. One of them would then stand, approach her, and place the talisman between her palms as she stood, head back, eyes to the heavens, before they returned to their place in the cardinal location. She would be the conduit of the spell.

Then the five would chant the words fivefold to represent each of them.

If it all worked, the talisman would be enchanted. A witch, *or a vampire*, with the activation word, could say the word and touch the talisman to the vampire. The effect would be instantaneous.

Reading it through again, Casey searched the faces of the others. Finally, she asked Sadie, "Why am I the conduit?"

The other woman gazed at her, her frizzy hair catching the rays of the sun and glowing a light brown around her face. "For a few reasons. First of all, being both a witch and a vampire, I thought you'd give more power to the spell in that position. I really wanted to ensure that both witches and vampires could activate the talisman. But, more than that, you're the most powerful of the five of us and can carry more of the load than any of the rest of us. We need this to succeed."

The others agreed, even Zen, though his face said he didn't like it. The five of them walked through the motions of the spell, pushing a pinch of their will through her so she could get a feel of how their powers would mix. It wasn't the full spell, but

Casey was learning what it would feel like to mix the five energies together. Being her first time leading a spell, she'd never mixed magics within herself like this before, and the emotions made her feel powerful ... and a bit ticklish.

The full spell would work best within three days of the full moon, which was the following Thursday, so they decided they'd wait. The first test was scheduled for Monday. Since she had time before her meeting with the werehawks, Casey went inside to shower and rest. She hadn't gotten enough blood the night before and she felt weak. The others wanted to remain outside in the sun, relaxing, and gardening.

Trudging up the stairs, a feather-light touch and caress in her most intimate areas made her miss a step and almost fall down. She grasped onto the rail, holding back a moan, as some intimate stroking hit a *very* sensitive spot. She shot a look over her shoulder and spied Damion following her in.

Casey bit her lip as a phantom hand squeezed her nipple. Her eyes threatened to roll back in her head. "What are you doing?"

"Well, sexy," Damion said, with a slow smile, "I just thought, if you'd like to change shape, we could share a shower, save some water, and you could have some blood you so obviously need. You're drooping ... it's clear."

Closing her eyes to remind herself *how* to breathe, she focused on her body and waited for the familiar numbness to flow out from her center and then the pins and needles to follow. Once it was over, the phantom hand grabbed her new member, grasping and pumping, and this time Casey did crash down to her hands and knees as the sensations invaded her body. She'd made it to the hallway with a moan, a wave of pleasure threatening to take her under. "Blood first!"

Warm hands picked her up. "Well, the next hour will be our turn to experiment with magic, and blood, and sex. I've always wanted to mix two of those, haven't you?"

Damion's words and his phantom hands put her over as he carried her into his room. He brought them into the attached bathroom, and they quickly washed. Casey was too drained for much shower-play.

"One of these days we'll have to see what we can do in here," Damion said, dark eyes gazing down at her. "But today I have other plans."

They ended up back in his bed, Casey on her back, Damion on his side, hitched up on his elbow smiling down at her. "Last time *I* got to fuck *you*, lovely Casey. Have you even done that with someone else?"

Eyes wide, she shook her head.

He leaned down and gave her a gentle kiss. "Do you want to try? I can imagine, the sensations of entering me twice, doing that while getting blood, it may be pleasurable for both of us."

She reached up and traced the side of his face. "This all could end in comedic folly, just so you know. But let's try it out."

Damion rolled to his back and reached over to a drawer in his bedside table. He grabbed out some lube and handed it to her. "Just start off slow. Get all the way in so we're both adjusted to the new sensation, and then bite me."

She smiled down mischievously. "What, you don't want random poking while my teeth are in you?"

He clasped her wrist holding the lube. "This may be a bad idea."

Leaning down to kiss him, probing his mouth with her tongue, enjoying the tingles that started to radiate down her body, she pulled back and waggled her eyebrows. "Too late, the plan is set."

He slung his right leg up to her shoulder and she prepared them both, using the lube on him and her. Then, slowly, she pushed her cock into him. His ass was tight, and everything about the situation was new and insane. As she pushed in, her boy trembled with the new waves of pleasure coming from the action. Seeing his cock grow thicker, she reached down and gave it a few pulls with her lube-slick hand.

Below her, his head tilted back, his body arched, and he moaned. Once her hips reached him, she collapsed over him, panting. Lining up with his neck, she let her teeth descend, then bit down, his blood finally flowing into her, a fine wine to top off the morning.

As she sucked, she slowly moved her body, rocking her hips, pulling herself out and then back in. She felt him jerk and quiver as her movements and blood-taking overtook Damion's senses.

Suddenly, she felt his phantom body take her from the back. He entered her from behind in a mimic of her actions, stretching her, filling her, demanding pleasure from her. As she pumped into him, he pumped into her. Her motions got faster, the blood making her dizzy with desire.

Her teeth ascended and she sucked his neck, assuring the wound closed, then pushed up on her elbows, giving herself more room to move in and out. Her hand, still slick with the lube, clasped his cock, moving up and down, mirroring her lower motions.

The room spun with the sensations from behind, up front, her hand, his moans ... Casey barely knew which way was up. Her body tightened just as she lost her seed within him, calling out her orgasm. Just as she came up for air, he spilled his seed over them both.

Carefully pulling out of him, she collapsed down, letting him pull her onto his chest. He gazed down his body. "We may need another shower."

Chapter 18

Jen and Riley pulled up with Kam just after noon in one of Cambia House's fancy house cars, available to anyone who lived there. They were bigger than Casey's VW bug, and the three of them could fit in it more comfortably. After meeting Casey at the door, they piled into the car and headed for the hiking trails.

They parked in the small parking lot and Kam spun in the gravel, kicking up pebbles, until she plopped on her butt, giggling. She gazed up to the sky. "Can we really go all the way up, Daddy? Riley?"

Casey knelt and gave her a kiss on the nose before helping her up. "Not all the way today, love, but we can come back. I love these paths, and I hope you love them too." She tapped her daughter's nose for emphasis.

As the four of them walked the trails, Casey wondered how long the hawks had been watching them. How else would they know that this was where Casey often went to think? Did they monitor all the paranormal folk in town or was she special since she was a witch and a vampire? How would they know that about her? A shiver ran down her back, not quite a premonition, but close.

Kam started the hike by running ahead, asking about all the plants and trees, identifying the ones she knew, and trying to catalog the ones she didn't. She bounced and spun as they went. Being a witch, Casey knew about plants, and answered every question that came her way. She understood her daughter's curiosity. The child soon got tuckered out, her three-year-old body quickly spending its energy on running and thinking. Casey put her on her back. Being a vampire, she had the highest strength and energy of the adults, especially with the extra blood earlier. Despite all that, the steep section right before the lookout point almost did her in with Kam's extra weight and wiggling body messing up her center of gravity.

Jen had carried a picnic basket from the car. She may have been human, but she was athletic and nearly as fit as a vampire. Once they got to the top with the small stone ledge protecting visitors from the stark fall, they went about setting up the blanket and food. There were sandwiches, cut up fruit and carrot sticks, juice, and water. In a small container at the bottom, Casey found chocolate-covered raisins.

They started eating and enjoying the food. It didn't take long before two hawks flew into the trees behind them, one had a bag strapped to its belly in a strange contraption. After a few minutes, Donovan came out wearing a pair of light gray pants followed by a woman in a yellow summer dress with white flowers on the hem. She stood tall like Donovan with matching dark bronze skin. She had shaggy, light brown hair that flowed almost to her waist and glowing hazel eyes.

If Casey didn't know better, she'd think they came from the same land Lucas did. Though Donovan was much taller, they had similar coloring to the vampire.

Casey stood and took the few steps to meet them. "Hi, I'm Casey. I'm glad you could take time to meet us."

The woman, several inches taller than Casey, who was almost six feet tall herself, seemed to judge Casey and find her wanting. "I'm Alicia, the leader of the werehawks. I've come to find proof of your claim that your child is the one from our prophecy and learn what you'll expect from us to break our curse ... which has been in place for thousands of years, child." She said the last word with a sneer.

Forcing a smile, Casey stepped back to indicate the blanket and food. "Would you care to join us? We could discuss while we break bread, so to speak."

The look of disappointment that crossed Alicia's face made Zen seem an amateur, but she nodded and sat next to Jen. Donovan sat to her left. Casey sat back down between Jen and Kam, who finished her peanut butter and jelly sandwich and smiled at the two strangers. "I'm glad you came out of the sky, lady, your arms looked so tired the other day, and I worried the fireworks would hurt you."

Alicia, who had been reaching for a ham and cheese sandwich, froze. Her hardened face turned to Donovan, who just shrugged. "I told you she saw us as people flying in the air, not hawks. It's one of the reasons I believed them." His voice was strained as he grabbed his own peanut butter and jelly sandwich, as well as some mango chunks.

Trying to project the same cool power Rowan did, Casey faced Alicia. "Who bound you to remain hidden? Was it the same person who set the prophecy?"

The disappointment coming from the older woman tickled Casey's nose, and she fought back a sneeze. "Are you always this foolish? Only a higher power can set a prophecy, and they don't care about free will actions beyond that. Of course our jailor didn't set the binding. As for our history, it is ours, not yours, child. We owe you nothing."

Casey fought the urge to rub the sticky scorn from her arms. "Will you share anything about your people? How many of you there are? Are you located only around here? Are you immortal like the vampires or mortal like the witches? Will you help us in our fight, or will you remain hidden and apart ... scared to be part of the paranormal world?"

Alicia took a bite of her sandwich and gazed at Casey while Donovan's mouth twitched. He seemed to be enjoying the show. Kam, getting bored, leapt up to explore. Riley stood and followed her.

Putting her sandwich on a plate, Alicia wiped her mouth with one of the cloth napkins they'd brought along. "Why would we tell you our numbers or locations, child? That would be idiocy. A tactical blunder. Do understand there are many hawks in the world. Millions of us." Casey fought to keep a straight face. She could read a lie from both her witch and vampire side, but information was information.

Quirking up her mouth in her apparent win, Alicia continued. "As for your fight, it is just that, *your* fight. We have no part in it."

That made Casey chuckle. "The fight is against H.O.A.P, Humans Only, Against Paranormal. Considering *you* are paranormal, it's your fight as well. So, let me summarize. You came here to *not* answer any of my questions, *not* to help us, really only to be judgmental and disappointed. You are above us in every way and condemn me for not being as old as you. I'm glad we've gotten all of that straightened out. Since you won't answer my questions, is there anything I can answer for you?"

Alicia's nose flared. "You are an impertinent child. We came in good faith to meet your daughter and get verification of her lineage as the thrice-born child. Without that, we are putting our own lives in danger. If she isn't who you say she is, we're all dead ... all the hawks."

Jen head tilted. "All of you? Over a million of you. And you indicated your jailor ... singular, is keeping tabs. He or she must be fantastic at what they do. The fact that Kam knows who you are as a hawk flying in bird form or a human sitting isn't enough? I mean, if nothing else, it should be a good start, at least good faith at you not being a complete—"

"Jen!" Casey stopped her friend from going too far.

Alicia turned her cold eyes to Jen. "No, human." The word came out as if it tasted bad in the hawk's mouth. "That just means she reads auras. It hasn't been done for hundreds of years, but anyone who can read an aura knows a werehawk from a regular hawk."

Jen shook her head. "No, she didn't just know which hawks were people by some aura, she knew *you* were one of the hawks when you walked out. She saw past the animal to the person. That's more than an aura. You know it and so do we."

Again, the flare of the nose. She started to stand. "Is that it? Is that the end of the proof?"

Casey shook her head. "No. I can offer more, but I'd like an olive branch. Give me something. If I'm going to be opening myself up to you, a prickly hawk who's done nothing but insult and belittle us, give us an answer or two."

Narrowing her eyes, Alicia considered. "We are not immortal, but we are long lived. Some hawks have been known to live as long as four or five hundred years ... even longer at the beginning. It is why we are so close to understanding our origins. My grandparents were in the first generation, and I've been around a long time, I've seen a lot. We saw you come to college, a witch hiding in plain sight, and were intrigued, but it isn't unheard of. Then when you were attacked and took on the mantle of vampire too ... you caught our interest. Two pieces of the three. We've followed all dual natured beings."

Anger began to boil low in her gut. The words were both truth and a lie. They'd been watching her longer, Casey could feel it behind the words, but the second mantle, this was why they'd been watching her extra closely. To have a thrice-born child ... a child of three halves, they needed someone like her. They'd been watching her for years ... hoping.

There was something more about her, but she didn't think she could get it from them. What was it about her, her specifically, that made them interested in her?

Biting back her anger, knowing it wouldn't help, she held out her hand to the leader of the werehawks. The woman gazed down at her hand like it was a viper. "What do you want me to do with that, child?"

Breathing deeply, Casey gazed directly into the hawk's disapproving gaze. "I'm inviting you into my mental glass bubble. From there I can show you proof of who I am, and why I know Kam is the one in your prophecy."

The hawk leader shot a glance over her should to Donovan who shrugged and mumbled, "Witches."

With a sniff of disapproval, she placed her hand in Casey's. Slowly, knowing she had to teach and guide, Casey brought the prickly hawk into the bubble.

It took a few minutes, but Alicia made it. Once there, the woman froze, then gaped at the room with its different areas. Casey had blotted some areas out, keeping part of her mind safe from this woman, but kept enough open that the hawk was impressed. "Where are we?"

Casey dropped the woman's hands. "We are in my mind, inside a glass bubble I created to protect my innermost memories. I have books for studying, a way to review memories, and, well, anything I may need or want."

Slowly pacing the room, Alicia's arrogance melted away. "Do all witches have this?"

Shrugging, Casey kept pace. "Probably, but I'm a mental witch, so mine is probably more elaborate. But we aren't here for a tour or information sharing on witches. You wanted proof and I have it to give."

Stopping, Alicia turned to face her, eyes huge with hunger; she seemed to want to learn everything. *Is she the information gatherer for her people as well?* "Right, proof."

First, they moved to the door. "This showed up around four years ago. If you'll notice, the runes are in an ancient language I'm trying to learn."

Alicia froze. "Who's teaching you?"

Casey shrugged. "One of the older vampires. Actually, the oldest alive, I believe. Lucas. The door didn't open until he came here with me. That's what triggered it opening and the book appearing."

Visibly agitated, Alicia's face turned to a sneer again. Then she took a calming breath and smiled. "Of course, it would be *him*. Show me the book." She sounded sweetly respectful, as if she couldn't bring herself to disrespect Lucas, even within the confines of Casey's mind.

Biting her tongue about being given an order and in all places, her mind, they headed to the oak table. Casey figured that this woman was used to giving orders. Alicia froze for the second time, gazing at the tome. "It exists. My parents told me about it ... it would come to be from one of the descendants of ... well, that doesn't matter. What was the prophecy, child?"

Casey's heart pounded. This woman knew more about her past, but something in the way she spoke let her know she wouldn't say more, not now. Opening the book to the first page, the prophecy sat alone, centered.

A child of three halves, combined of the immortal and hexed, will bring the unity or destruction of the ancient clans.

Alicia traced her fingers over the words, the only ones in the book in English, then raised her focus to Casey. "Okay, child, I believe you. Here is my contact number. We will discuss more later, but for now, I must get the word out to the other werehawks that we can come out of hiding."

The words and thoughts Alicia tried to hide shifted through Casey's mind. There were six clans, four in America and two in Europe. There were less than four hundred hawks worldwide. Alicia should know better than to think private thoughts when in the mind of a witch ... especially a mind witch. Casey filed that information away; she could place the locations on a map later if it seemed necessary.

Guiding Alicia out of her mind took less effort than bringing her in. The two werehawks said their goodbyes, making sure to let Kam know they were leaving. They didn't give much attention to the humans. Then they were airborne again, strange contraption strapped to the body of, Casey assumed, Donovan.

Once they had left, the four cleaned up and made their way back to the car, snacking on the chocolate-covered raisins on the way down the mountain. At the car, they found Lucas waiting for them. "Casey, I need to discuss with you what you were doing today."

She handed Kam to Jen. The girl looked ready to take a nap, and after a bath she'd get one. *How did she get half a tree of leaves on her?*

Casey walked over to the older vampire. "I'm glad you're here, I wanted to talk to you. We were meeting with werehawks. Have you ever heard of such a thing? Absolutely crazy!"

Quirking his mouth to the side, he shook his head. "I've heard of them, Casey, love. You need to be very careful around them. They aren't what you think they are."

"What do you know of them? Did you know they have a prophecy centered around Kam?"

He placed a hand on her upper arm, shaking his head. "This doesn't surprise me. She's quite the girl. Now, I'm not going to interfere, it isn't my place ... not anymore. I just want you to be smart, as you often are."

Again, she wanted to pin down how old Lucas was, figure out what he really knew, but knew it was both a rude question and one he wouldn't answer. Instead, she shifted to another worry. "Have you seen Blake? Do you have any ideas on how to help her?"

Smiling, he nodded. "I have a donor who's reached the point she's earned vampirism. I'll be misting her into Blake's room tonight to let her do the honors of draining her down. First life's blood should shift Blake into an emotion vampire. Living in a group home, she should be fine."

Casey snorted at the truth of that statement. The only thing better would be teaching at a middle school.

Giving Lucas a quick hug and kiss on his cheek, she thanked him. Then they were off. She had her date with Rowan tonight, and she had to get to Cambia house to start baking cookies.

Chapter 19

Jen parked in the garage of Cambia House, and they headed in. They all laughed over Kam's antics on the walking trails after meeting Alicia, the head of the werehawks. The young girl had flapped her "wings" the whole way down, convinced she could fly like a hawk, that is, when she wasn't stuffing her mouth with the last of their food. The kid was cute in her exuberance. When they got inside, they found Rowan in the hallway waiting for them. His warm smile welcomed the group home. "You're early for dinner."

"Well, I promised you dessert. If you've arranged dinner, I need to start baking. There's a rest period before the actual baking with these cookies I'll shower and dress while they dry." Casey began figuring out the timing for each step she needed to take before dinner as she tried to skirt around him.

One side of his mouth quirked up. "Okay, you start your dessert, then come up to my rooms for the shower. I'll have a dress brought up."

Rolling her eyes, she went to the kitchen and found the ingredients she'd requested. She started sifting almond flour and powdered sugar. She then mixed egg whites and regular sugar to stiff peaks. Folding the two until the mixture slid from her spatula, she put the mixture into a pipping bag and made circular cookies atop parchment paper on two trays. As she was getting done with the procedure, Rowan came into the kitchen. She took each tray and banged it on the counter three times to remove air bubbles.

When she was done Rowan wrapped his arms around her waist. "Are you making macaron cookies?"

With a straight face, she shook her head. "Of course not. They're called bang bang cookies, named for banging the trays on the counter."

He leaned in and whispered in her ear. "I thought they were named for what we did last time we ate them."

A warm heat rose through her body at his words, and she twisted in his arms to give him a kiss.

Chef Monica thwapped her on her backside. "Not in my kitchen you don't. Out, both of you!"

She laughed and shot a glance at the chef over her shoulder. "I'll be back down to finish these off in a bit."

"Out!" Her finger pointed towards the door.

Laughing, she ran up to Rowan's private floor to shower. In his room, she ran into something new hanging from the ceiling in the center of the open space. At first it looked like a weird black plant holder, but as she got closer, she realized it appeared to be two seats and two sets of handles. It was some sort of swing. As she touched it, she noted it was slightly padded.

Rowan entered, and she heard the door lock. She turned to face him. His gaze was hooded, and he had a small smile on his face. "Take off your clothes, my lovely Casey."

His words flowed over her like silk, and the command in his voice sent a zing of sensation straight to her core. She immediately started to tingle, and heat burned low in her belly. She bit her lip and held his gaze. "You first."

He stepped into the room, unbuttoning his shirt, and slipping it off. His hard, sculped chest and abs drew her focus and she licked her lips before yanking her eyes back to his. He'd made it halfway to her. "I'll warn you now, anything you're wearing when I get to you may not survive the night." He removed his belt with a swish of sound, and it clanked to the floor. Slowly, he started unbuttoning his pants when she realized what he meant. She quickly pulled off her shirt and jeans.

When he got to her, she was as naked as he was. "I see you've found my new gift for you, love."

Her breath hitched. "For ... me?"

He chuckled and picked her up, placing her on the first swing seat. Grabbing her face in both his hands, he kissed her deeply, his spice and mint scent enveloping her. She felt him get harder and longer as he pushed against her stomach. Wrapping her legs around him, her muscles tightened in anticipation.

He pulled back, slipping out from her between her legs, and she grabbed onto the upper hand hoops as her body swayed in the swing. The sensation both exhilarated her and felt odd. Her heart raced at the instability of where she sat.

He clasped her hips and pulled her towards him, leaning in to gently kiss one nipple. Then, backing up, he rubbed his hands down her thigh towards her knee, one hand on the inside, one on the outside, until he reached her foot. Lifting her foot to his mouth, he kissed the sole, then placed it in the lower loop—a stirrup, she realized. He did the same with the other foot, again starting with a kiss to the nipple.

Her breath hitched with his motions.

Her body was primed for him, the apparatus she was on opening her wide, and rotating her at will. He stood watching as if she were an art piece to appreciate. Then he knelt, grabbed the seat of the swing, and brought her most intimate body part to his mouth. She realized, in this, he had all the control. A groan escaped her.

His tongue gently licked up her folds, barely touching her. The muscles in her lower body contracted tighter with need as her hands clenched, gripping the small hoops reflexively. A moan of desire and anticipation intermixed with her panting. He let his tongue enter her, sliding in, then out, before licking up, to lap over her clit. She trembled as she balanced in the swaying swing.

Her body tried to arch up, but she didn't know how to move in the swing. The sensations were building—heat, and the excitement of this new, unknown position. Then he thrust fingers in her, sucked in her clit, piercing her with teeth and it was too much. She screamed, her body bucking back. Pleasure washed over her in a wave.

Fingers spasming, her hands slid from the hand hoops and fell, but the second swing seat caught her near her shoulders. She writhed with the building sensations. She laughed at the fear she'd felt while falling, and *oh, gods, what is he doing now?!* He was ... an eruption of her body and all she knew was the explosion of her orgasm as he played her expertly.

When she yanked a bit of herself back, she saw he stood, and felt him inside her. A new wave of heat started within her. One hand at her clit, the other on her breast, he built a new pool of need and desire within her. She hadn't yet got her breathing figured out. "Oh, gods, Rowan!"

The hand on her breast pinched the nipple and the thumb on her clit was insistent as he let the swing help with the timing of his thrusts. And then her head fell back, and the ocean of sensations hit her again. His mouth, hot and wet, bent down to her breast, his hands holding her so that his last thrusts were in his control. He pumped in and out, the wave of the swing adding to the surrealness of the moment. And then he shouted her name.

Suspended from the ceiling, her world fractured, Casey reveled in this new toy. His warm hands slid up her body to help her sit up. "Wrap your legs around me, love."

She did, and he pulled her from the contraption.

They took a shower together. Satiated, they used the time to clean themselves, only sharing small touches and kisses. Rowan had transferred some of Casey's preferred shower soaps and shampoos up to his private shower, so she wasn't left to using only his items. That had happened once. He had claimed her by scent to the rest of the house, but his need to prove she was his had calmed down. That need he had only proved even old vampires could act the fools when newly in ... like.

Casey wasn't sure if she was ready to face a bigger concept than a school yard, 'this is mine.' She knew what her heart felt but didn't want to push their relationship too fast. Rowan was an old vampire, and he'd just moved from bachelor to live-in girlfriend ... most of the time. The next step would probably take a few hundred years.

Once out of the shower, she found a black tank dress, subtle and nondescript. It was tight on top, but the skirt flared to her knees. She wore black heels to match. She dried and made sure her curls were still bouncy and did basic make up. Afterwards she headed down to the kitchen to finish the cookies.

She put the two trays in the oven and whipped up some butter cream, a chocolate, and a lemon batch. When the timer went off, she pulled out the cookies to let them cool. Then she piped the butter cream in each. Some chocolate and some lemon. Next time, she'd make the s'mores version they'd tried and Rowan had loved. The variation she'd just made seemed to work out okay this time, but she knew these cookies were temperamental. A few people came through to check out her work, and the overall verdict was a thumbs up.

Chef Monica approved, and decided they'd go on a monthly rotation. That way, she could try a different flavor each month, play around with the recipe and see what worked.

Casey returned to Rowan's apartment for dinner. Though she'd cooked, Monica would find someone else to serve.

Entering Rowan's suite, she found the swing had been removed and in the center of the room was a table with a candle, a vase, and a single red rose. Standing by the table, Rowan had dressed in a black tux with a pale green shirt that matched his eyes. He looked heart-meltingly perfect, and Casey forgot how to breathe as she gaped at him.

Smiling, he walked over, placed her hand on his forearm, and led her to the table. He pulled out her chair and got her situated before he took his own seat. The meal had five courses, each more decadent than the previous. As they ate, they discussed their plans for the future, not only concerning Jude, but work, the coalition, Kam, her parents, and her coven ... and other future plans.

Rowan pointed to the extra room. "I figure we can convert that into Kam's room. She'll be close enough to us to be safe but also have her own room."

Casey smiled. "Is this floor the safest for her? If anything happens, I know the third floor is best, but that room doesn't have any windows ... is it safe for a kid?"

She could see the wheels turn at the thought. "I see your point. If there's a fire, how does she get out without a window ... except that the girl can mist."

There were times she wanted to forget that about her daughter. "That's true. So, she's safe even without a window. What about a door or other privacy measures? You take secure calls all the time. Three-year-olds, four-year-olds ... you get my drift, they aren't known for keeping secrets. She'll start talking about what she's heard."

He sat back. "Why do I get the feeling you don't want her up here? Do *you* not want to be up here?"

Her chest hurt. "That isn't it. I ... it isn't about me or what I want. I just think she'd do better in my old room."

His face began to close down. "And where do you think you'd best end up?" His voice was soft ... closed off.

She bit her lip and stared at her plate. She knew the right answer as a mother but couldn't give it. Her heart had been his for too long. She finally gave the only answer she could. Her voice was small as she said what was in her soul. "Wherever you are."

Playing with her hands, she hoped she hadn't pushed him too fast. They'd been enjoying their physical time together, and he wanted to claim her as his, but that didn't mean the same thing to vampires as it did to humans. And, at the end of the day, he'd been a vampire for a very long time, and she wasn't that far from being human.

She heard his chair scrape back. *Is this it? Is dinner over? Did I say too much?*

He walked over to the other side of the room. *Maybe he just needs a few seconds from me.* Casey looked up to watch him. Then she saw him by the wall of electronics and a moment later *Take my*

Breath Away started playing. He returned to her and held out a hand. "Dance with me, Casey?"

She gazed up at his handsome face and gave a slight nod, taking his hand. He pulled her into his arms, placing his hands on her back. She placed hers on his upper arms. They swayed to the music.

They danced through *Every Time You Go Away* and *Crazy For You, Lady in Red* and *I Wanna Dance with Somebody.* When *Is This Love* came on, Rowan stopped moving and grabbed both sides of her face. "This isn't a question for me, Casey. I've been waiting for you, I think maybe my whole life. Then, I waited to make sure what I was feeling, what we were feeling, was real. I waited the better part of four years. What I'm feeling is a connection I've never expected. When you're here, I want you by my side, with me."

Is this love or am I dreaming? Is this the love I've been searching for ...

Rowan stopped their motion, leaned down and kissed her, soft and full of love. Then he slid down to one knee, grabbed her hand and kissed her palm. Slowly lifting his pale green eyes up to hers, his face softened with a slight smile. "Casey Strega, witch, vampire, person and mother extraordinaire.

Would you do me the honor of adding wife to your list of titles? My wife, to be exact. I love you."
Am I dreaming ...

Chapter 20

The next morning Casey was still groggy, but she made it down to the cafeteria by eight. Despite being early for vampires, there was a line to wait in before getting eggs, toast, and coffee. She sat in the corner, too tired from lack of sleep to want to socialize. Her mind was a-buzz and she had to try to compartmentalize until after their raid on Jude's compound.

Halfway through the meal, Tonya sat next to her. "I'm really asleep right now. If you take my blood, I'll just go back to bed versus walking around. It's too early to do anything else because it's before ten. You look like shit and in need, by the way. I know your day will be hard, so don't fight me. Here, just take my arm now, there's like, no one even in here to see."

Casey was going to refuse, but the arm was pushed into her face. Glaring, she bit down, and her soul began to sing with the needed blood. Closing her eyes, she let the strength flow into her as she took in what she craved. As her body shifted to heat and desire, a moan escaped her, and Tonya giggled. "Alright, two more pulls, and I'm off to sleep."

When Casey was done, Tonya gave her a quick kiss on the cheek, and sauntered off. When Rowan entered the cafeteria, he headed over to her and gave her a deep kiss. "I hear you're off on a mission this morning, love. And you taste of blood, which is good for your strength, especially after last night."

She leaned in, wrapping her arms around his lean form. Cuddling in to gain a different type of strength. "It's been a hell of a week. I have some debriefing for you and Sydney both about the werehawks I neglected to get to last night. For some reason, I was preoccupied. Oh, and I forgot to tell you we may have figured out the spell ... so distracted last night ... not my fault." She smiled sleepily at him. "Hopefully, that can happen tonight or tomorrow."

Kissing the top of her head, he held her in tight arms. "After the op, you can fill me and Sydney in on everything. Right now, you need more coffee."

Before she could respond, Sydney's voice called from across the room, "Casey, you're here, good. In the study room. We need to plan this out, and what you're doing now won't help."

Her face burning, she pushed away from Rowan. Casey grabbed her plate, returned it to the kitchen, filled her mug of coffee, and trudged into the hallway. She caught up with Sydney and followed her to the study room. The others were all already there. They were all wearing black jeans and black turtleneck shirts. Casey had dressed in the same uniform that morning as well. She'd even borrowed a black knit cap from Tilly to cover her bright bleach-blond curls.

Casey sat down next to Jaxon and across from Jen and her mom Gwen. Micha was sitting at the end of the table. Sydney placed her hands down, gazing at each person individually. "Today is about stealth and information gathering. We want to learn what's inside the compound, maybe learn how many people are part of Jude's organization. For some reason, he's trying to take out his own kind ... as well as other paranormals. We need to figure out why."

Jaxon pursed his lips. "Do we know anything about what to expect in there? Is it all one big place, are there multiple floors? Anything?"

Micha shook his head. "Sorry, man, I should've gotten more from one of those sentries, but I was so worried about Cyran, I just grabbed him and ran. It didn't even occur to me to read their minds."

Sydney held up a hand. "I'm glad you didn't. That wasn't part of your mission. Of the six of us, I don't know that anyone but Casey can really get in and out undetected. We all can change memories, but read them, watch memories, learn from them ... she's the best out there for that. And she doesn't love doing it."

Casey shook her head. "It feels like a violation."

Jaxon's face darkened. "Will you do it for the ultimate safety of our kind?"

Sitting back, she considered him. "If that were the case, yes, I would, but how do we determine whose mind I violate? It's a slippery slope we're talking about. I'm hoping our stealth will be enough to garner the information we need."

Sydney nodded in agreement. "Okay, if there *is* an upstairs, Jaxon and Casey, that will be the two of you. A basement, Jen and Gwen. Find a lab, find files, find anything with facts we can bring back. We need to know what we're fighting. Questions?"

When no one had any, they went to the garage and got into a black van. Sydney drove with Micha directing from the passenger seat. The rest of them sat in the back, holding on for dear life. Jen sat next to Casey. "You know, this black monstrosity of a van feels like we're traveling down the road in a huge metal whale."

Casey laughed. She wondered when they'd have time to joke again. The thought of the mission made her body tense with stress.

They parked on the side street near the entrance to the warehouse after circling it once and discovering that there were two openings. Only one was used as an entrance. Along the other side, to the right, was a service door that could fit a semitruck's trailer. That garage style door was closed and padlocked shut. No one had seen any of the guards when they canvassed the building.

Quietly, they slipped out of the van, and Sydney entered, leaving the door slightly ajar. There were no sounds of fighting. It all seemed too easy. The rest of them followed her after waiting the allotted time. When Casey entered, she saw what looked like a box of a room, maybe fifty feet by fifty feet. There were two rows made out of boxes of other random stuff coming towards them from the opposite wall, which made a sort of aisle down the center of the room. The wall to the left looked like offices, but they went up to a second floor with more rooms and a catwalk. Behind the door they'd entered were the stairs up to the second floor.

Sydney waved to get her attention, pointed at her and Jaxon, then the stairs, then up to the offices. She knew her assignment but gave a curt nod before ascending. The stairs squeaked so she had to slow down to try and avoid the noise. Jaxon followed suit.

At the top of the steps there was a small walkway that skirted around the two rooms which each had doors and windows. The structure was solid and didn't make a sound as they walked and looked through the first window. The lights were out, but Casey could see a desk and a chair. Papers were stacked on the desk in neat piles. Jaxon tried to open the door, but it was locked. Putting out her hand, Casey called the whole doorknob apparatus to her, lock, and all. Jaxon gaped at her for a moment as the door swung soundlessly open.

Jaxon had on a backpack, and they searched a filing cabinet and started stuffing as many files into the backpack as they could. Then they shifted to the desk and collected what they could find from there as well. The area was imposing, but there weren't as many papers in it as they expected. Despite that, the backpack couldn't hold as much as the cabinet and desk had to offer.

Gazing around the room, frustration bubbled up in her. "There must be another office."

Jaxon nodded his agreement. "Let's check out the other room."

As swiftly as they could, they moved down the walkway. As they slid down the catwalk, they checked over the rail and saw the others taking down boxes and cataloging what was in each one. The next door they came to was again locked. Looking through the window, Casey saw a person on the bed asleep.

She wasn't ready to face Jude yet. Turning to Jaxon, she shook her head. "Whoever it is, they're asleep."

Squinting for a better look, Jaxon surveyed the room through the window again. "I don't see any papers either."

A small sound came from the room. "Help me ... please."

Jaxon froze. "What do we do?"

Casey sighed. "We walk away. It's probably a trap."

He nodded. "I know you're right, but what if you're not?"

The voice came again, very feminine. "Please, Casey. I know you probably hate me, but you're my only hope. I need your help before he comes back ... please."

The voice felt like scraping nails inside her brain. A knife of premonition down her spine, and she shivered ... she knew this was bad news. They had to walk away or face disaster. She couldn't stand it, but somehow knew the trap had been sprung, things were already in motion. Despite that ... *I have to try. For years she'd been my friend. What if*

*there's a spark of that friend somewhere in her?
Am I being a fool?*

"Please, Casey." Fingernails on a chalkboard would be more welcome than that voice. Friend or no, the betrayal was still raw.

Facing Jaxon, Casey said, "It's Kailey. It has to be a trap. We must move on."

"I'm sorry, Casey, but there was so much pleading in her voice. I know she's the enemy, but what if Jude turned around and betrayed her? We know he's an ass. He's capable of anything."

Casey was shaking her head as he kicked down the door. As the door flew open, Kailey appeared on the bed, naked and tied down. She writhed, as if in ecstasy. "Please, Casey, I need you, I need you now. He's gotten me so close but said only you were allowed to finish me off." She moaned. "I've been waiting for you; he knew you'd come. He'll keep me like this, forever wanting, never achieving ... always waiting for you. Please, Casey ..." She looked up, eyes piercing Casey, emotional manipulation coming from her in a feeble attempt. "You have to fuck me."

Jaxon got close when the gunfire began below. Taking a quick glance, Casey saw that the first floor was starting to fill with fighters, but she couldn't get distracted. Each pair had a set of instructions, and hers was up here, watching Jaxon's back.

Casey cursed. "A fucking trap! Jax, we have to go."

Jaxon turned to her, eyes wide. "I'm sorry. I know I should've listened." Spinning on his heel, he ran to her, leaving Kailey behind.

Voices started to scream, two in particular rang out. Sydney's came first. "Gods above you'll not die! Casey!"

Casey was already running to the catwalk. As she ran, she heard Gwen's voice. "You fucking ass, you killed my daughter! You do not get to keep her body."

When Casey got to the railing, a set of keys flew at her face. She caught them by instinct just as she saw Sydney with a prone and dead-looking Micha, and Gwen with a dead-looking Jen. Both misted away.

Standing there with the keys, she looked down at a sea of guards, who all pointed their guns up at her. Jaxon grabbed her arm and yelled in her ear, "Mist! To the van! Mist, Casey! Now!"

She misted, just as she saw from the corner of her eye, Kailey, naked and sauntering up behind them, with a gun in her hands, lifting it up to point at her head.

Chapter 21

Jaxon drove. "Where do you want to go? Casey? Casey! Where?"

She sat with her head in her hands, elbows on her knees, bracing herself as the van tore through town ... their shark van, as Jen had labeled it, in waters full of fodder they had to navigate around. "Do you know where Velvet's house is? Near campus?"

His whole body tensed. "Yes, but that's a bad idea. I know you want to find Jen, but we're not strong enough. We have no idea what we'll find there."

Continuing to massage her temples, she fought back the choking depression over her best friend. Dead. How could she be dead? The warehouse was empty, the surrounding streets had been empty, everywhere had been empty. They'd all done a sweep, mental, physical, everything—they'd searched. Then, suddenly, dozens of guards everywhere. How was that possible? Jude didn't have that kind of power, not in general, not at all, and especially not against her.

She played back the scene, over and over, but couldn't see it, couldn't feel it. No matter how her mind replayed it, she couldn't figure out how it could have gone down the way it did.

"Casey! Where are you? Talk to me." Jaxon sounded pissed and stressed and ready to crash the van to get her attention.

Slowly sitting back, she watched the city stream by in a haze of colors, lights, cars, and faces. "Just take me home ... the Cambia House home. We'll check in with Rowan, see if Micha survived, report to Sydney, and go from there. Rowan can call Gwen and demand Jen's body. She's one of ours, and she can't be dead." She felt the heat from her tears streaming down her cheeks as something inside her cracked open. She began to shiver uncontrollably.

She tried to breathe, but only random chaotic sounds came from her, and she was getting lightheaded. When she shot a glance at Jaxon, his face was blotchy, and he openly cried, too. "Cambia House. Thank you." He flicked the turn signal, slowed down, and turned. "I just couldn't make my mind up or figure out where to go. All I could think about was her. I love her, Case, did you know that? I've been wanting to tell her, but didn't want to scare her off, but she's amazing, and I love her, and now she's gone. Gods, what am I going to do?" His words were said so softly, she barely picked them up over the roar of the traffic around them—or was that the blood pounding in her ears?

It didn't take long for them to drive up to the house's garage. Once they'd parked, they made their way inside. The shock of the morning made them move numbly and robotically. Tonya met them once they'd gotten to the main corridor and led them to Rowan's office. He was there with Sydney, drinks, and food.

As they walked through the door, his head popped up and he smiled softly, pointing to a couple of chairs in the sitting area. "Sydney has filled me in on her impressions of today's mission. As she tells it, there was no indication that anyone was in the compound, and then, in a blink, there were dozens of guards, maybe upwards of fifty. Some magic that none of you detected. Let's start there. Do all three of you agree on that part?"

Casey and Jaxon nodded. "Whatever spell Jude had used was beyond anything I've seen or felt before. I'll have to call Hildegard and my grandpa, see if they know what he used. That isn't something small, or anything I've ever heard of. It was powerful ... it was power!" Her body shook with the enormity of it.

Rowan's lips pressed together, and he looked frustrated. Casey didn't blame him. Just thinking about the implications of Jude having a full coven working for him, working for an organization whose sole purpose was the end of paranormal people, made her blood boil. How could he collect so many or alter their mental pathways so completely? Humans maybe, but witches? She couldn't believe it.

Rowan turned to them. "What did you discover on the upper level?"

She shook her head and looked at him desperately. She couldn't think about her mission when she didn't know about her fallen comrades, about Jen. "What about Micha? Jen? We have to know."

He looked down at his hands, sighing heavily. "Micha didn't make it. He was younger than Cyran and the mix of silver and herbs hit him hard. He was hit with three tranquilizer darts, each more concentrated than what they used at your graduation party. Sydney was about to mist to your daughter for her magical blood, when the med staff said it was too late. As for Jen, we don't know. I've called Gwen, but she told people in her house that she was not to be disturbed. She gave specific instructions that if you or I called or barged in to tell us she'd get in contact soon. No one was to enter her suite of rooms on punishment of death."

Anger. It was a welcome change from the empty sadness she'd been feeling. Hot spikes of anger shot through her system, and she felt like she could breathe for the first time since she'd seen her friend misted away. Picking up one of the mugs of coffee, she took a long drink, savoring the flavor. She grabbed a second and handed it to Jaxon.

Turning to Rowan, she put down the mug and sat back. "Is there anything we can do?"

His face hardened. "No, not while she's in the center of their house. We can't storm in. We have to wait."

She felt like she was a pot of boiling water, ready to boil over, a tea kettle, ready to shout its anger, but she tried to tamp it down. "We have a bag of papers. They may be useless, but they were what we found in his office. When we left, things were still quiet. I'm pretty sure the trap was set off when we went into the room with Kailey. She was in a bed calling for us, saying she was sorry. Once our backs were turned, she got herself free and had a gun. She was the only thing in the second room, hell, the only thing on the second floor. Once we entered that room, all hell broke loose down below."

A small growl escaped Rowan at the traitor's name. "She was tied down? What was the point?"

Jaxon sighed. "To lure us in. She said Casey was the only one who could help her. Casey saw the trap. I wanted her to be changed, back to her old self. Once we crossed into the room, I think that's when whatever spell hiding the people uncovered them."

Shaking her head, Casey thought about the logistics. "I bet they were misted in at that point."

Sydney coughed, nearly choking on her coffee. "Misting in four dozen people at once? Who has that kind of power?"

Casey shrugged. "I don't know, but when you walked the building, not only did none of us sense them, you didn't run into any of them. They weren't just hidden from us, they weren't there. I know it's impossible, but we have to consider it."

Rowan steepled his hands in front of his face. "So, what you're telling me is, we have two possible answers for today's debacle, one more outrageous than the next?"

Laughing at how crazy that was, Casey tossed him the bag. "Yeah, but we brought you some reading material."

His eyes danced. "Aren't you just the best gal a guy could ever ask for."

Sydney stood. "Well, that's my cue to leave. Jaxon, want to help me figure out our next attack on chez Jude?"

He stood, eyes glowing. "We're going back?"

She reached the door. "Fuck yeah. We'll bring an army and take the jerk down. Now that we have some basic information, we know what we're facing. I think, if we can get our ducks in a row ... you know, herd cats, we can go in sometime next week."

Face going hard, Jaxon followed the acting head of security. "Good, I want to bring them *all* down."

When they were alone, Rowan's focus centered on her. "What are your plans, love?"

Face falling, Casey stood. "I'm going to head up to my old room for a bit. I want to decompress. I know you need to review the papers. I may call my grandpa later about if he's heard of this level of magic."

He nodded. "Let me know. If you head out there, I'd like to join you."

Standing, she left the office, then slowly made her way up the stairs to her old room. Closing the door behind her, she locked it and curled up on her old bed. Closing her eyes, she dropped all the walls she'd been holding in place.

Jen. Gods above, how can I do this without Jen? She'd been there since I started down this path at the start of college. That first day when we met in the dorms.

"Hi. I'm Casey. I'm going to be your roommate." The girl was fit, with frizzy red hair she tried to contain in a ponytail for move-in day. The heat of the day, the work from moving so much stuff, meant that she had a ring of red around her face ... it was pretty cute.

Timid but determined eyes gazed back at her. "I'm Jennifer ... no, Jen, call me Jen. I'm ... God, I'm messing this up. I'm not a weirdo. Okay, again. Hi, I'm Jen, nice to meet you."

I knew from the start I'd like her. At least, once she calmed down and let herself be her true self. We had a few rough times as Jen learned how to not always be a loner and stop spouting out the hate her dad had filled her with. In the end, we'd become sisters. Jen had helped me through my trial, she'd supported me when I thought I was alone, she stood by me through every twist and turn life has thrown at me. And in the end I was facing Kailey instead of protecting her. She's my best friend, my sister ... and she's gone.

Gods above, I'm going to have to tell Ginger ... A fissure cracked open in her soul and tears flowed. Casey hadn't told anyone about Rowan's proposal. It had been spontaneous; he didn't even have a ring. She had planned to tell Jen after the op, ask her to be her maid of honor. The two of them bungling through all of it ... *what will I do now?*

The sound of her own sobs shocked her, and she tried to push herself up, but she was shaking too hard. Rolling to her back, she covered her face with her arms and let her emotions flow.

Chapter 22

Sunday morning, Casey woke up in bed next to Rowan. Her grief a hallow pit inside her. She knew she had to keep moving. Slipping out of bed, she showered and dressed in a jean skirt and a pale green button-down sleeveless shirt. White ankle socks and white tennis shoes finished off her outfit before she ran down the stairs to the main floor of Cambia House.

Entering her favorite study room, she sat by the phone and called the witch house. "Hello, Sadie speaking."

She closed her eyes to center herself. "Hi, Sadie. It's Casey. I crashed at Cambia House last night, it was a rough day yesterday. I need to go out to ask my grandpa and Hildegard a question today. I was thinking of bringing Kam with me. Could I come pick her up?"

There was a pause and muffled talking. It sounded like she put her hand over the receiver end of the phone. Finally, Sadie came back to the phone. "Apparently Riley had planned on taking the kid to the beach today and Kam would be devastated to miss out. When we asked if she'd want to go with you, she disappeared—" there was muffled talking in the background, "—ah, misted, with a cry of disappointment. Riley explained to us why she was upset."

Biting her lip, Casey thought. "Okay, I get it. I was hoping to have some time with her, but this trip may not be enjoyable. The beach sounds like a bunch more fun. Thanks, Sadie."

There was a smile in her voice when she answered. "Of course, dearie. Tell your grandpa and our fearless leader about my spell and that we're testing it on Monday. We're working on the counter-spell and may have something ready for

Tuesday or Wednesday evening, assuming the first spell works."

Casey heard Riley in the background tell Kam she shouldn't mist just because she disagrees with something and if she does it again, no beach. "Okay, Sadie, thanks again. I'll see you tonight."

Hanging up, she used a push of her energy to call in a cup of tea from the kitchen. She took a sip of the chamomile and mint tea, then dialed up her grandpa. "Daana residence, Parker speaking."

She smiled at his formal greeting. "Hi, Gramps."

"Honey child, what are you doing calling this early on a Sunday?"

Leaning back in her seat, she filled him in on what had happened the previous day at Jude's warehouse. "I want to come out, maybe bring Rowan. I was hoping you and Hildegard could help us figure out if a witch or a full circle of witches could've done what I saw."

There was a pause. "We'll look into it while you drive up, child, but I doubt we'll find anything. Once you're here, we'll review your memories, but I'm guessing that you're right, it's beyond anything a single witch, or even a full coven of witches could do." The worry in his voice traveled down the line.

She sat, holding the phone to her ear, when he spoke up again. "There's more, isn't there? I can feel it through the line. My premonition has been buzzing for a few days, and it's had a few flavors."

A smile broke through her musings. "I'll see you in a few hours. You'll have pizza from Tony's? You know I'll be starving." Tony's made the best pizza in the world, and thinking of it made her stomach grumble.

He huffed a laugh. "Sure, if that's what you want. Are you bringing your girl? I'd love to see her again."

She sighed. "She was promised a day at the beach and couldn't be convinced a day driving in a car was a better alternative. Next time."

"What a shame. I guess I'll have to suffer with just you. Love you. See you soon." There was a pause. "And drive safe."

"Love you too, Gramps."

She hung up and thought about her next call. She knew it had to happen. She couldn't put off telling Ginger any longer ... she too had a right to know.

Her hands trembled as she punched in the numbers she knew so well. After a moment Ginger's groggy voice came over the line. "This better be important."

Casey bit her lip. "Hi, Ginger. I need to talk to you. Any chance you can come over to Cambia House for a bit?"

"Case? No. I'm busy this morning. What's up? Is it about that op you were hinting about on Thursday? Did something go wrong?"

A knife to her heart would hurt less. "Yeah, Ginge, something did. There was a trap, we didn't all make it out ... Jen ..." Casey's voice broke, and she took a sobbing breath as she tried to get more words out.

"Oh, God no. Jen didn't make it?" Ginger's voice cracked, and Casey could hear her sobs. "Tell me I'm wrong Casey, tell me I didn't hear you correctly."

"I don't know what to do Ginger. She was my rock around here, my best friend, my sister. She helped me so much. And she's gone." Casey's whole body shook as the wound opened up, and she cried.

She and Ginger spent time reminiscing about Jen, sniffling, and crying, laughing, and trying to heal enough to survive the day. Once they'd exhausted an hour, they hung up. Tea cold, Casey exerted a tiny bit of energy to warm it so she could let the warmth sooth her. She finished it off and carried the mug back to the kitchen. She debated grabbing breakfast when arms wrapped around her from behind. The scent of spicy mint enveloped her, and she leaned back into Rowan's embrace. "Where'd you slip off to this morning?"

She rotated and wrapped her arms around him, letting her hands play with his curls. "I needed to call into witch house, let them know I was okay, and I'd be back tonight."

His arms locked and his smile dropped. He touched his forehead to hers. "I know that's the arrangement, but ... is there any way we can work around it? I *really* want to figure something else out. Having you away half the time isn't our biggest issue but isn't my favorite setup."

Not wanting to disappoint him, but also knowing she had two duties, she didn't answer right away. "I told my grandpa I'd come out to talk with him and Hildegard today. I mentioned you may be joining me." She pulled back to be able to gaze into his eyes. "I know you said you wanted to come but I wasn't sure if you'd be free."

His fingers dug into her hips, keeping her close. "As long as we can drive one of my cars and not your death-mobile, I'd love to drive out there with you. I insist even. I want to know what's happening ... and I'd like to discuss a matter with your grandpa."

Her eyes narrowed. "With my grandpa? Hmm. Whatever, I'm hungry. I'm going to grab some food, then we should go. Though I want to check in on Cyran first."

He leaned in and kissed her. "Food, you visit Cyran, I'm going to call Gwen, and then we can depart."

She walked into the cafeteria and grabbed a bagel. She toasted it and covered it with cream cheese and jelly.

After she ate, she headed down to the medical suite in the basement. Cyran was lying in bed, but he was awake. "Hey, beautiful."

She grabbed his hand. "How are you feeling? It looks like rumors of your death have been greatly exaggerated."

He struggled to sit up, and she moved to help him. "I still feel like shit. They must've used a larger dose this time ... more concentrated. Or it's because I was hit a second time."

Unable to stop herself, she gave him a quick hug. "Probably all of the above. The tranquilizers *were* more potent, but a second hit can't've been good. You were dead. I ... gods, Cyran, don't do that again, okay? My heart died with you. Just ... don't."

His hand lifted, and he wiped a tear from her cheek. "Hey, look, I'm still alive. Still kicking. I hear Micha didn't make it back on Saturday ... or Jen."

Swallowing her tears—she didn't want to start crying again—she nodded quickly. "Yeah. They came out of nowhere, Cyran. It was weird. We have to figure this out before we can go back in."

His other hand came up, and he cupped her face. "You've got this, Case. You all have it. You're a great team. Have confidence in what you can do together. Not to mention, Jude's an idiot. He'll mess up." He pulled her in and gave her a chaste kiss. "Now, go kick some ass, okay?"

She laughed. "Got it, boss."

After a few more minutes, she backed up, and a piece of her heart began to heal. She wasn't sure how he'd come back from the dead, but there he was, alive and kicking. He'd survived. When she got to the main corridor of the house, she automatically moved towards the front door. Rowan's hand shot out and grabbed her arm. "Oh, no. My car, remember? Your car is a death trap, and with a toddler, I may accidently send it to the car smasher and replace it with something safer."

Her face dropped. "You wouldn't dare, the Green Chameleon is a classic!"

His brow shot up. "So is an Audi."

Chapter 23

The drive to her grandpa's place was swift. They discussed the call with Gwen or lack thereof. She was still not taking calls. The people of the house said she was locked in her suite of rooms with the message that she'd call when she had anything to report.

Casey debated sharing her fantasies of kicking down doors and not taking names. She was pretty sure Rowan would laugh, but wasn't positive, so she kept the images to herself.

Their talk moved on to the call with Ginger and she decided once they'd returned to the city they'd figure out a way to connect. Casey needed to find closure and she needed Ginger to be there. She'd invite Jaxon along too. The three of them deserved the time together.

After that, they tried to lighten the conversation with discussions of Jude, his compound, and finally Casey's new job.

When they arrived at the big house, Grandpa pulled into the driveway behind them, both cars kicking up small pebbles. He had a large gravel area for cars in front of the house, and they parked next to each other. He got out holding boxes with steaming pizza. She and Rowan rushed out to grab the boxes and followed Grandpa inside.

The pizza sat in the center of the table—ham and pineapple, meat lovers, and a pesto and chicken pie. Casey gathered plates while Grandpa started a pot of water for tea.

Rowan smiled. "Anything I can do?"

"No." Grandpa said gruffly, a twinkly in his eyes. "You're a guest."

"Sounds good." Rowan sounded amused. "I'll just sit and be impressed by how seamlessly the two of you move to get things done."

Once the water was ready, Grandpa poured hot water over black cherry tea. He placed the teapot between two of the pizza boxes, and everyone sat. Casey was about to grab a slice when Rowan stared Grandpa in the eyes. "Parker, can I have a minute of your time ... in private?"

Casey slumped back in the seat and glared. "This isn't necessary, and the pizza's getting cold."

Pursing his lips, Rowan stood. "I believe it is. Not only that, you can wait another five minutes to eat your food."

She gaped at him. "Five minutes?"

Grandpa laughed as he led Rowan out the back door, shutting it firmly. Resting her head on the wall behind her, she shut her eyes and tried to imagine what they were discussing. The stillness of the room was interrupted by the crunch of wheels on gravel. She assumed it was Hildegard, and continued to sit and wait, trying to relax. The scents of the pizzas made her stomach growl.

She listened as the car door opened and closed, but instead of Hildegard's normal gait coming to the front door, she heard it retreating. Just what she needed; Hildegard involved in whatever conversation Rowan was having with Grandpa. She was about to leap up to stop this nonsense, when the sound of the back door opening jerked her up to a sitting position. Three sets of footsteps entered the house.

She watched as they came in and took seats at the table. Hildegard gazed at the pineapple in disgust before taking one of each of the other two types. "I don't know about this green pizza, Parker, but I'll try it. Your insistence on pineapple makes your overall judgement suspect." Her German accent was thick as she critiqued him.

Chuckling, Casey took one of each type, then asked Hildegard, "Did Grandpa tell you about why we came down today?"

Her flat stare turned to Casey. "Of course, Fräulein Strega. I know what you told him."

Casey finished off her first piece of pesto pizza, then debated if she liked it enough for a second slice. "Have you ever heard of magic that could act like that?"

The coven leader shook her head sadly. "No. I can't see witches being able to do that. Moreover, I can't see them falling for an idiot like Jude. I know he convinced you, but I can't see it working on a larger scale. He convinced you to like him as a person, but you'd never do magic against your own best interest."

It was nice to know that there was a level that Hildegard didn't think she'd slink below. It was something at least.

Grandpa's smile turned wide. "Should we discuss what happened the other night while we're eating? We can get back to Jude afterwards when we can visit your memories."

Casey froze with the pizza halfway to her mouth. "The other night?" She spoke hesitantly, not quite sure what he meant.

Her grandpa's smile got wider, and his eyes began to twinkle. "Yes, honey child, you know, Friday night. Now that the proper channels have been taken, will you do your job as my granddaughter?"

Thinking back to Friday and what happened, she bit her lip. "I haven't told anyone yet."

He reached across the table and grabbed her hand. "And why not?"

She felt Rowan's hand slide to her knee while she continued to focus on Grandpa. "It's just so big. So many changes so fast ... it's a bit overwhelming."

Hildegard finally had had enough. "What are you two talking about?"

Casey, still holding Grandpa's hand, shifted to face her coven leader. "Rowan asked me to marry him ... I said yes."

Her face transformed. The strict German leader, the terror of all who knew her, softened, and smiled at her. "Congratulations, Fräulein Strega. You'll have to rearrange your time at witch house, either drive in each morning or mist over. I can't imagine you'll want to sleep away from your fiancé, much less your husband. The others will understand."

Casey jaw dropped at how simple she'd made that. "I ... I ... I ..." she stuttered. "I thought I had to live at witch house."

With a shake of her head, the strict leader was back. "You always complicate things, child. Just give time to the witches. Remember your roots."

She wanted to scream and dance and run around. So many emotions shot through her at once. Her hands started to shake, and she shot a look at Rowan, who sat back coolly. His smile was full of laughter and love.

Grandpa's eyes narrowed. "I did notice you aren't wearing a ring. I have your grandmother's upstairs. I'd be honored if you'd consider wearing hers. If not a wedding ring, then as an engagement ring."

Emotions choked her up and tears streamed down her face. All she could manage was a nod. Grandpa stood, slipping out of the kitchen, returning a couple minutes later with a simple gold band with a small diamond surrounded by six tiny sapphires. It looked like a blue flower. "Grandpa, it's beautiful."

He smiled. "She'd be thrilled if you'd wear it, honey child. But call your parents once we're done eating. They have a right to be at the top of the list of who hears the news, don't you think?"

She slid it on her finger. It was a bit tight for her ring finger, but it fit perfectly on her pinky. She'd get it sized for the correct finger later. Gazing up at Grandpa, she blushed. "Of course. Yes."

As they ate, she filled them in on the spell Sadie had created to bind Jude. Hildegard pursed her lips. "It will be tricky. She's planning on utilizing your strength, which isn't a bad idea, but it's the only way it'll work. Using the full moon will help as well. Tell her to call me on Tuesday with the results."

Casey agreed and went back to eating. She knew she was being utilized for her strength but didn't realize it was the only reason the spell would work. She wasn't sure if that made her excited or terrified about the whole ordeal.

Once they'd finished eating, she called her parents, who gave their blessing. The group then moved into the living room. She sat on the couch, Grandpa and Rowan sitting next to her. She was planning on bringing all three into her glass bubble. Hildegard wouldn't need help or physical contact, the other two she'd bring in herself, and the touching helped.

Once in her bubble, she created extra chairs and brought them over to her screen. She played the memory of entering the warehouse. She increased the sensations she felt, so they could feel how empty it was. No one was there. They weren't hidden under a mirror shield; they just weren't there. That left misting in.

After Jax entered the room Kailey was in, the gunfire started up on the lower level, and the place was full of emotions and sensations. A sudden filling of people.

Each person wanted parts of the memory played again, felt again, experienced again. In the end, there were no answers.

Casey and Rowan spent the night, discussing possibilities with the leaders of the witches. Casey told them about the werehawks. Hildegard had heard of them in an old story from her childhood. They were part of the origin story of all paranormals, she explained. She agreed to find the book for the next time Casey visited.

Rowan suggested talking with Lucas again about their origin stories. Hearing that they were part of both the witch and the vampire beginnings, Casey began to think it may be a good idea to add it to her lessons.

Though the four had talked late into the night, Casey and Rowan only left the next morning with Grandpa's and Hildegard's blessings, no answers. The four of them hadn't figured out how an army could suddenly appear from nowhere.

Chapter 24

On the car ride home the next morning, Casey kept gazing at the ring on her finger. "Should I take it off until you've announced it to the house, or the media, or whomever you think you need to tell?" Her heart clenched at the idea. Now that the ring was on, she never wanted to take it off.

A small smile played across Rowan's face as he kept his eyes on the road. "No, keep it on. I like that you're wearing it." He paused as his face tightened in concentration. "I know that you still need blood, and that your donations will lead to other things, but your heart is mine, and that's what I care about." He shot a glance in her direction. "Remember that. We're vampires, and in the end it's your heart and love I want."

Biting her lip, she gazed at his profile. She wasn't sure how she got to be so lucky. She loved this man, and he loved her, and it was amazing.

For the rest of the ride they discussed other ways Jude could've brought the group in. It bothered her the more she thought about it.

After just over an hour, he pulled up to witch house. Getting out, he came around and took her hand. They walked up the stone path together, checking out the flowers and the garden off to the side. At the door, they knocked, though it wasn't necessary since Casey was living there. Since she had Rowan with her, she felt it was more respectful.

Seconds passed and Casey raised her hand again, either to open the door or knock, she wasn't sure. Damion answered the door, saw them, and smiled. His eyes widened as he saw the ring on her finger. Stepping outside, his face froze, and he shut the door. "Is this a congratulations, then?"

Smiling shyly, Casey nodded.

Damion eyes looked sad as he smiled at them. "Kudos! I'm happy for you. Have you figured out what you'll do about your two weeks with us?"

Pressing her lips together, she considered him. "Hildegard suggested I sleep at Cambia House and either drive in or mist in each morning. I'll spend the time here and sleep there, unless there's a particularly late night and sleeping here just makes more sense, like tonight."

Damion nodded. "Yeah, that makes sense."

A tension was building up in Damion, and Casey wasn't sure why. Finally, Rowan sighed. "Damion, we're getting married, but she'll still need blood donors. I'm not ignorant of what that means, especially in a vampling as young as she is. I would love to restrict her interactions with others, but that isn't practical."

Damion's eyes bulged and his mouth gaped open. Casey fought to keep a blank face as she realized what had been plaguing Damion. Then her face heated, and she could only imagine the color. She reached over and placed her hand on Rowan's arm. "Actually, I'm going to try to save any of my female with male fun time for you. Damion likes when I'm a male, so it's very different."

Rowan's brow raised. "I kind of like that. It gives me one thing with you that's special and mine. I prefer you in this form personally, so if that's his preference, it does give me something special."

Throwing his hands in the air, Damion gaped at the two of them before grumbling, "Vampires!" Then he spun on his heel to head back inside the house.

Leaning down, Rowan kissed her, then led her to a bench on the porch. She felt his need for more time alone with her. "Thank you for that. I wouldn't have asked it of you, but it means a lot."

She looked to where Damion had been standing. "It isn't much, but it's what I can give you."

His hands tightened on hers. "When I was young, I was oldest, but not the oldest son. I couldn't inherit the farm; I couldn't take over for our father. I was put in dresses, my mother decorated my hair with flowers, and eventually my brother tried to arrange a marriage for me. Throughout it all ... it felt wrong ... *I* felt wrong."

"You never told me he arranged a marriage."

He huffed out a laugh. "A friend of my father, over twice my age. The man was rich, and we needed the money." He gazed at the clouds in the sky. "I once told you I became a blood donor to bring money to the family ... and that was a truth, but only part of it. I needed an escape, and the vampire house gave it to me. It gave me a place to not wear dresses, not be a pretty girl, not be ..." His pale green eyes deepened as he shifted to look at her, desperate for understanding. "I had to escape from being me."

Casey squeezed his hand, then leaned in to kiss him, whispering, "I love you ... all of you."

He swallowed, remembering a pain from hundreds of years past. "After Ashby made me ... and I learned how to shift ... it was so freeing. Even before then, Ashby let me dress as I pleased. I didn't understand men's clothing, so I did wear dresses, but the clothes provided shifted slowly to trousers as Ashby realized that was what I preferred. He sent someone to pin up my hair. And then, one day, I was a vampire, and a could make my body look the way I had always felt. Gods above, do you how elated I felt the first time I shifted? I cried. When my body shifted back, I wanted to hide in a dark room until I could make the female bits go away again. And for you to recognize that this is what is important to me ... to see me and know me."

Leaning down he crushed her mouth in a bruising kiss, demanding in its need. She returned his kiss to let him know she saw him and loved him, everything about him.

Once emotions calmed, they headed into the house. Kam was in the backyard painting with Riley. Casey stuck her head out back. "Hey, Kam, do you want to go to the park with me and Rowan?"

She leapt up and faced Riley. "Can I Riley?"

Riley rolled her eyes. "She's your Mom, er, Daddy. If she says you can go to the park, I'm fine with it, just help me clean up first."

Kam started 'helping' Riley to tidy up. Casey wasn't sure if the actions caused more mess than they cleaned, but Riley praised her efforts.

Afterwards, Casey started to carry her to the bathroom when she misted away. Riley growled low, "Kam, what have I told you about misting when you have two working feet!" She turned to Casey. "I swear, I'm starting to be able to sense where she lands, she mists so much." And she ran off to find the wayward girl.

Clean and in fresh clothes, Kam was ready to go. Casey and Rowan walked with her the three blocks to the neighborhood park. There was a metal slide, three swings, some monkey bars, and a merry-go-round. The day was cool and the clouds dark, threatening rain, so there weren't other families cluttering the area.

Kam ran off to climb on the bars, then she swung on the swings. Rowan pushed Kam while Casey sat next to her, matching her pump for pump. Soon, they were both high enough that their chains wiggled at the top, and Kam squealed in delight.

Next, the small girl darted off to the slide, but the sun had heated up the metal contraption and she yelped at the top. Placing her hand on the apparatus, Casey used a push of magic to cool it to a reasonable level, then Kam ran in a circle of ladder, slide, and back again for longer than Casey thought could actually be fun.

She and Rowan sat in the shade of a tree on a bench and watched her until she misted into Casey's lap and giggled. Poking her nose, Casey said, "Kam, love, you shouldn't mist all the time. We're in public and we don't want people to see."

Her eyes widened. "But Daddy, it's so much faster."

Rowan leaned down and kissed the top of her head. "It is, my sweetest girl in the world, but it isn't always safe. You need to trust us adults that we want to keep you safe, okay?"

Sighing, she slumped into Casey. Casey's arms wrapped around her in a tight hug. Tucking her hair behind her ear, Casey kissed her cheeks. "I missed you, Kam. As did Gramps. He wants to see you soon." She gave her a big hug. "And I love you."

Kam's small arms snaked around Casey's neck. "Love you too, Daddy."

Sitting back and pulling her daughter tighter on her lap, Casey squeezed. "I have something I want to talk with you about."

Kam's eyes got big. "What is it? Do I haffa go away? Like Mommy did? Is it cuz I mist when I'm not s'posed to?"

The words were like a punch to her gut. "Gods, no, darling. Never. I'm keeping you forever. Rather the opposite. Rowan wants to marry me, become my husband. I wanted you to know right away before I tell the others."

Kam's searched Casey's face, then rotated to gaze at Rowan. Her investigation took just as long. Finally, she smiled. "Does this mean I'll have two Daddies?"

Chapter 25

On the way back to witch house, they stopped at an ice cream shop. After sampling all the flavors, Kam selected chocolate marshmallow swirl. Casey agreed with her choice, so they both got a sugar cone with a scoop. With a dubious eyebrow raise, Rowan choose cookies and cream.

The sugary walk back was full of laughter, and by the time they returned to the house, Kam was covered in chocolate. Rowan watched the girl spin down the walkway. "She's wearing as much as she ate!"

Casey watched, amused. "And a happier girl you've never seen. Now, shower? Or the hose out back?"

They entered the house, and Riley laughed at how covered Kam had gotten herself. "Okay, squirt, to the bath. Bubbles and colored body crayons for you!"

Checking the time, Casey realized she only had two hours before she had to get to the Sand Hill Girls' Home for work. She asked everyone to join her in the living room. "Riley, I want you in on this as well. Kam can head up to the bathroom and you can meet her there." She had too much pent-up energy to sit and she kept rubbing her finger, nerves playing havoc with her system. "Rowan and I have some things we need to do back at Cambia House before I have to work today, but I wanted to let you all know about some changes."

She spun on her heel as she paced the room. Casey decided this would go best if she focused on one person, so stopped fidgeting and stared at Riley. "Rowan proposed to me Friday night, and I said yes."

The room erupted with noise, but she tuned it out. Her heart pounded as the news became more and more real. She surveyed everyone's face before returning her focus to her friend. "It's been decided that I'm moving back to Cambia House, and I'll drive or mist in each day. I'll only sleep here on nights like tonight when we're working late."

In a dry tone, Zen asked, "Who decided this? Your vampire lover?"

Frustration eating away at her nervous happiness, Casey swung around to gaze at the irate witch. "No, if you must know, it was Hildegard. To be honest, it makes a lot of sense, and I'm not sure why the lot of us, all smart witches in our own right, hadn't thought of it before. However, if you have an issue about where I sleep, I'm sure she'd be happy to discuss it with you."

His blank face gave nothing away.

Shaking her head, she shrugged. "For now, we need to figure out our next move. I have a meeting with Sydney and Rowan in twenty minutes to get all the information on the table."

Zen sighed. "Vampires only?"

Rowan smiled. "Well, as it goes, Casey is a witch first. I'm not sure if you realize that. But if you are speaking about one or two of you, then come. You're welcome. All you ever had to do was ask ...

it was the main reason you relocated down here, no? The more minds figuring out this thing with Jude, the better. Who wants to come with us? With Casey's job starting so soon, we need to leave right away."

Zen's eyes widened a bit at his ploy being called out. Damion rose. "I'm free. The others are doing more to study the counter-spell to the binding and set up for tonight. My part is good to go."

Riley watched as everything went down. "I need to wash Miss Ice Cream Monster. Then I'll get everything packed up and head over later. Is there a room ready for Kam?"

Casey bit her lip. "I was thinking she'd have my old room, but it isn't ready yet. We need to finish moving all my stuff up to the extra room Rowan has, maybe let Kam pick out a color to paint, then let her set the room up how she wants. Do you think having her own dorm-like room is too much?"

Riley nodded. "I don't. I'm across the hall, there are others close by who'll love to be near to help her. And with you sleeping here tonight, I'll have her sleep with me tonight. I'll take her over now, get some help, and see what we can do today and tomorrow with moving you out and her in.

With vampire misting, we may be able to get the room painted today, and mostly set up by tomorrow."

Casey froze. "You'd do that?"

Riley glared. "What do you think I've been doing? I'll send you a nanny bill later. Now, off to bathe and pack. We won't be far behind you."

It felt like a weight had been lifted from her shoulders. Casey ran over to give Riley a hug and then she and Rowan walked to the door and out to the cars.

Once at Cambia House, they gathered in Rowan's office. Cyran managed to climb the stairs from the medical suite, not as the head of security, but to know what was going on. He was feeling better, and they thought he may be back to full health in a week. Sydney and Jaxon joined them. Rowan's sitting area was large enough for them all to sit.

Before they could start, Kam misted in. "Daddy, can I have a cookie?"

Casey gave her a hug. "What are you doing here? You should be with Riley! Get back to her, and no cookie until after lunch, dear heart. You already had ice cream."

Turning to stare at Cyran, Kam's head tilted. "That's the one who was on the ground. He took my blood. He's better."

Casey gave her a squeeze. "That's right. It seems your blood helped to heal him."

Kam bit her lip. "Would more help? Riley shares her blood with me, and I feel stronger. Would my blood make him stronger?"

Everyone in the room froze. Casey wanted to scream 'no,' that Kam was a baby, and no one would take her blood. But it had worked before where Rowan's hadn't. Her heart started beating hard, and she hugged Kam to her chest. She realized everyone watched her.

Cyran's gaze dropped to the floor. "I get it. I wouldn't want anyone taking blood from a child of mine. She's so small."

Emotions pounded through her veins and her eyes moistened. She wanted to help Cyran, but she also wanted to protect her daughter. Heart beating faster, she buried her head in Kam's hair. The small girl smelled of the outdoors, the sun and wind. This was her baby, and though she may not have raised Kam, the small being was still precious, and needed to be protected.

Kam vanished from Casey grip. Casey jerked herself back before she fell forward and saw Kam standing in front of Cyran holding up her hand. She'd opened up her thumb on her own tooth. The metallic scent of blood filled the air. It had been covered up by the scents of her daughter's hair and the smell of child. "Just take a few drops. Maybe it'll help." Her voice, small and childish, rose at the end, like a question.

Cyran dropped to his knees, taking Kam's hand. Before he took the offered blood, he caught Casey's eyes. She gave a quick nod, refusing to look away. He lifted the child's thumb to his mouth and sucked off the pooling blood. Then he licked the wound closed.

His breath caught and his eyes widened in shock. "Oh my gods." His breathing got faster, like he'd run a marathon. Taking Kam's face in his hands, he kissed each of her cheeks. "You are a doll. Go, get a cookie. Tell Riley Cyran gives you permission, and then find your favorite paint color for your new room. Whatever color you want, you get."

Before Casey could protest, Kam misted away.

Cyran gazed up at her glaring at him. "She just donated blood. Sugar is always the proper way to refuel."

Casey huffed in annoyance. "You took, like, three drops of her blood. She's lost more running home from the park."

He bounced up to his feet. "I know, but her blood is magic, Case. Your daughter, the child of three halves ... I get it now. I feel amazing."

Rowan cleared his throat. "You may feel better, but I'm still going to wait on the medical professional's report before reinstating you. I don't want to take any chances on losing you. Now, let's get through our talks before Casey needs to leave for work. Where do we start?"

Casey stood from where she'd been crouching. "I think we should start with the good news."

That got everyone's attention. Sydney's dubious look said it all, but in case Casey didn't catch on, she asked, "You have good news?"

Biting her lip, Casey nodded. "Well, I hope you think it's good news. Rowan," she shot him a glance, but he just leaned back in his seat and smiled. Taking a breath, she started over. "Rowan proposed." She pursed her lips, still unable to say all the words she wanted. She finally ended with, "I said yes."

For the second time, a room erupted. This time it was much louder, and the talk lasted longer. Everyone wanted to see the ring and had questions. Once they'd gotten through that, Casey filled them in on her plans to try to create a binding spell with the witches that evening. Finally, she filled Sydney, Jaxon, and Cyran in on the werehawks.

Sydney told everyone about the compound and what had transpired on Saturday. "I would like to go back in on Friday or Saturday. If we can get a group from all the vampire houses—well, I don't expect any of Velvet's, but the other three—we'll have some good vamp power. Then there are the witches, especially if your spell works. And, Casey, if you can get any of the werehawks ... just think, a three-pronged paranormal attack. There is no way Jude can prepare for that."

They all contemplated what it all would mean. Just as they were about to break up the meeting, a new vampire misted in. "I heard you were preparing another attack ... we're in. That asshole has some payback coming, and it's coming from the top."

Standing there, looking ready to fight, were Gwen and Jen.

Chapter 26

Casey sat in her car outside Sand Hill Girls' Home. She had to go in, but her mind was reeling. Jen was alive ... alive.

Gwen had made her a vampire before the bullet and loss of blood had killed her, but then the herbs in the tranquilizers almost did her in. It was touch and go, and Gwen wasn't sure if she'd done the right thing.

Jen had never wanted to be a vampire, and once they had time to talk, Casey had to figure out how traumatized Jen was about this decision Gwen had taken away from her, but right now ... *right now* Casey was just thrilled to have her best friend back. She knew she'd have to take Jen's side in whatever emotion she was feeling about the transition, but until she knew for sure, all Casey felt was relief ... and a bit of joy.

When Gwen and Jen had misted in, Jen still looked weak. Casey searched her body and found a bit of silver hiding in her gut. She pulled it out, and it helped. Then they called in Kam, and for Jen, her best friend, her sister, she allowed Kam to give her a bit of blood. The process was the same as she had done for Cyran, and Jen improved more.

They learned that Velvet had weakened after Jude's defection, and Gwen had taken over as head of the family. The fact that she had the power to take over and lead the family—as young as she was— was impressive.

After the meeting, she and Jen had gone to the study room and called Ginger. Casey knew they couldn't wait on making that call. Ginger sobbed over the phone, then laughed. The call hadn't lasted long, but it had been needed ... for all of them.

Casey hadn't wanted to leave, but this job was new, and she couldn't get fired. Taking a final breath, she opened the door to the cool breeze and headed for the house.

She knocked on the door and Phillipa answered, leading her to the dining room. She found all the girls already around the table. Casey instantly recognized a difference in Blake. Smiling wide, she gave the girl a wink. "Hi, Blake. You seem happier today."

Ducking her head, the girl stood and started handing out plates and napkins. Veronica was in the kitchen finishing up plating the meal. "I feel much better. Thanks for noticing ... and thanks for ... well, everything."

Casey nodded. "I'm glad I could help. You actually helped me—well, us—as well."

Once the plates and napkins were handed out, she grabbed the rest of the flatware. "Lucas went and spoke to my parents. The lawyers said I'll be released tonight. I guess my parents are wary. Someone named Gwen is coming over at nine to pick me up. You'll still be here; do you know Gwen?"

A huff of a laugh escaped Casey. "Yeah, I know Gwen. She's my best friend's mom. She's a good ... person. You'll do well with her. Lucas is right that she's the best person for you to go with. This is the right decision. You'll be in good hands."

Blake visibly relaxed.

Tammy, having gone this long without talking, a feat Casey hadn't thought was possible, finally had too much. "I can't believe she really was innocent of her crimes. Like, yo! Everyone claims that. And you believed her. Why her?"

Veronica brought in a bowl of salad, a platter of baked mac and cheese bubbling with a broiled top that looked and smelled divine, and garlic bread. She noted the chunks of actual baked garlic on the bread this time and bit back a laugh. "I've always had an affinity for hearing truths and lies. It's why I decided to study criminal psychology."

Sitting and staring at Casey with an accusatory glare, Veronica raised an eyebrow. "I've always heard that vampires could hear or taste lies."

Casey shrugged. "I always heard it was the witches. It's funny how rumor always puts it at the feet of the more convenient paranormal." The truth was, not all vampires, nor all witches could hear a lie, but Casey seemed to get it from both her sides. She could always hear it as a witch, but once she turned vampire too, her ability increased. It was almost like she could feel the lie before the person spoke it.

Casey filled her plate with a bit of everything. The garlic bread was much better, and she snagged a second slice.

After lunch, they had their group session. Most of the girls spoke about what they'd done over the weekend, ways they were working on coming together as a community, and their family day on Sunday. Veronica continued to be hostile.

Betsy, who'd decided to sit on the floor, rolled her eyes. "Just because your family didn't come this week, don't take it out on the rest of us during session. My family never shows up and I'm never a bitch."

Veronica's nose flared. "We aren't supposed to use that kind of language. She needs to get a punishment."

Casey knew she was losing control, but secretly agreed with Betsy's assessment. "Veronica!" she said in a stern voice. "You need to focus on you and your issues and let me worry about Betsy. She's up for session today—"

"Well, that's certainly a punishment," Veronica mumbled.

Casey took a slow breath. "And so are you. I will work with each of you individually on how to interact within the group. Since we were close to the end of our session anyway, why don't you all take a half-hour to unwind, and Veronica, I'll start our sessions off with you."

The girl got up and slammed out of the room. The others sat and watched her, even Tammy, her best friend. It wasn't until her footsteps faded from the stairs that the others stood to leave. Only Tammy stayed behind. When it was just the two of them, Tammy slumped. "Her dad is part of this organization, and she's worried about him."

Casey rubbed her temples. "Will she get upset that you're telling me this?"

Tammy shrugged. "Don't know, don't care. Her dad is part of this thing called Hope, or something. I don't know what it is, but she keeps on trying to get me to join with her. She's like, it will bring hope to all the humans. Like, having vampires and witches ruins any chance of hope for humans,

I dunno. Anyway, her dad was supposed to come, but he called from the hospital on Saturday. I guess some vampires attacked their stronghold. They killed a bunch of them, the vamps, you know, but he was one of very few of the humans who got hurt."

She really didn't know what to say and her head was beginning to pound, but she doubted Veronica would tell the story any better. "Can you give me those details again?"

Scrunching her nose, Tammy shrugged. "Her dad said a group of like a dozen or more vampires attacked their stronghold. Then the humans attacked them and killed all but, like, two or three of them. They have specialized guns, I guess. In the fight, two or three humans did get hurt. Her dad was one of them. He ended up in the hospital."

Casey bit her lip. "Got it. Thanks for letting me know. At least I know where her anger comes from. She knows that I'm friends with vampires, so she sees me as an enemy no matter what."

Tammy stood. "Pretty much. My uncle, his name is Thomas, Tom for short. He belongs to one of the houses, Lucas's, the one Blake mentioned. He's like me, a bit scattered. He's not, like, my dad's brother, he's my great-grandfather's brother, but calling him my uncle is easier. Anyway, I've grown up knowing about vampires. I don't know them well, but they're just people ... you know, who live longer."

Casey struggled to not react at the name of Tammy's uncle. It was the vampire who lost control at her scent. Witches smelled particularly good to vampires and before Casey understood that, she worked at one of their parties, and Thomas attacked her. Casey didn't know she'd been attacked until she'd met Jude, and he'd informed her she was a vampire. Much like Blake, she didn't know about or remember her transition.

Watching Tammy walk away, a shiver ran down Casey's spine. Calling Tammy's family scattered was only the beginning. Casey got up and searched for Cindy. She found her in the kitchen, sitting at the long table. "Hi, can I ask you something?"

Looking up, the leader of the house smiled and nodded at a seat on the bench across from her. Casey grabbed a glass and filled it with water before joining her. "I was wondering if I could set up a work-study for Delilah and Phillipa?"

Sipping her tea, Cindy gazed at the juncture of the ceiling and wall. "Why?"

With a small push of will, Casey closed her eyes and sensed. She knew that there were no girls in the kitchen or near them, but that didn't mean that there weren't air vents leading to the kitchen. The den, however, was a private space. If it wasn't, the girls wouldn't talk with her in there. "Can we speak in the den?"

Cindy gave a slight nod and followed her into her makeshift office. Closing the door, they each sat. "Did you know that the two girls were witches?"

Cindy nodded. "You get a feel for that sort of thing around here. What you did for Blake was pretty amazing. I can tell when a girl is something more, but I don't have the connections you do. I see that ring you're wearing. It's on your pinky, but am I to assume there's an announcement coming?"

Casey smiled. "Yeah, Rowan proposed."

A brow rose. "How will you keep your own special nature from the girls then?"

Shrugging, Casey said, "I don't know. I didn't mean to initially. I'm not embarrassed, it was more a game to see what they would do to ask appropriately. Delilah and Phillipa already knew I was a witch; they've known from day one. I want to get them studying with the small circle my coven keeps here. They need training."

"And you want to call it work-study?" Cindy took a sip of her tea.

Casey nodded. "This way, they can choose to tell or not tell what they are. It's safer."

Cindy sat for a few more minutes, she looked to be in thought. She drank tea as she considered the situation. "Would this option be open to other witches who found their way into our home?"

Smiling, Casey felt a weight lift from her shoulders.

Chapter 27

Kam finally fell asleep ... probably. Casey was in the living room reading a book and had been listening to the girl playing in her room. She was supposed to be asleep, but the random crashes told a different story. The upstairs had been quiet for the last twenty minutes, so all the adults who had been waiting were hopeful.

"Daddy! I'm thirsty!"

Groaning, Casey went to the kitchen to get a small cup of water. Riley intercepted. "You need to get ready with your small circle. Let me take care of

Kam. Our original plan was a sleepover at Cambia House. Why don't I take her there? Then there'll be no interruptions."

Letting her head fall onto Riley's shoulder for a moment of rest, she let her friend take the water, and head up the stairs. Halfway across the living room she heard Riley say, "Hey, kiddo, what have I told you about misting?"

Kam's voice came quiet and shaking. "Only do it when it's necessary."

Riley voice got softer as she headed up the stairs. "Righty-O, kiddo. You didn't need to mist down for water; you knew it was coming up to you. You need to listen to me, to us, when we tell you things."

Kam's small voice floated on the air. "Sorry, Riley."

The rest of them had already changed into clean white robes and watched as the sky darkened from a dark blue to something inkier with white stars. Casey quickly slipped into her robe and grabbed her walking stick. This level of magic would need the extra boost of both ritual and the power of the stick. It felt like Zoryda winked at her in anticipation.

Sadie stood. "Okay, witches, it's time."

They all moved to the shrine room. In the original house blueprints, it was probably a walk-in pantry, but the witches used it for spell components. Casey grabbed the eight white candles needed for the spell. The robes had large pockets in which she could store the candles. She'd light them with her magic. Tilly grabbed a small piece of rowan wood, two to three inches long, the talisman. She lifted the robe's hood to cover her head and waited on the others. She had to be the last one out. Once she touched the candles, the spell had officially begun for her.

Tilly was the first out, followed by Zen, Sadie, Damion, and then Casey. She hadn't seen the rest of the spell's parts and hadn't known what everyone's roles would be. As the first one out, Tilly stood in the position of leader, where Casey held the spot of the pillar. If she fell, Damion would take her place, standing second in power. Tilly, as the leader, held the third strongest power level in the spell. Interestingly, Casey hadn't known the rankings, actual or perceived, before this moment. She'd have to ask the others about it later. Were their placements for this spell only or how they actually felt the ranks were?

Once they left the house and entered the patio, a cleared slab of cement, open to the sky, clean and prepared for tonight's spell, they all became components of the spell. Tilly stood at the west point, the point of water, the panther on her walking stick standing tall and proud. Next, Zen took the southern spot, representing fire, his wolf appearing ready to strike. Sadie came to a stop to the east, air, her bear standing on three paws, the fourth ready to swipe away a foe. Damion, in the final position, took the impact of the spell and their strength, the northern spot, the location of earth. It also represented midnight and the full moon. It was why the spell was planned for nightfall and why they all knew the spell would work best under the full moon or within a few days of it. His tiger lowered atop his walking stick, ready to pounce.

The four of them positioned their walking stick in front of them in unison, with the stick standing perfectly vertical between their palms. Once the circle was locked, the magic would flow strong enough the sticks would stand on their own, balanced on their sharp silver points, holding, filtering, and guiding their magic. Without the aid of their familiars, this level of magic could crack part of their mental abilities, leaving them impaired.

Casey slowly approached as the final member to enter the spelling ring. She circled the others once counterclockwise to place the cardinal candles a foot behind each witch, twice to place the intermediate ones and form an eight-pointed circle, and thrice to light them each with a tiny push of her will. The she reversed her direction and, with the words to build a circle, traced the circle four times, once for each member inside, the four cardinal directions, and the four phases of the moon. Reversing course once more, she chanted the words to lock them and the magic inside. Stepping inside, she felt a pull on her power as the circle closed behind her with enough of a snap to depressurize her ears. She began to hear popping sounds every time she swallowed.

Moving to the center, she realized the others chanted quietly, part of the spell she didn't know. She planted her feet shoulder-width apart, placed Zoryda facing out, her protector, intertwined her arms, joining her palms, and raised them to the sky, lifting her face with them. The next phase of her chanting began.

She felt the others move around her, their words a counter-melody to hers. At some point the rowan twig was slipped between her palms. The dance continued, and she felt her body fill with the combined magic of the four other witches. A tingling started in her feet and inched up her legs as she began to lose feeling with the spell.

The tenure of the chant increased as the four sat back at their cardinal points. Casey saw from the corner of her eyes when they threw their hands to the sky, faces high, singing out to the heavens. The magic held their walking sticks in place. The tingling was at her waist. She was glad for the stable stance of her central pillar position. Her breathing was getting chaotic as she maintained the spell, the others' words cascading through her, filling her, numbing her.

The spell came to a fever-pitch, their individual parts coming together to form a single line they all chanted out in unison. It was repeated three times and then they all went silent. All that could be heard was their rough breaths over the still quiet of the back yard. Then a swell of power gathered from the edges of the circle. It expanded in and funneled up through Casey into the sky in a fountain of blue and silver. If felt like pins stabbing her in a thousand places as the magics rushed through her body ... tiny knives, then swords.

When it was finally done, she collapsed, her vision tunneling to pinpricks of pale blue and she struggled to remain conscious. She knew her walking stick still stood, the spell was still working. Her body shook as she choked out, "It will fall back down. Beware!"

A moment later, the magic plunged down, swamping them all. It filled her back up. She held the rowan stick in the waterfall of power, chanting the final lines to seal the magic in. This spell was brilliant, but a waste of energy. It would kill them all if they had to do it too many more times.

As the magic finally dissipated, Casey pushed herself up to a sitting position, reaching out to grab Zoryda before she fell. Casey massaged her temples as her head pounded. She let her head fall between her knees and she just breathed in the clean air. The wash of the falling spell cleared away the circle, lock or no. Too much power for the circle to hold in.

After several minutes of breathing, she realized the others were talking to her. Shaking her head, she sorted out what they'd been saying. She lifted her head and found Sadie in the mix. "Your spell was a mess, but it worked ... at least, the stick has magic sealed in it. We can take it over to Lucas tonight to see if it does what you designed it to do."

The others' faces all transformed into content and happy forms. Damion's was a bit apprehensive. "Are you up to the trip?"

She nodded. "Yeah, I just need to stand first."

Tilly stared up at the starry sky. "How about a bit of blood? I know that's usually a whole production, but could you just, I dunno, take a sip before we leave?"

Casey shot a glance at Damion, whose eyes darkened with lust. Biting her lip, Casey nodded. "Yeah, sure. I can control myself, and I think after that," she waved her hand vaguely, "blood would be a good idea. I can probably get a bit now, and more later ... after we visit Lucas."

Tilly smiled. "How about I give you some now, and Damion can top you off afterwards?" She smiled at her with a nod. She glanced at Damion— his smile was much less innocent.

The others headed in and gave them privacy. Casey chuckled. "Just let me have your arm. You've had a hard night too; I won't take too much."

Tilly's smile brightened. "That wasn't bad for the rest of us. It was really hard on you, but we just got to watch the magic beat up on you. Zen won't be able to complain about your abilities after that. You were freaking amazing, Case."

The compliment from a former teacher gave her warm fuzzies. Carefully taking the offered arm, she bit down and took as little blood as she could get away with. She knew she was in trouble when it took five pulls for it to feel pleasurable. That spell had hit her hard. She took an additional three, then cleaned off Tilly's arm.

Tilly looked pale, but strong. "Did you get enough?"

Casey stood. "Yeah. I'll be fine. I'll get more tonight, and if I'm still in need, living at Cambia House, I'll always be able to find a donor. We're just going to drop this off and come back, right?"

Smiling, Tilly stood, and wavered a bit. "Right."

Guilt washed through her. "You, maybe, should stay here. Drink some juice, have some sweets."

Tilly wanted to go, but in the end realized it was better for her to stay behind. Damion and Casey went alone. They arrived at Lucas's place, and were welcomed in. Like Cambia House, it was large, to accommodate vampires and blood donors both, but his house had more paintings, sculptures, and art, as if it had been collected over many more years.

In the foyer, there were paintings that looked as old as time itself. One was of a black lab and a white cat with jewel green eyes. They were running in a wooded area with a lake in the background. The cat gazed out towards the person viewing the artwork and there was sharp intelligence in the animal's eyes.

On the opposite wall, there were a series of smaller paintings of Lucas as a kid, though his hair had a purple tinge. Some of the paintings had him with the same black dog, another with three other kids, all young, and a third in a field with a dragon in the sky flying high above him. He must have had that last one commissioned. It was fantastic.

Lucas met them and saw Casey's interest in the art. "My mother's artwork from when I was a child. I never imagined it would survive the years." Again, she wanted to know his age, his story, but knew, deep in her heart, he wouldn't tell her, at least not today.

He led them to stairs that wound down to the basement. Along the walls to this private area there were more paintings, but these were more fantastical. The dragon again, in flight, but in more detail. A unicorn, shining white, with iridescent wings, a griffon—until she got to a painting of man with violet hair walking into the darkness of the forest, these painting almost felt like an homage to the witch's familiars. On and on the images went, each painting beautiful, each one a fantasy.

At the bottom of the stairs there was a locked room with a single vampire. Taking the stick, Casey said the release word, and touched the stick to him. His eyes bugged out and he slammed himself against the wall, sliding to the floor. "Lucas, what have you done to me? This is so much worse than the silver. I feel horrible. Am I human? Did you have them unmake me? Oh, gods! You made me human!"

The vampire began crying as he curled up on the floor. Lucas's eyes narrowed, then he pulled Damion and Casey out. "That was remarkable. I'll let you know if it wears off, but his aura is still vampire, so you didn't unmake him. If ... when you come up with the unbinding, we will fix him. I believe this punishment will do the trick."

They left. Casey thought about Lucas's ability to read the vampire's aura. But after seeing that reaction, Casey knew, after Jude, she never wanted to be part of a vampire binding again.

Chapter 28

Casey sat in the front room with the other witches. The response of the vampire they'd bound still played out in her mind, chills ran down her spine.

"How bad was it?" Tilly asked, her elbows on her knees, a cup of tea in her hands, cold for how long it had gone undrunk. All her attention hung on Casey and Damion's story.

Damion shivered. "It was rather awful. He thought we'd undone his vampirism, as if we have that power. The spell worked better than I thought it would. We really need the counter for the spell." He shook his head. "I'll do the spell again to bind Jude—that vampire needs stopping, he's gone too far, attacking everyone—but beyond that ... I'm not comfortable using it."

A shiver slithered down Casey's spine. "I agree. Not only is the spell wicked powerful, I don't know how many times we can do it as a small circle coven."

Zen sneered at her. "Are you afraid?"

Casey's eyes narrowed, but before she answered, Sadie's voice whipped out like a throwing star. "Would you stop it? I'm ready to talk to Hildegard about replacing you. I don't know what issue you have with Case, but she is the only witch I know strong enough to pillar the spell or the counter. Do *you* want to try? It would kill you, Zen. Gods above, stop being an ass."

Casey worked to keep a blank face and, gazing at Damion and Tilly, it looked like they battled the same fight.

Zen grunted. "Whatever, I'm going to bed. It's late." He stood and walked out, tall and proud.

Once he was gone, Sadie slumped. "Sorry for swearing ... he just ... gah ... he's so frustrating.

Anyway, I don't think we can work that level of power every day ... or, well, night. Since we need to work around the full moon, let's plan on Wednesday for the counter spell, to make sure it works, and not leave that poor vampire suffering. Then we can repeat tonight's spell on Friday."

Everyone agreed with the plan and the discussion broke up as they all headed to their rooms. Damion grabbed Casey's hands and pulled her up. She could feel how low her reserves were, and she swayed a bit. She made it up the stairs and into his room before leaning on the door and using the last bit of oomph she had to shift her parts from female to male.

He came over, sensing when she was done, and tipped her chin up. "You okay?"

Looking up into his dark eyes, she gave a small smile. "I will be."

With a mischievous glint, he grabbed the hem of her shirt and pulled it up, stripping off her top. He gave her flat chest a quick glance before letting his eyes roam down and then he groaned. Casey was learning he was a chest and abs man. "If you get the rest of your clothes, I'll get mine."

She smiled. "Sounds good." She kicked off her shoes and pushed down her pants and panties. As she bent, a phantom hand began stroking her and she almost toppled over. Her hand shot out and she grasped the side of the bed.

Making a sound of pleasure, he slapped her ass, hard. "I like you in this position, but I have other plans for you tonight."

Her breathing hitching, she licked her lips, and with the help of the bed managed to straighten. His phantom fingers never relented. "Gods above," she panted. "How are you doing that?"

He wrapped his arms around her from behind, then turned her around. "A magician never reveals his secrets. Now, grasp me." She did. He was thick, hot, and soft as silk in her hand. She tried to match her actions with the phantom hand on her cock. Then his arm circled around her waist, pulling her in so they were close. The scent of him made her fangs descend. He kissed her just below her ear. "Feed, Casey."

He didn't have to ask her twice. She bit down on his neck and his blood flowed into her, giving her life, and power. After a few sips, it filled her with heat, adding to the ecstasy building from what he was already doing to her and what she was doing to him.

His blood flowed into her, and her head swam as the sensation of hands on her body and blood filled her. One more pull and every muscle tightened. She swallowed, then cried out, quickly licking his wound closed. Only Damion's arms holding her up kept her from collapsing onto the floor.

He placed her on the bed. "Scoot up to the pillow, unless you want to be on top?" Not knowing what was about to happen, she shifted until her head was on the pillow. He moved on top of her until he was straddling her, but not so that his mouth was lined up with hers. Looking up, she saw his long thick dick, ready for penetration.

Looking between their bodies, he winked. "Ready for this?"

She licked her lips and nodded. Grasping him, she guided him into her mouth. She started with the end of his cock and slowly moved more and more of him in until he reached the back of her throat. He was large, and she used her hand to make sure she wouldn't gag. Sucking hard, she began moving him out and back in. His moan and rough breathing were a pleasure all their own. Using a free hand, she let it travel up to play with his more sensitive areas.

Suddenly, he grasped her cock in his actual hand. Stroking it, he lowered his head around her. His tongue licked and sucked, his hand at the base helping with his rhythm. His phantom hand suddenly entered her ass slowly, finger by finger. The sensation felt slick and stimulated her ... everywhere. She bucked up in surprise. He was ready, moving with her. With a deep chuckle that vibrated through her core, her whole body quivered with desire.

Heat began to boil in her center. Building from every corner of her being.

He continued to suck, finding a rhythm. She mimicked his motions, the build of sensations of having three sensitive areas stimulated, because who knew her mouth could be so sensitive to this, almost too much. It all added to the ocean of heat building in her gut.

They moved, her body a bow string. She dipped a finger, then two, into his ass, trying to give him what he gave her. His moans and groans vibrated through her body, heightening the sensations. The pressure of his mouth, the speed of his motions, the phantom feeling, it grew to a crescendo, until she orgasmed with his cock deep in her throat. The ocean of heat exploding.

She cried out, hearing him cry out as well. He filled her mouth before collapsing onto her, and she swallowed his salty seed before he rolled away. Flopping on his back next to her, he sighed contentedly. Breathing heavily as the sensation ebbed through her, she closed her eyes and enjoyed the feelings.

Sitting up, she slid from the bed, grabbed her clothes, and was about to mist across the hall, when Damion stopped her. "You could stay here tonight."

She sighed. "I could, but if I'm sleeping with a guy, I'd rather sleep with Rowan. And if I shift in my sleep, you don't want to wake up with me with naked female bits."

A shiver ran through his body. "Fair enough. If you only always had male parts, you'd be about perfect."

Casey smiled. "Maybe if I'd fallen for you before Rowan ... but you do make an excellent blood donor. Witches are better than humans."

He sat up. "Well, good. We can have a standing arrangement. You come to me since Riley is helping Kam. I am the least threatening to your upcoming nuptials."

Laughing, she misted away. When she reached the room she shared with Riley, she found her friend sitting up in bed reading. Shutting the book, Riley raised an eyebrow. "This is an interesting way to come to bed."

Casey bit her lip. "Sorry. Give me a second and I'll shift back."

Riley shook her head. "No worries. Come and lie down. I've never really investigated this side of you."

Swallowing hard, Casey climbed into bed. But then Riley's hand was in her face. "Wait, what did you and witch boy do? Did you do butt stuff? Like, should you go wash first?"

Laughing, she pushed Riley's hand away. "No, we did mouth stuff. Actually, let me go wash my hands." Running to their attached bathroom, Casey washed her hands. Not knowing what Riley planned, she rinsed out her mouth as well before returning. Lying down, Riley leaned on one hand, the other touching her face, and her chest. "This is so weird. I mean, I've seen this, but not on you. You're so ... male." Her hand went lower, and she started playing.

Casey groaned. "Gods, Riley, before you start something, how much are you going to ask of me? I mean, you do know where I just came from."

Her mouth twitched up. "I don't think I said you could ask questions, did I?" And she leaned down and aggressively kissed Casey. Taking both wrists in her hands, she pinned them above Casey's head. Pulling back, she said, "I want you to imagine you are in my bed, there are slats, and your hands are holding onto them. No moving. Understand?"

Casey watched as Riley slipped from the bed to remove her black tank top and panties. Crawling back up, she grasped Casey. "You know, for a girl, you have a great dick. It's thick, and hot, and long enough to be dangerous. It's a real chick dick." She began playing with it and the balls below.

Casey squirmed, heat building, and Riley eyed her. "Do not move those hands, or there *will* be a punishment." Not knowing what this hot wire of a woman would do for punishment, Casey tried to not move as Riley explored. Her eyes threatened to roll up as electricity shot through her body once again.

Straddling Casey, Riley lowered herself onto Casey's cock, slowly sliding Casey inside her. Riley was tight and wet. The warmth encasing her ratcheted up Casey's need and she groaned. Riley placed her hands on Casey's chest so her thumbs and fingers could play with Casey's nipples. Casey matched the rhythm of Riley's rolling hips.

Riley's breathing was getting rough, as was Casey's. Riley eyed her. "Okay, one hand, right on my clit. Take me home. The other, on my breast."

Following directions, trying to focus on Riley's needs as her own fireworks were ready to explode again, she made sure to hear Riley's scream of pleasure before she finished off herself, bucking up as her orgasm shot through her. Riley landed on top of her, and Casey's arms wrapped around her.

As the two of them cuddled, Riley wiggling to lie next to her, Casey did a final push of will to shift back to her normal appearance. Once her body was softer, Riley moaned in pleasure. "That was fun, but you're a better pillow when you're soft." And then a soft snore escaped the vixen.

Chapter 29

Wednesday morning, Casey woke up with Rowan. It was her first morning in this bed where she had no other option within Cambia House to sleep. Kam had her old room. After spending Monday and Tuesday with a gaggle of vampires and donors, she had a light purple room with a dragon painted on two of the walls for protection. Or so she claimed.

They kept the same bed and dresser Casey had used, but there was a chest full of toys, old and new.

All of Casey's possessions were strewn in the extra room until things could be figured out. That would be done in another week when she wasn't spending all her free time with the witches.

Stretching, she curled into Rowan, gave him a hug and a kiss on the cheek, and tried to climb over him. He held on. "Where do you think you're going?"

She smiled down at him. "To shower. Dress. Get to the witches and then my job."

He pulled her down into a deep kiss. Apparently, morning breath didn't scare him away. Once he was done, he said, "Shower, yes, dress, if you must, though you naked could be fun for the day, but we have a meeting with the police. Call the witches, ask one of them to join us for the meeting. Then we need to call Lucas, Cynthia, and Gwen. The meeting will be at ten."

Collapsing on him, resting her cheek on his chest, she let the worries of the day wash over her for a few minutes. His arms tightened around her again, but when she pushed up, he let her go. She moved to the shower. She had barely gotten wet, when his lovely self joined her in getting clean.

She picked a pair of acid washed jeans, a dark gray t-shirt, and a black blazer for the day. Heading down for breakfast, she stopped in Kam's room. Her daughter played a game and still wore her pajamas. "Let's get you dressed, and we can find breakfast!"

The girl leapt up and flew into Casey's embrace. They found her a pink skirt and a white shirt with a rainbow horse on it. In the cafeteria, they found pancakes, sausage, hash browns, and scrambled eggs. Casey wasn't sure what warranted such a feast, except celebrating it being Wednesday, but she loaded up two plates and headed to a long table to eat.

Soon, she was joined by Lucas, then Gwen and Jen, then Cynthia, and finally Rowan. It didn't take long for her to surmise why the breakfast was as elaborate as it was. Riley made her way down, saw how many people were at the table with her and Kam, and swooped in. "Hi, Kam. Want to stay here with Daddy and all these adults or go play on the obstacle course? I'm guessing a new one will be set up soon."

Kam's eyes widened. "Jen, do you wanna see my new room?"

Jen's smile blossomed. "I'd love to. Why don't we go up to the room, then you and Riley can go play?"

Kam jumped up and danced before running around the table to take Jen's hand and drag her from the cafeteria. As they got to the doorway, Kam stopped and looked up at Jen. "When did you become a vampire, Jen? You weren't one last time we played. Does this mean you get to train with me? Can we be partners?"

Jen shot Casey a desperate look before being pulled out of the cafeteria. Cyran, who'd joined them, gazed after them. "She reminds me of her Daddy in the number of questions she asks."

Cynthia, the information gatherer, laughed a belly laugh at that. Lucas smiled. Gwen, who hadn't spent much time with Kam, looked confused. "Her Daddy? Who's her Daddy?"

Casey snorted. "I am."

Gwen stared at her for a few seconds before it clicked. "By gods, I'm slow this morning. I probably need more coffee. This family has got to be the strangest of the four. You fathered the child, not mothered her. And she calls you Daddy?"

Smiling, Casey nodded. "Her choice, not mine."

Jen returned, sitting back down to finish her breakfast. Gwen watched her, face softening with love and concern. "If you fathered Kam, and she calls you Daddy, once you and Rowan marry, what will she call Rowan?"

Dropping her fork, Jen's focus shot to Casey, looking hurt.

Casey bit her lip. "Jen, I ..."

Her friend's face hardened. "I've heard, I just wanted you to tell me."

Casey's hand shot out to Jen, but Jen shied away. Casey sighed. "I've been wanting to tell you, it's just ... things have been a bit crazy."

"Too crazy to make a phone call?" Jen's eyes hardened.

Shoulders falling, Casey tried to make Jen understand. "You were the first person I wanted to tell, but it happened when everything else happened. And then I didn't know how I could get married without you there, by my side. Because I wanted to formally ask you to be my maid of honor." Casey dropped her eyes to her coffee, not wanting to put any pressure on Jen. "But you don't have to if you don't want to." She finally looked back up.

Eyes widening, Jen just gaped. "You what? What do you want me to do? What do I know of weddings or being a maid of honor?"

Casey shrugged. "What do I know of being a bride? I thought we could mess everything up together. It'd be more fun that way."

After a few seconds, Jen's face broke into a smile. Finally, she reached across the table to clasp Casey's hand. "Okay, yes, I'd like that. We make great messes together."

Everyone else at the table seemed to relax once their hands linked—everyone but Rowan. "I knew you two would work things out."

Elbowing him, Casey rolled her eyes and faced Jen again. "Would you want to grab lunch tomorrow? I don't have to work, and I'd like to catch up, just the two of us."

Jen nodded. "Yes, I've missed you. I know it's only been a few days, but, gods, it feels like a lifetime."

After eating, they moved to one of the study rooms. Rowan's office was big, but the study room would accommodate more people. As they tromped down the hallway, Damion came in, followed by the chief of police.

Once they were all situated, the chief of police began his debriefing. "Because of the girl that Casey found at the Sand Hill Girls' Home, we've been looking for Jude Malvado. We got a second hint from another girl at the same Girls' Home on Monday when we learned that the father of one of the girls is a member of H.O.A.P, Jude's organization. This led us to his warehouse."

Everyone in the room gaped at Casey, who shrugged. "My new job has some interesting benefits."

The officer laughed at her choice of words. "We raided the compound looking for Jude. We didn't find him, but we did find both Kailey and Velvet, who have both been taken into custody. Despite their incarceration, neither are talking. We also found boxes of silver bullets and tranquilizer darts. We emptied the warehouse of both and are planning on destroying the drug."

Casey wondered if they were destroying or researching the drug for a weapon against vampires. Humans had never had a way to fight such a strong enemy, and now, thanks to Jude, they did. It was great that Jude and company had lost all their stock, but now the government had the chemicals and could reverse engineer the weapon.

Searching the faces around her, she saw passive acceptance of what the officer had said. There was nothing she could do to fight this ownership of the drug, so she mentally shrugged and listened to the next part of his story.

The chief faced the heads of the four houses. "The warehouse was empty of men when we raided it. There was no sign that anyone had even been there recently, except the two women. My men took the product and emptied all stock from the lab. It will be hard for them to recreate what they had with such an empty compound ... including a dismantled lab."

Nodding, Rowan held out a hand. "I would like to thank you for the job you did. You have, once again, made our streets safer."

The officer gazed at each of them, searching their faces for something. "Do any of you know where the vampire Jude Malvado is?"

They all shook their heads. Cyran, who'd stayed silent, pounded the table with his fist. "I wish I knew where he was, sir. That jerk has done a lot of damage to his own people, and I, for one, would really like to know why."

The officer nodded. "Thank you. I doubt there is more I can do here, so I'll be heading out. If you get a lead on him, do not go after him, let the authorities know. It's our job."

Once he was gone, the meeting could really get started.

Sydney held up a hand. "I think we need to go in on Saturday morning, say eleven. The witches will create a new binding stick tonight."

Casey shut her eyes, thinking about the spell. She'd planned on having the counter-spell, but they decided they needed to focus on Jude first. The counter-spell could wait a few more days. Part of that was after a conversation Sadie and Lucas had had.

Gwen glared at the table. "Then why not go in tomorrow?"

Damion sat back. "Because I, for one, would rather the witches be functional when they head in to help. We are good, we can throw spells, but not if we lay out that level of spell work the night before. We need time to rest, especially Casey. You don't understand, this is a full coven spell that we're doing with five witches. It's only her power level, which is amazing by the way, that's letting us accomplish this."

Gwen's eyes narrowed. "Is it that big a spell?"

He gave her a charming smile. "Would you like to come over tonight and watch? We were planning on doing the counter-spell tonight. We really want to release Lucas's test vampire. We don't like what it's doing to him, but we think the raid on Jude's compound is more important. And when I say we, I mean Lucas, who convinced us we could reprioritize. We need to wait a day between each spell, and the spells must be done within three days of the full moon, which is Thursday."

Lucas stared at Damion for several seconds, his eyes bright with excitement. "So, you'll do the counter-spell on Sunday?"

Damion shrugged. "Or Saturday, if we feel up to it."

Lucas nodded.

Cynthia smiled around the table. "So, Friday, each vampire house should bring the head of the family and one to two other strong vampires. The witches will bring their small circle. And, if Casey is clever, she'll convince and collect the werehawks.

We'll all gather and enter the empty compound ... and?"

Gwen smiled. "Being his new master. If he doesn't come on his own, I'll call Jude in. And trust me, *that* won't make him happy."

Chapter 30

When the meeting broke up, Casey stopped Lucas. "Could I have a few minutes of your time before I need to be at work? I have a call I need to make, but then I have a request that may take a few minutes."

His brow rose and his head tilted. "I have an engagement back home, but if you'd care to join me, I have some time."

She thought about it, then agreed. He sat back down at the table to wait for her to make her call. She dialed the number for the werehawks and asked for Alicia. Someone else had answered, but when she'd given her name, it didn't take long to get the werehawk leader on the line. "I'd like to fill you in on everything that has been happening."

The cool, disapproving tone chilled her. "Why, child? Will you expect something from us?"

Casey took a calming breath and bit her lip to stop herself from snapping back. She saw Lucas's face harden in disapproval at Alicia's tone. "Expecting, no, hoping, maybe. There's a lot going on, and I'd ... we'd, like you to both know about it, and have an opportunity to be a part of it. You won't know if you don't come speak with me."

There was a shuffling sound. "Very well. You work today. Donovan and I will be at the look-out tomorrow, say, ten in the morning. You can bring one of your human friends, unless that daughter of yours wants to come, then bring them both."

There was a click as the line went dead. Sighing, she replaced the phone receiver on the base. She wasn't sure what she thought about the fact that the werehawks knew and followed her schedule so closely.

She flopped back in her chair and huffed out air. At the end of the table, Lucas chuckled. "That went well."

Her head flopped to the side. "Too bad you don't know more about them. I could just foist the dealing of the werehawks on you ... or anyone. I'm not really sure how I ended up having to deal with them ... besides being Kam's parent. This damn door in my head."

Lucas stood. "Shall we head back to my house?"

Casey grunted as she stood. "Yes, please, absolutely. I can drive you if that would be okay."

"I thought we'd fly. I don't think you've traveled by my house's specialty. You can mist back to get your car later."

Excitement coursed through her, and she smiled. They started walking to the door. "How will we keep people from seeing us?"

"There are a few tricks. We could mist above the clouds, fly really fast, or, my friend, you could put a mirror shield around us."

In the courtyard between the house and the gate, Lucas wrapped his arms around her. Casey's heart began to pound fast as she pushed out a bit of will to wrap a mirror around them, making them invisible to anyone watching. In a woosh, they were in the sky, cool air flowing over them. She squealed in delight as they quickly made their way to Lucas's house.

Once they'd landed and she knew there weren't people watching, she dropped the shield and they headed into his home. Again, she paused to gaze at the paintings that were so expertly rendered. "You said your mom painted these?"

He let his focus shift from image to image, lingering on some longer than others. "It's been so long; I don't often stop to really appreciate them like I should. I miss them, the people, the animals ... though we'll see Jacque in a second, and he was there and knows everyone from these images as well. Let's head up."

He ended so abruptly, she sensed he didn't want any more questions asked. She worried about what she came here to ask.

At the top of the stairs, they entered a large conference room with a cherrywood table. A beautiful man with light brown curls that framed his face stood to greet her. As he walked through a beam of sun, his hair glowed blond, like an angel.

His skin was coppery like Lucas's, but his eyes were a pale green, similar to Rowan's, but with a bit more blue.

He lifted her hand to his mouth and gave it a kiss. "Lovely to meet you. I am Jacque, and you are?"

Her cheeks warmed. "I'm Casey."

"Ah, my savior from your very own graduation party."

She realized he was one of the first vampires she'd pulled silver from, and a smile blossomed across her face. "It was my pleasure! Nice to meet you up and walking around."

Lucas moved to Jacque's side and gave him a quick kiss on his cheek. "Welcome to our rooms, Casey. Now tell me, how may I be of service?"

She scrunched up her face, wondering why she wasted her time on such frivolity. "Part of me thinks this is silly, but I keep hearing I need to know this, and that you're the best to ask. Can you tell me the origin story of the vampires? Do you know it? The ongoing joke is you were there."

Jacque's eyes twinkled, and he smiled wide. His beauty made her catch her breath. "How about I go get some tea, and you can fill her in?"

Lucas grabbed his hand. "How about you stay right here with me, you call up some tea, and the three of us talk. You, my love, are older than me."

Jacque turned to Lucas. "How much are we telling her? Not all of it."

"There are secrets in our world," Lucas began. "And I believe if we ask, Casey can keep a few more. She's a witch, after all, and knows about keeping witch secrets. Now, let's all take seats at the table and see what we can learn about where vampires came from. Maybe not the full story, but enough to help with the current situation."

Lucas pulled out a chair for Casey to sit at the head of the table and he and Jacque sat together next to her on one side. Casey felt a push of will from Jacque, and there was a pot of tea and three cups. Her jaw dropped. "You're a witch."

Jacque smiled. "Yes, ma'am, my whole life."

"What are your specialties, if you don't mind me asking?"

"Fire and conjuration. It's why you weren't called in to help here once I'd healed. I could pull the silver out of anyone who needed it, though we mostly keep my origins on the down low."

She laughed. "Maybe you can teach me fire magic. Zen, our local witch, is a bit of a ... well, we don't get along." Jacque looked shocked at the request. Casey threw up her hands. "Never mind, I'm just being silly. Is this the secret you'd like me to keep? I can absolutely not tell anyone that you're a witch."

Both vampires nodded. Lucas smiled. "Let's discuss the origin of vampires, or at least the folktale."

Disappointment caused Casey to slump. "The story won't be real?"

A half-smile flitted across the old vampire's face. "Let me tell my tale, vampling." He sipped his tea. "Many years ago, the Hall of Treasures of one of the Kings of Demons was looted."

Casey jerked. "There are demons? Like for real demons?"

Jacque reached across Lucas and rubbed Casey's hand. "Let him tell his story, it's better that way."

Lucas just rolled his eyes at her. "The demons, lower-level ones, and not the brightest in the hellscape, stole a few items, including one that enhances power, one that allowed them to gate to

Earth, and one that allowed the demons to share their power with humans.

"The ability of humans to summon demons was also lowered. This was the only reason it was noticed in hell.

"The demons used their newfound ability to create ..."

Lucas stopped and stared at Jacque. "Are we sure we want to do this much background? I could start the story later. Most of the books start late. I could grab one of them and give it to her to read to Kam."

Jacque shrugged. "Didn't you tell me she's been having meetings? Isn't there another one coming up? Shouldn't she have all the information she can?"

Taking a sip of tea, Lucas slumped back in his seat. "Gods above, fine. But this isn't going to end well. I wanted this day for years, but now ..."

"I know, my love, I know."

Lucas gave a curt nod and placed his mug on the table. "The idiot demons portaled up and started imbuing their abilities to humans. Their creations were ... most were nasty pieces of work. Once the demons and the angels realized what was happening and sent representatives to deal with the aftermath of this creation, it took many years to find and clean up the disaster.

"In the process of fixing this mess, the angel opened the ability of magic in humans, starting the first of the witches. The angel and demon representative together created the first vampire, very much by accident. He had all four of the family traits. As he created new vampires, his 'children.' Each only had one of the traits.

"Together with the witches, the demon, the angel, and the vampires, once the first had matured to adulthood, worked together to eliminate the nastier werehawks, because that is what the idiot demons had created.

"In the end, the werehawks who weren't out to kill were allowed to live, under the prophecy you were informed of by Alicia."

Casey stared at Lucas. "How do you know all this?"

Lucas shrugged. "The story is one I've known about for a long time. Vampires of my family have had to watch over the werehawks to ensure they follow the rules of the prophecy."

Her jaw dropped. "So, you did know about them?"

Jacque laughed out loud, a belly laugh. "Sorry, this is all rather fun for me. He ... we ... haven't told this story in ... well, ever I guess. It's been a long time since I've ever really thought about it. It's nice to think back on times gone by."

Lucas shook his head. "I prefer bathing inside. That lake was cold."

Casey took a sip of tea and tried to sort her thoughts. "I don't know how you can create an ordered story for the masses out of that. Wait! What about the flying unicorn?"

Lucas's head dropped to his hand while Jacque chuckled. "Do you want the real story, or one you can share with others?"

Her head swam with everything they'd told her already. She wanted to run out and tell all of this to Jen, but she'd promised to keep most of it secret. "Why don't you tell me what I can share? I'd like to tell a story to Jen the next time we're together. I think she deserves that much, not to mention Kam."

Lucas gave her an understanding smile. "We have just given you a lot to take in. Well, the angel flew down from heaven on a flying unicorn, and the 'good' demon, the one who helped control the werehawks who were trying to destroy humans, came in on a dragon. They each had their own stead."

"Ah, and the real story is *more* fantastical than that?"

With a chuckle, Lucas stood. "I believe if you can learn to read that book in your head you'll get much more of the story, my dear. Now, can you mist home, or do you want me to take you?"

She gave each man a quick hug, her head stuffed with thoughts she still needed to sort through. "I'll see you tonight for the spell." And then she left.

Chapter 31

Wednesday night's spell was going to be big. They'd done it on Monday, and Casey knew the other witches were prepared for the enormity of the power this time. Mentally, she was. Physically ... she was pretty sure she could handle the spell again. The moon would be up at about ten to eleven, around the time she got off work.

Her day had been quiet. Her individual meetings had been with Tammy and Phillipa. Tammy told her and Veronica's story. They'd been walking downtown, and Veronica saw someone she said she knew from her childhood. The two started exchanging words. Their fighting got louder and then physical. Veronica pulled Tammy in, and before she knew what was happening, the other girl was on the ground not moving. Tammy learned later she was in intensive care in the hospital.

Veronica admitted later the only thing she had against the girl was she believed she was a witch. She didn't have proof, just a hunch. Tammy had felt sick after learning that but had no one else in lock up.

During Phillipa's meeting, they discussed how life at Sand Hill Girls' Home was going. Phillipa filled her in on the training she and Delilah worked through in the intro primer Casey had given them. Phillipa had brought a list of questions the two girls had compiled.

Before leaving Sand Hill Girl's Home, when the girls had headed to their rooms, and Casey had a few minutes alone with Cindy, she requested that Delilah and Phillipa be allowed to join her for the spell. "It's a big one. It will show them what they'll be working for. It isn't something they'll be able to do any time soon, only full witches working with a circle can carry this kind of power, but sometimes seeing witches in action lets us push through the harder times."

Cindy gazed off into nothing. "And the spell has to be done under the full moon?"

Casey nodded. "It's a hard spell, like I said. It's usually only done with more witches. It's such an odd curiosity that others in the community are coming to watch. If you let me take them, I'll make sure they get back here once it's done."

The older woman nodded slowly. "Okay, but let's not tell the others. No reason to borrow trouble."

Twenty minutes later, Casey found herself with two young witchlings, driving back to witch house late Wednesday night.

Delilah, stuffed in the back, practically vibrated. "I can't believe we're going to go to a séance."

Casey snorted. "Um, that isn't what this is. If you're going to call yourself a witch, you may want to not use that word ... just saying. You're going to observe a full-on spell. Just be forewarned, there will be witches and vampires around. You'll be in the company of a lot of power ... and powerful people. Just stay relaxed, observe, and you'll be fine."

Phillipa sat in the seat next to her, hands stuffed under her legs, eyes glued to the street ahead, with her heart beating erratically. "How powerful? Should we have changed? Should we be nervous?"

Casey had approached the girls while they were in the garden alone. When Casey mentioned this outing, both girls were excited to see an actual spell, but now that they were close, Phillipa's fear filled the car. "You're dressed fine."

In the back seat, Delilah sniffed. "What's that smell?"

Casey considered how to answer the question. "What do you smell?"

Taking the turns that would lead to the old neighborhood where witch house was located, Casey focused half on the girls, half on driving. The lots in their neighborhood were large and private, which allowed for magic circles in the back yard.

Delilah rubbed her arms. It almost looked like she hugged herself. "It smells peppery," she wrinkled her nose, "and a bit sour."

In the front, Phillipa sniffed the air, her brow furrowing in confusion. It wasn't always easy to smell your own emotions. Catching Delilah's reflection in the rear-view mirror, Casey nodded.

"Good. You're attuned to emotions. Not all witches have the same abilities. You're smelling Phillipa's fear."

"I'm not afraid!" Phillipa's response came so fast, her words tripped over themselves.

Delilah leaned forward, sniffing first Phillipa and then Casey. "I get it. That's really cool."

Yanking her hands out from under her legs and turning to face her friend, Phillipa's face reddened. "I'm not scared."

Pulling up in front of the house, Casey turned off her car and rotated in her seat. "It's fine. Tonight will be a lot. You'll meet several vampire house leaders ... actually, you may meet all of them. It's okay to be nervous. We'll go in and I'll introduce you to a human. She normally watches my daughter ... who is hopefully asleep. Tonight, the human, my friend, will help you two figure out where to go. She's a bit like Betsy." She faced Phillipa. "Just breathe."

Phillipa still looked nervous, but they all got out of the car. They headed into the house and found everyone in the living room. There were the four other witches, Rowan, Lucas, Cynthia, Gwen, and Cyran. Everyone. Everyone but Jen had come to watch the spell. Raising her eyebrow, she stepped into the room with her charges. "So, you *all* decided to come to the show?"

Lucas chuckled. "How often are we invited to see this level of magic? It's been years for me, and I miss it. As for the others, they've never seen anything like it. It'll be good for them to see, learn, and understand."

She gazed at Lucas and considered his story from earlier. She thought Jacque would've enjoyed joining them, but he was in hiding. "You've seen a large witch spell like this?"

A smile bloomed on his face. "Certainly, but it's been ..." His gaze softened, then he shrugged. "I miss it. Thank you for the invite."

Biting her lip, she thought about the full spell. "Of course, but you know then that no one can interrupt until the end, no matter what you see." Her gaze fell to Rowan. "No matter what you see. I'll be fine. If you charge in, we'll just have to start over, and then things will get dicey."

Standing and ambling over to her, Rowan slipped his hands around her waist. "I can control myself; I promise." He dipped his head down and gave her a kiss. "I won't try to save you, no matter how harrowing things seem to get." He kissed her again, deeper.

She felt the two baby witches behind her freeze, and she smiled into his second kiss. Pulling away, she introduced them. "I'd like you to meet Delilah and Phillipa. They are two of the girls from the Sand Hill Girls' Home. They got in trouble when their magic blossomed, and they didn't even know they were witches." Hearing footsteps on the stairs, Casey spun. "Riley, perfect. Can you help these two figure out where to go while the rest of us do the spell? I want them both to learn how witches live, and how a spell really works ... a big spell."

Riley smiled. "Do they know anything?"

Shaking her head, Casey said, "Nothing. They didn't even know they were witches before setting things on fire."

Riley, coming up to them, hooked her arms into theirs. "Fire? Cool. With me, witchlings, let me give you some beginning lessons."

Sadie stood. "Okay, it's getting late. Witches, it's time to get this going. There are chairs in the back and a cord. We're asking that the observers don't cross that line. It will help us to forget you're there and to focus on what we're doing."

After that, the running of the spell started off close to how it did the first night. Experiencing it once before, the motions were smoother. Having an audience, tension ran through Casey like she was on a running course.

Delilah and Phillipa started to whisper when the walking sticks stood on their own. She remembered the first time she had seen that. A corner of her mind gave way to the warmth of the memory. The power of the sticks always impressed her. When she became a full witch, her thrill at the walking sticks morphed to awe when she realized the animal toppers were more than decoration, but full-on familiars with abilities of their own.

At the point she stood pillar, face to the sky, staring up at the moon, one day from being full, the connection to the celestial body was stronger, almost pulling her off her feet. The chanting a tether from the other four witches, through her body, to the massive rock in the sky. Her breath came in gasps as she spoke the words.

As the invocation came to an end, all four chanted in unison, the connection was electric. She felt the pull as if they were a lead to the stars. The wave that crashed through her did lift her up, and she hung suspended as the magic swirled through the heavens, spinning and mixing. Her arms extended out for balance. Her walking stick floated up, then rotated, parallel to her arms.

She didn't crash down this time. She watched, enchanted by the colors swirling above her. As the magic came back, she saw the crash before it came, and knew there was nothing she could do. Holding the talisman, she chanted the holding spell as the wave brought her to the ground hard, tearing through her, the other witches, and the circle she'd created.

Lying in the center of the circle on her side, she waited for her body to stop pulsing from the magic that used her as a conduit. All her focus was on the tiny stick of rowan. She felt hands on her shoulders. Turning her head, she saw Zen and Damion helping her up. Once Casey was on her feet and stable, Sadie smiled.

The four of them moved to the spectators. Delilah stood. "That was amazing. That was, like, totally not a séance. Will I, or um, we be able to do that one day?"

Tilly came over to the two girls in teacher mode. "Maybe. That depends on the type of witches you are and your power level. Casey is incredibly strong. She just did the work of, what ... two witches?"

Zen, who was heading into the house, mumbled. "More like five or six."

Snapping her head to him, Casey's jaw dropped. *Since when does he have anything nice to say about me?*

Laughing, Tilly patted her shoulder. "He may be a bit of an arrogant jerk, but he knows what he saw."

The vampire leaders approached. Gwen gave her a quick hug. "Okay, I get it. I see why you wouldn't want to do that the night before an op. Did you get a meeting with ..." Her eyes darted to the two witchlings.

Cyran came up to Delilah and Phillipa. "Riley, why don't you collect Kam and let's drive these two home. I'm guessing Casey and Rowan have some discussing they need to do and may be home late."

Riley shrugged. "Sounds good. But if the girl is up half the night, you're playing with her. I'm tired."

Cyran laughed. "Deal."

Delilah tilted her head. "Since your walking stick is rowan wood, does it hold the spell you just created?"

All the witches still in the backyard froze. Closing her eyes, Casey reached out to Zoryda. The dragon laughed in her mind. "Silly witch, of course we do. We hold the spells we create, and the counter-curse. It is what we do."

Wanting to scream at her ignorance, Casey calmly asked her familiar. "How many times can you bind a vampire?" Her dragon, holding still in front of so many strangers, laughed in her mind. "You've run the spell twice. I can do the spell twice and the unbinding twice, as can the others. You witches need to utilize us more." The admonishment was severe.

Biting her lip, Casey turned to Riley and Cyran. "Thanks for taking these two home. Delilah, Phillipa, I'll see you Monday. I don't have to remind you to keep this to yourselves. You can create journals in your glass bubbles if you want to write about it ... keep it private."

Once gone, Casey told them about what Zoryda had told her. Excited, they wanted to test out the unbinding right away. Before they left, she told Gwen about her meeting with the werehawks the following morning and asked the vampire leader to let Jen know she wanted to meet her at Cambia House at nine the next morning.

Once that was decided, they moved to the counter-spell. All the witches wanted to go with Lucas to test the unbinding. He suggested bringing the vampire in question to the witches' backyard. After some debate, they agreed to meet at the park a few blocks away.

It took a few minutes to get everyone there. As soon as Lucas had the location in mind, he misted away and brought the vampire who had been under punishment. He was pale and had lost weight over the last few days. Landing in the park, he cowered at the sight of all the vampire leaders. "What now? Am I to be executed? Were my crimes so bad?"

Lucas lifted the man and kissed him on each cheek. "Your punishment is coming to an end, friend. You will not kill a human or next time you will follow their fate."

The man blanched but nodded. "Yes, sire."

Sadie, the creator of the spell, stepped forward. Her walking stick, topped with an eagle, proudly in her hand. Standing next to Lucas, she closed her eyes and focused for a few minutes. It didn't seem like anything was happening, but a slight glow began to emanate from the runes on the shaft of the rowan wood. Gently tapping the back of the eagle to the shoulder of Lucas's vampire, Sadie said a single word.

The vampire's eyes widened, and he gasped. He began breathing fast as he stared at the stick and Sadie. Slowly turning to face Lucas, he said, "It's back ... all of it. It's back. Thank you, Lucas, thank you, my sire."

Chapter 32

There were dragons, griffins, and flying unicorns ... where did they come from? She watched as they all flew above her as she lay in purple grass. But it wasn't grass; it was too soft. Standing up she thought she was on a—

Opening her eyes, Casey felt small kisses trailing up her shoulder to her neck. Letting out a sound of encouragement, she tilted her head away, giving more access. She stretched out her body, rubbing herself against him languidly as heat began to warm her.

"Morning, love," she said, rolling to capture Rowan's lips, exploring his mouth with her tongue, enjoying the feel of his body as he leaned into her.

Sliding her arms around his waist, pulling him somewhat on top of her, she deepened the kiss. She wrapped a leg around him, locking his body to hers. He pulled up from her. "What time will Miss Clark arrive?"

Rolling her head to see the clock on the small table, she saw it was just before eight. Groaning at how early it was, she squirmed to get more of him touching her. "We have time. She won't be here until nine."

His hands caught hers and held them. The side of his mouth twitched up in a tiny half-smile she adored. "Excellent." Leaning down, he kissed her deeply enough to leave her breathless.

Suddenly, he was gone. She sat up and saw him heading for the closet. He smiled at her, slow and wicked over his shoulder. "You're wearing too much, my love."

She wore a tank top and panties. Scooting to the side of the bed, she went to follow him. He returned with a pillow and ... something. She wasn't sure. When he got close, he tossed the pillow onto the bed, and pulled her in for another kiss. Then he slipped off the tank top. He moved away, and she felt him tie something around her head. Opening her eyes, she couldn't see anything. "Rowan?"

His mouth on her breast made her toes curl, her breath catch, and sensation zinged from her nipple to her core. "Gods above." Her hands went to her face, not to remove the blindfold, just to touch the velvety softness of the material cutting off all light.

As he sucked, she felt her underwear slide down her legs. She felt exposed. She knew Rowan was the only one there, but without her sight, it was so much more thrilling. Her breathing became faster, ragged. One of his hands began to play with her other breast, rubbing and teasing, while the other slipped around to her ass.

Then he was gone. Her body sang with the sensation. The nipple that had been in his mouth, cool from the moisture he left behind. She couldn't see or hear him, and chills ran down her body. She stood, not knowing what to do with her hands. Anticipation had her clenching her inner muscles. He could do anything to her. The thought had her *wanting* him to do everything.

His warm hands grasped her upper arms from behind and he kissed the back of her neck. She moaned in anticipation. Her sense of the room was shot because of her internal focus of her body.

His voice flowed into her, hot and seductive. "Climb up onto the bed. Kneel where I guide you."

Scooting forward, she felt the bed. She climbed up and got on her knees. He had her rotate, so she was pretty sure she faced the head of the bed. "There is a wedge pillow in front of you. Bend over and rest on it." His voice continued to seduce her.

Following his directions, she leaned over. The pillow he'd brought out was some sort of triangle pillow and the highest point came to her waist. She leaned over, resting along the long side of the soft material. She heard as Rowan open a flap—it sounded like Velcro—on the side of the apparatus. The sound played havoc on her system. He placed Casey's wrist against the soft, yet sturdy structure. He re-secured the strap, first on one wrist, and then on her other. She was wet with wanting from the few actions he'd already taken.

She was on her knees, face down, hands bound, blindfolded. His finger traced her spine down to her ass, sending chills through her body. Then he bit her ass and she yelped. He chuckled. "I would take my time, Casey, love, and see how far I could push you with this, but we really don't have unlimited time this morning. You look delectable right now. Are you okay with how I have you?"

She continued to breathe faster than normal, but that was the excitement for what was going to happen next. After taking stock of everything, she said, "Yes, I'm good ... really good." The last two words came out husky and low.

He smacked her ass, and she yelped then moaned. He rubbed where he'd slapped, and his own breathing stopped being silent. She felt him climb up behind her. His hand reached between her legs, touching her, stimulating her, entering her. Her body sang with need. "Gods, my love, you're so wet. I could fuck you now, and you'd be ready for me. You really are enjoying this. One day we are going to have a full day of play, not this quick rush job."

As he spoke, his fingers continued to alternate between stroking her clit and penetrate her. "Oh, you *liked* the sound of that. You can't hide anything with my fingers fucking you. You like things a bit rough. We may have to go shopping together, find items that make your breath stop all together. Live out your fantasies, my love."

Casey wasn't sure she knew how to breathe anymore. His fingers were creating shockwaves within her body. She writhed against his hand, which moved slowly, masterfully orchestrating her needs, but not enough. She wanted more. He shifted his hand away and slid his dick in. His first thrust was slow. He held her hips since she had no way to brace herself.

Then, once he established the angle, he found a rhythm. He pounded into her, using her body roughly. Tied down and blind, all she knew was his cock as it thrust into her, claiming her. He slapped her ass, and she screamed in pleasure.

His voice flowed into her, took over, demanded obedience. "Cum for me, Casey. Orgasm, scream with my name on your lips."

It didn't take long for her to break, the buildup exploding out. As he commanded, she yelled out his name as he pushed her over the top, thrusting into her deeply. Her head.

Once he found his climax, he did a final thrust, and collapsed on her, both of them trying to catch their breath.

He kissed her back and after a few seconds removed her blindfold and then her wrist bindings. She didn't move, couldn't move. Between the release and his weight on her, she wanted to stay where she was forever.

He slid his hands under her shoulders and, sitting back, brought her up with him. She made sounds of protest as he placed her on his lap. "We should go shower before the day begins."

Scowling, she rotated and wrapped her arms around him. Sliding her legs so they straddled him, she said, "Are you sure we need to shower right now?" She wiggled on his lap, not ready to let the moment end.

His eyes moved to the clock, then he kissed her languorously. His hand snapped out and she heard something hit the floor. His arms went under hers, and lifted her off him, sitting her next to him on the bed. His eyes flitted down then back up. "I don't appear ready for a second run."

Smiling, she pushed him until he lay back. Staring at him, she realized he was small enough at this moment to fit completely in her mouth ... that was new. She grabbed his balls and lowered herself, slipping his cock past her lips. As she sucked and played, she could taste herself on him. Pulling back, she slid his dick from her mouth, and he instantly began to grow and thicken.

His hand lifted off the bed, reaching for her. She was situated at an angle from his body, and within reach for him to explore. As she continued to suck and enjoy herself, his fingers found her sensitive areas and began their own tender strokes.

Thinking hard, wanting the advantage, as his fingers began to cause her brain to short-circuit, she thought she might know how Damion did the phantom fingers. Testing her theory, Casey tried to stimulate Rowan's ass before she lost all ability to use magic. She began with a small pat, a request.

He bucked up. If she hadn't moved with him, she would have deep throated him. Growling deep, Rowan grabbed her and threw her to the bed.

"I'm not sure what that was." He snarled, an edge of danger in his voice.

"A bit of magic. If you're interested."

"Hmm. I'll let you know when I'm not."

Sliding between her legs, he thrust in again, as Casey let her magic roam, her phantom hand doing what her pinned hands could not.

Leaning down. Rowan moaned, then kissed her deeply, penetrating her mouth with his tongue in time with his thrusts. Wrapping her legs around him, she lost herself in the sensation, the feel, the minty smell, that was all him.

The heat that had been building didn't take long to explode again in an erotic ending to their morning play.

Chapter 33

"Is she why you decided not to bring Kam along?" Jen watched as Zoryda flew high in the trees as they made their way up the hiking paths.

"Yeah. The familiars are supposed to be unknown. You know because you helped me figure things out. I'm assuming the hawks know because they've been watching me. If they've seen us up here, then they know about her." Casey gazed up at her small dragon stretching her wings. "I love Kam, but I've been with her or working for the last two weeks. Zoryda hasn't been able to get out and fly."

Setting a brutal pace, Jen watched as the dragon soared. "It's too bad Kam can't know about her. Your daughter would be in love."

They'd made it to the last part of the climb where the trail got steep. They focused on making it up the path, and not the rules that kept a three-year-old from learning there was an actual dragon she could play with.

When they got to the top of the hill, they sat on the wall of the look-out point and gazed out over the town. Jen swung her head from Cambia House to campus and back again. Casey was about to ask her about the last few days and what she'd gone through, when she saw the hawks approaching. She decided to grab Jen's hand and give it a squeeze. When Jen's focus shifted to her, she smiled. "We'll talk at lunch." Jen gave a small smile and then the hawks flew in.

It only took a minute for them to shift and dress. Donovan only wore dark linen pants, his sculpted body a magnificent display. Alicia had slipped on a gray tank dress with a pink belt. Walking out with no shoes and such free clothing, you'd think they'd be at a disadvantage, but no, they oozed royalty and disdain for the two vampires waiting on the half-wall.

Alicia eyed the ground. "What, no picnic this time?"

Jen mouth quirked up in a half-smile. "We weren't sure what you'd want. Do you want to stand, sit, eat?" She was playing host.

Sniffing the air, Alicia tried to call her bluff. "Well, child, you aren't a human anymore, are you?"

Jen stiffened. "I was attacked on Saturday. It's part of what we want to discuss with you, once we get the *how* figured out."

Sneering, Alicia eyed the two of them. "Well, then, a blanket, green or brown, to better fit in with the surroundings. White wine. And a cheese and cracker plater."

Sighing, Casey closed her eyes. The blanket was tricky. There was one in Cyran's room, and she hoped he wasn't using it. The wine was simple, there was a stock in the kitchen with four glasses. She'd told Chef Monica of her plan, and the picnic basket was set up on a table. She would put everything on the counter, Monica would load the basket, then she'd bring it to the meeting spot.

She grabbed two kinds of cheese and a box of crackers to the table with the bottle of wine. Then she found the blanket she wanted and brought it to the mountain top. It was folded neatly and smelled clean. She and Jen laid it out.

Once it was down, the four of them sat. Alicia's smile grew. "Ah, nice. A blanket, but no food?"

Turning to her, Casey smiled. "I thought we'd start talking first. I didn't know you needed everything right away."

Smirking, Alicia shook her head. "You can just admit that you don't have refreshments for our talk."

There was a small mental tap. It came from Rowan, letting her know the food basket was ready. They didn't often reach out mentally, but small pushes were possible. He told her the closer they got as a married couple, the stronger their link would grow.

Sighing, Casey said, "If you really want the food and drink now," she pushed out her will and conjured the picnic basket from the kitchen, "then we can have it now."

Jen pulled out a gold platter and began arranging the crackers, three types, and cheese, four types, all sliced perfectly. Monica must have called in help. Then she pulled out four wine glasses and one of two bottles of white wine. Opening it up, she poured for each of them.

Checking in the basket, Casey saw the last of the macaron cookies she'd made in a box at the bottom. She wondered how Monica had managed to save them from being eaten for a whole week. She must have a refrigerator no one knew about.

Taking a slice of cheese and a cracker, Alicia took a bite. Then she sipped her wine. Next to her, Donovan dug in. Alicia's mouth twitched. "Not bad, witchling. Now, why are we here?"

Casey wanted to put down her glass, but there really wasn't a good place. "Jude, one of the vampires of Velvet's house ... do you know the leaders?"

Jen, stiffening next to her, mumbled, "Old leader."

Donovan leaned back and placed his glass on the small wall, then rested on his elbows, stretching his legs out in front of himself. Alicia watched, taking a sip of her wine. "We know about the vampires. We know who Velvet is ... we didn't know she'd been dethroned."

Eating a piece of cheese with cracker, Casey shrugged. "We offer you information, but we also ask for your help. Tomorrow morning at eleven, we are going to go in to take Jude down. We have the cooperation of all the vampire houses and the local witches. If we can get the werehawks to help as well, we'll have a full paranormal force to let him know he's in the wrong."

Face hardening, Alicia took a sip of her wine. Her every move oozed with disappointment at the young pups who were being daft. "Why would it take so many to bring down one dolt of a vampire?"

Case bit her lip to keep from snapping. She took a long breath. "He has help. I don't know who or what, but he has someone helping him. When we went in on Saturday, a group of about fifty soldiers appeared out of nowhere ... just appeared. It was like they misted in, but no vampire or witch can do that. We need a force that can handle that kind of power."

Alicia froze and Donovan's face hardened as he sat up straight, his relaxed posture gone. The hawk leader's eyes narrowed. "You have no idea what could move forces like that?"

Shaking her head, Casey leaned forward. "Do you?"

The two werehawks faced each other in a silent conversation. With a curt nod, Donovan grabbed some food, then leaned back again.

Alicia took a cracker and cheese and eyed the two vampires. After a few minutes, she took a long breath. "Long ago, before I was born, there were stories about other creatures. Ones who didn't live on our plane of existence. Humans, and sometimes other beings, would summon them. It didn't happen often, but it did happen."

Casey could hear Jen's heart begin to beat faster. Her friend leaned forward. "Are you talking about demons and creatures from hell? I mean, that's the only kind of being *I've* ever heard of being summoned, and that has only been in books, not, like, for real."

Casey's mind whirled as her conversation with Lucas and Jacque began to parallel today's. She focused more intently on what Alicia said. Did the woman know her own origins?

Eyes narrowing, Alicia shot Jen a scalding glare. "Child, do not speak so openly. If that arrogant vampire *has* summoned one of those beings, it could be anywhere. They are crafty and can listen to the wind. We know ... they are very powerful. I can give you more information, but not if there is one of those ... beings ... hanging about. None of us are safe."

Feeling like a bucket of cold water had splashed through her, Casey made fists to hold back her frustration. "Does this mean you won't help us?"

Gaze penetrating through her, Alicia's voice was a knife. "Oh, no child, we'll help. This beast must be sent back to its pits of hell, literally, and you lot aren't strong enough or wise enough to do it alone."

Tired of being treated like an idiot, Casey sipped her wine and gave the werehawks a flat look. "Do you know as much as you do because of your origins?"

Alicia bristled, Donovan lifted a single eyebrow, and Jen shot Casey a confused stare. First to get herself sorted, Alicia snapped, "And what do you know of where we came from, child?"

"I know enough. I know how the werehawks were created and the start of your prophecy. You forget the book I have and the stories it tells. The history it gives me. You belittle me and give me no credit, but that doesn't take away from my knowing things. So, I ask again, given your origins, do you have a way to track that which has been summoned, *if* that is how Jude is doing what he's doing? Would that creature be tracking you?"

Before Alicia could snap back, Donovan placed a hand on her shoulder. "No, we can't track anything, and it probably doesn't care about us. We've been in hiding, surviving until your daughter was born. Now that she's here, everything has changed. It's a new world for us."

Alicia jerked out from under his hold. "If this is what that ass of a vampire has called up to help him, then we'll help. After that, who knows? Eleven tomorrow morning. Call with the details, we'll be there."

She gave a signal to Donovan, and the two shifted out of their clothes and flew off without another word.

Chapter 34

Casey and Jen made their way down the hill, sloughing off the disdain of the werehawk leader. When they got to the bottom, they headed to a pay phone to call Ginger, deciding they wanted her there for their lunch. It had been too long since the three of them had hung out, and Ginger hadn't seen Jen since she was declared not dead. Then they found a local bar that had great burgers.

They got to the bar before Ginger and found a table in the back. Ginger arrived a few minutes after them. At some point over the last few days, while she'd been working, Rowan had gotten her grandmother's ring sized, and it took Ginger two seconds to spot the ring on her finger. "Oh, my god Casey. What is that on your hand? Talk to me, tell me everything."

They ordered burgers, fries, and soda, and while they waited for their orders, she told her two best friends about the night Rowan had proposed.

Jen got a bit misty, but Ginger's eyes got calculating. "That's amazing. All out of the blue? Like, so romantic. Jen is your maid of honor, of course. We are friends, but the two of you are thick as thieves. But she is *not* helping you pick out the dress. I can't even imagine what the two of you'd come up with if left alone. I'll be one of your bride's maids and the wedding planner. Now that that's set, do you have a date picked out?"

Taking a slow sip of soda, Casey tried to decide if Ginger had taken a single breath in all of that, her words tripping out faster than anyone she'd ever heard speak.

Ginger kicked her under the table. "Case, date?"

Shaking her head, she said, "Oh, right, no. Not yet. This week's been crazy. But, yes, you as wedding planner sounds just insane enough to work. Wedding party, absolutely. Plan away, insane lady, plan away!"

Ginger beamed.

Biting her lip, Casey looked to Jen. "We actually aren't here to talk about me and the wedding. That will be next time. Jen?"

Shaking out her hands, Jen leaned over and gave Ginger a hug. "I've missed you Ginge. But I have to tell you a story. Case is right, this week's been hell."

Ginger sat back. "What's up?"

Jen grabbed her soda and drank half of it down. She shifted her gaze to Casey, then back to Ginger. "Last Saturday a group of us went into Jude's warehouse to figure out what was going on. One of his asshole guards shot me with both a silver bullet and a second with a tranquilizer ... they can't tell vampire from human, or they were covering their bases."

"I know all of this. You were dead. I cried, my heart broke, and now ... wait, it was more than a medical miracle?"

Casey looked over the Ginger, whose hands were shaking. She'd put down her drink and her hands were inching over to Jen. Jen saw the motion and gave a small smile. She took the offered hands. "I was partnered with my mom, and she misted me out. The only way to save my life was to—" she took a shaky breath, color draining from her face, "—was to turn me ... like her ..." Jen gulped and pointed to Casey with her chin. "Into a ... um ... vampire."

Ginger, who knew Jen as well as Casey, threw her arms around Jen's neck. "Oh, Jen, are you okay? Talk to us." She pulled back and reclasped Jen's hands. Casey, sitting on the other side of the booth, watched, unable to do much more.

Sensing her feelings, Jen reached out so Casey could be connected as well. "Honestly, I don't know what to feel. This isn't what I wanted. If I help turn one of the blood donors, I won't need to drink blood anymore and I can feed on emotions. Working in a school, that should be easy ... I mean, how many students feel angst about gym class? But the choice was taken from me in the first place. It sucks. I totally get what you were feeling freshman year, Case."

A tear ran down her cheek as she stared down at the booth. "I didn't want to die. I'm really glad I'm still here, that I'll be part of the next fight, that

I'll be in your wedding, Case, and yours one day, Ginge. It's just ... now I'm this as well."

Casey winked at her. "And we'll be in yours one day."

Jen snorted. "Time ... give me time, Casey Strega!"

Casey squeezed her hand and closed her eyes. "Okay, let us help. You helped me, gods, you helped me through so much. I wouldn't be here today if it weren't for you. Anything I can do, I'll do. So will Jaxon. He almost didn't survive when he thought you'd died. Do you *know* how much he loves you?"

Her eyes, red with crying, turned up to Casey. "Can we be together even if we're from different houses?"

Casey nodded before answering. "Of course. You *are* part of our family. You can live with us regardless of which type of vampire you are. I don't care. Rowan won't either. Gwen may have an issue with you not staying under her roof, though."

She shook her head. "No, I can't stay there. The whole house needs to be cleansed. Gwen is starting the process, but Velvet and Jude did a number on the family. I can't stay there, it's too much."

Their food came, and for a few minutes silence descended on the booth. Then Ginger put her burger down, wiping her hands on a napkin. "You know, Jen, my place is huge. I rented a two-bedroom apartment because I loved the view. If you're worried about staying at Cambia House, stay with me for a while, just until you get things figured out."

Jen lowered the french fry she was about to eat. "Are you serious? I mean, I know that living with vampires, especially right now when there's so much training I need, it's really important for me, but I need some time to get my head around what's going on. If I could spend a bit of time, a week or two, away from it all ... it would help."

Smiling, Ginger dug in her purse and pulled out a ring of keys. "I always carry my spare on my ring, so I don't lose it." She unwound the spare and handed it to Jen. "Here, take it. You know where I live ... where *we* live." Taking a sip of soda, Ginger turned her calculating stare to Casey. "Now can we plan Casey's wedding? I mean, how many things do

I need to fix to get to the fun bits? You know if she's involved, she'll just mess it up anyway."

All the warm fuzzies Casey felt suddenly turned to dread.

Chapter 35

Casey sat in the study room reading a book and drinking tea. She'd been in the room for just over half an hour and the solitude was welcome. It was just before one in the morning, and she waited for Lucas. She had a lesson on obscure old languages and prophecy translation. She hadn't had one in a couple of weeks, and she felt learning the language of the prophecy book was too important to skip again.

While she waited, she read a book about people who bonded with dragons and who lived on a different planet. They flew the skies to protect their world. She tried to imagine what it'd be like to be away from all this stress and worry and be able to fly on the back of *her* dragon.

The door opened and Lucas walked in. His smile was wide as he took the seat next to hers.

She waved her book at him. "Can you imagine flying on the back of a dragon, being able to speak to them?"

His mouth quirked. "Sounds fantastic." He grabbed a mug and poured himself a mug of tea. "Jacque says 'hi.' Are you ready for a lesson on old languages?"

Closing her book and putting it aside, she took a final sip of tea and smiled at him. "I am. Once we're in my glass bubble, can I ask a few questions ... not about the prophecy book? Oh, and give Jacque a hug from me."

He shrugged. "Of course. Are the questions private?"

Wrinkling her nose, she considered his question. "Private enough, but it'll be easier in there." She tapped her head.

She took his hand and with a tiny push of will, pulled them both into her mental landscape. As always, she gave him a few minutes to nose around. He loved her private sphere. She'd created a study area for him, with a small bookcase and beanbag chair. When she was studying at her oak table, he spent time reading books he'd found in her library.

Once he'd made sure all 'his' things were still in place, he joined her at the longer study table. "What did you want to talk about?"

She waved him to sit. "I spoke with the werehawks—"

His whole body tensed at the mention of the beings he so obviously didn't like. "I told you everything I can about them. Beyond that, I can't help you with them."

All the muscles in her body tightened. "I'm not asking you to help with them, Lucas. My story just starts with them."

He slumped back. "Sorry, go ahead."

Huffing out her annoyance, she nodded. "Okay, we were talking with them about what happened on Saturday, and they think it involved," she paused. She thought what she was about to say sounded foolish, and she hated sounding childish in front of this vampire she respected. Taking another breath, she forged ahead. "They think the only way Jude could do what he did was if he had a demon helping him. It made me think of your story. Having demons come up twice in two days couldn't be a coincidence."

Straightening in his seat, Lucas's right brow rose, though she noted a bit of tightening around his eyes. "I didn't get the full story about Saturday; can you show me?"

They both shifted their seats to face the screen she used for her memories. She called up the debacle from the warehouse. He watched the screen, and she watched him. There was a small shift in his focus as the action and sounds played out. He only wanted to see the memory once before he felt he'd experienced enough.

They faced each other across the expanse of the table. Lucas's face was blank. "You are correct that no vampire or witch, single or coven, could have moved that army of men for Jude. As for what did, I don't know. I have a guess, but unlike the werehawks, I'm not going to give theories and state them as facts. Tomorrow morning, when we go into the compound, we will know for certain."

Placing her hands on the table to keep them steady, Casey gaped at him. She knew he knew something but wasn't sharing. "How should we prepare?"

"You've all prepared brilliantly, my dear. Now, let's begin our lesson." Lucas grabbed the prophecy book. "This book grows more important each and every day. How much of it can you read?"

He was holding things back, she knew it. She could feel the secrets like a pressure in her chest. With a sigh, she decided to drop it and move on with the lesson. She rubbed her temples and looked at the book. How could she focus on this old tome when so much hung in the balance tomorrow? Growling to herself in frustration, she knew she wouldn't be able to bully him into answering any questions. She gazed at the weird symbols on the page and glowered at them. "If I don't think about it, I can read most of it. It's like my brain wants to read the words, and they just come to me. I don't really understand why. When I think about it, none of it makes sense."

Lucas chuckled, beaming at her. "That makes perfect sense, my dear. The language is very old and wants you to read it. It makes more sense for you to understand it instinctually. Read the book, Casey, then tell me what you read."

She searched the page, reading. She got lost in a story, incredible and unbelievable. It bled into a second story and a third. Page after page, she let the words sink into her, fill her. After a minute, an hour, a day, she pushed the book back. "Are the stories in this book true?"

Lucas shrugged. "I've never read the book. It's been locked in your mind, and the mind of your predecessors since the very first witch to walk to Earth. No one but you has ever read the stories to know if the stories are real."

She sat back. "How do you know that? How *could* you know that?"

He shook his head. "That's for our next meeting. Today, you read the stories. I want you to think about them. Then next week, we'll discuss what you've read."

She bit her lip. "I'm related to the first witch? I wonder what she was like ... how did she meet the angel from your story yesterday? Was she nice? How well did she adapt to suddenly having magic in the world?"

Lucas shook his head. "We should end for tonight, it's getting late. Like I said, we can discuss the stories later and your ancestor and *his* wily ways then."

Chapter 36

The vampires, the witches, and the werehawks, met two blocks away at an abandoned building the werehawks spotted on a flyover the day before. Each of the vampire leaders brought people. Casey recognized Jacque and Thomas, Lucas's men, and Gwen with Jen, since they didn't trust any of Velvet's people yet. Rowan brought Jaxon, Sydney, and Cyran. She didn't recognize the vampires that came with Cynthia. The information house was secretive to a fault. There were eight werehawks, including Donovan and Alicia, and all five witches showed up carrying their walking sticks, primed and ready to fight.

As soon as the hawks landed and changed, there was a tense moment as Lucas stared at them. Alicia stepped up to him. "We bear no grievance with you, King of the Vampires. Our fight died out long ago and we've moved on, changed over the years. We know you've monitored us, culled us, protected us from ourselves, and we give you all honor for that which you have done since our inception. With the coming of the thrice born child, we hope to fully come out into the light, and maybe one day call you an ally, if not a friend."

After that, all eight of the werehawks took a knee, and bowed down to Lucas. He watched them, seeming to stand taller. "I truly hope that you speak true, Alicia, leader of the fallen. It has been many years, and the battle is tiresome. If the prophecy holds true, then I will call today the end of the genesis that began," his hand made a rolling motion, "long ago."

Head still bowed, Alicia quietly said, "Thank you, King of the Vampires, Marquis of the Legions below, and Voice of the Elders." Then, all eight hawks stood. "We give allegiance to you, and whomever you feel deserves our loyalty."

His face still flat and serious, his stance that of a prince of old, Lucas gazed at them. "Today we follow Rowan and Casey. They are the leaders and the ones to whom you should give your loyalty; they deserve it. Without Casey, you'd still be in hiding, still be in danger from the prophecy. I've heard how you've been treating her despite the hope and life she offers. It is a disgrace and a throwback to years forgotten to history. She is the bringer of the thrice born child that you've been waiting for, and you know that! Do better!" The last he boomed out as a command that had them all staring at him as if he were their ruler.

As the group watched, Alicia shifted and approached Casey. Bowing low from her waist, she took Casey's hand and pressed it to her forehead. "I apologize for any slight I may have given the mother of the thrice born child."

Casey mumbled, "Father."

Alicia's eyebrows furrowed in confusion but continued. "We will work, as the Marquis has commanded, to be better partners in the future. Today we will be successful in bringing the betrayer down to show our strength and dedication in our side of this battle and all future battles. We are no longer what we once were. We've spent years proving this and will not ruin that now."

The confusion around her grew, mumblings about the King of the Vampires, but something in the words tickled the back of Casey's mind and reminded her of one of the stories she'd read the night before. Nodding, Casey shot Lucas a wary look before steadying herself in front of the leader of the werehawks. "I look forward to witnessing the rise of the werehawks in their new position on the side of good."

She saw Lucas's nod of approval as well as Alicia's stunned gape of disbelief before Casey turned her back on them both. "Okay, everyone. Sydney has a map and a battle plan worked out. Let's group up so we can get this jerk."

Jen stepped up next to Casey, grabbing her hand. She whispered low in her ear. There was enough commotion, Casey was pretty sure no one else would be able to hear her. "What the hell was that all about?"

Shrugging, Casey answered as honestly as she could. "I only understood about a quarter of it. The werehawks messed up a long time ago. It has to do with their origin. I don't understand all of it. This is their redemption. Lucas knows about it, I'm not really sure how. That's it, that's all I've got."

Jen yanked her arm. "But those words you said ... how did you know what to say?"

She sighed. "I don't know. I've been studying this book of prophecies; it must have been something I read last night. It just got stuck in my head and I spit the words out. Why, did I actually sound smart and not like a fool?"

Punching her arm, Jen dragged Casey towards the debriefing. Everyone would be grouped in sets of two or three, depending on their comfort level and if they were used to working with other people.

Casey was partnering with Rowan and Jaxon. They would be misting to the upper level. She'd use her mental magic to slow Jude's people down while Jaxon and Rowan protected her. The others were each given their assignments and partners, some misting in, some going through the door. When it was time, they walked to the street the warehouse was on and got ready to enter.

On the signal, they misted. Standing on the catwalk, Casey looked around. She saw the other groups mist into the further reaches of the large warehouse. She heard the door on the wall to the right open and saw the rest of her party enter. The main area was emptied of boxes. None of Jude's people were there.

Gwen moved to the center of the large empty space and called out, "Jude Malvado, I call you to me. Come here *now*!"

Casey felt the pull. She'd never seen or experienced a vampire master call one of their vampires to them, but the sensation was intense. Every vampire in the room faced Gwen as the call was sent out, except Rowan, Lucas, Jacque, and Cynthia. Interesting.

There was a buzz in the air, then Jude showed up in his tight black jeans that looked painted on his body, and black long-sleeve button down shirt. With a purr, audible from across the warehouse, his hand reached out and he traced Gwen's jawline. "Well, hello, darling. I see you've taken on the mantle of house leader ... good for you, good for you. But before you can keep it, you'll have to manage *my* people." And he lifted his hand and snapped.

The room filled with men, dozens of them. It wasn't fifty this time, but closer to one hundred, or more. The fighting began.

The men brough guns, stupid in such tight quarters where they'd as likely shoot one of their own. In contrast, the vampires were fighting to disable—it was one of the training exercises Cyran ran: If humans attacked, how do you knock them out without killing them?

From her vantage point, Casey tried to put the human army to sleep, a bit of mental magic. She couldn't do anything widespread without taking out friends as well as foe. She knew at least Damion was trying to do the same thing she was doing.

As she sat taking humans down, one mind at a time, Rowan and Jaxon were her bodyguards, defending her. A group of men ran up the stairs, and her guards made sure none of them got to her.

She wanted to watch what they were doing, but she couldn't afford the distraction.

One of the werehawks got hurt, and the squawk that came from their human mouth was the same as that from a bird's beak. As if she were watching a movie and someone hit pause, everything, including her own actions stopped. She could barely breathe.

Casey recognized the atom slowing spell Tilly had taught her. She began to unwind the spell around her, frustrated to be caught by Jude's ally. She was not going to let some charlatan win. She knew in her heart, anyone who could freeze a fight this large was the real deal, but she couldn't let that intrude on her thinking.

Pushing with all her might, she found a crack, and wiggled through it. She was determined to find her way out. She started with getting more air. Next, she got to where her hand would move, just a little. Her head, she could rotate it. She checked out the people around her. Finally, a tiny body wiggle.

Anger giving her strength, she forced her chin to her chest and finally saw Jude, a knife to his throat, a trickle of blood dripping down his neck. The look of death in Gwen's eyes.

A motion caught her attention. Strolling in from the door was a tall man. He had long violet hair that went past his shoulders in waves ... the same color as the painting in the stairwell to Lucas's basement room. His dark skin was almost the same color as Lucas's, but that was all they had in common. As he surveyed the room, Casey saw his eyes were turquois and had a slitted pupil. *Who ... what is he?*

With a final push of her will, she broke through his spell. She wasn't sure she'd have been able to do it if he hadn't been holding over a hundred other beings. She stood and looked down. "Who the hell are you?"

Gazing up, his beauty hit her like a weapon. "Why, my dear, I *am* hell. The Prince of Hell to be exact."

Chapter 37

He snapped his fingers and Casey was standing in front of him. He'd cleared a circle around them, moving the others away. "How did you escape my spell, love?" His finger traced gently down from her temple to her chin. "You *are* a lovely one."

She bit her lip, then glared up into his utterly perfect and beautiful face. "It was magic. I just unwound what you did around me. Pitiful, really. You need more lessons, if I were to be honest." Casey babbled, but she stood in front of a demon, a real demon. Days ago she didn't know they existed, and now this one traced her face and was the living embodiment of beauty.

Gulping, she realized she still held her walking stick. *I could club him with it. I wonder if that would do anything more than piss him off.*

Quirking a smile, he leaned in close as if to kiss her, but didn't. "You remind me of someone I once knew, maybe even loved. I wouldn't with your stick, bad idea." He gazed up at her familiar. "Hello, sweetie. Aren't you the spitting image of my Shark?" He gave her Zoryda a pet, even though she was still in her wooden form. A purr in the back of her mind told Casey she enjoyed it. Catching her gaze again, his bizarre stare seemed to pierce straight through her. "What's your name, young one?"

Eyes narrowing, Casey took a step back. "Young one?" Her brow rose. "Is there a thing where giving a person like you my name means you own my soul? I don't think so! I don't know if I can trust someone who can move armies, freeze wars, and is as pretty as you."

His eyes widened and he smiled. "Do you really think I'm pretty?"

She rolled her eyes. "What do you want?"

He winked. "I want to know why one of the people on your side sounded like a wounded bird."

She lifted her hands, palms up. "We fight as three, the vampires, the witches, and the werehawks."

Freezing, the beautiful man gazed at her, the sniffed. "You are more than a witch. What are you, girl?"

"I am a witch and a vampire." She backed up another step, not trusting this beast.

Closing the distance, he traced her lips with a finger, then tickled his fingers down her arm, barely touching her, until he could take her hand in his. "How did you learn of the werehawks?"

Wetting her lips, she knew, she *knew*, deep in her heart, she couldn't lie to this creature. He'd know. He'd know a lie faster than she did. "My daughter. She recognized them flying in the sky. More than just as hawks. She saw them as people."

This time when he leaned in, his mouth came down on hers in a brutalizing kiss. Demanding, thrilling. Without meaning to, she leaned in, ecstasy curling her toes at the mere touch of this man's lips on hers. Oh, gods, what was he? She tried to bite back her moan of pleasure.

He broke off the kiss and stepped back. "It's true, you fathered the thrice born child, and this idiot didn't even know. He's in breach of contract." Gazing at the room, he shook his head. "Well, it was fun." Snapping his fingers, the humans all disappeared. Eyes widening, the man—man? Demon?—spotted Lucas and his smile turned genuine. "Heya, kiddo. You know, you could summon me once in a while. I miss you." His gaze shifted to Jacque standing near Lucas and winked at him as well. "I'm glad you're still with him. He needs you to stay human. I don't want him to come home too soon. I was sorry to hear about ... ah, but now is not the time, is it?"

Turning, Casey realized Lucas wasn't frozen. He shrugged, eyes wide, not speaking.

The creature winked at Lucas. "Have you communicated with your mother lately? She worries about you."

Sighing, Lucas shook his head. "No. You know I haven't ... not since ... not for a while."

Taking a few steps to Jude, the man said, "Being in breach of contract, you are mine, from now until your last breath." And in a flash, the two were gone. There was a cacophony of sound as everyone in the room was released.

Turning to Lucas, Casey had a million questions to ask him, but he took Jaque's hand and misted away.

Interlude

Jude stood in a large cavern with many other beings. Looking down, his normal clothes were gone. He no longer had his tight black jeans, and his customary black button-down shirt that hugged his sculpted body. Around his waist were two twined gold cords. It looked like there was a basic clasp at his hip that would release them. They held up two simple but fine pieces of red silk, one in front and one in back. The silk was barely wide enough to reach across either his front or his back, though it reached down past his knees.

He lifted up the ends of the cloth and examined the markings that lined the material. Rune-type lettering stretched across the bottom of both the front and back pieces. Uncertain if it represented words, ranking, or decorations, he let the hem fall. Swallowing, he realized the barely-there silk was the sum total of his coverings.

With an unsteady breath, he took stock of the others in the room and noted that every creature around him wore similar attire, though not everyone wore red. Some wore green, others blue. Most of the beings he recognized as human looking, but not all. His breathing got ragged as he realized he'd made a huge mistake.

Mind short-circuiting, he wasn't sure what he was supposed to do. He was about to approach one of the others when the demon he'd summoned appeared in front of him. The violet-haired creature looked like a man, but more ... so much more. He was beautiful with his odd turquoise slit-pupil eyes. "Well, well, well, don't you look different. Follow." He walked towards a door. Jude debated not following but decided against it. He didn't know where he was or what the punishment would be for disobeying. He hurried after the Prince of Hell.

In the hallway, the demon, almost too handsome to for words, spoke. "You'll be serving as my new slave until such time as I release you ... which won't happen, or until I've used up your life energy, which will take a long time, as you *are* a vampire."
In a test of power, Jude tried to mist ... nothing happened. He reached out to feed off any of the emotions around him ... nothing. Fisting his hands and glaring daggers at the back of the head in front of him, he wondered if it were possible to kill a demon.

The man in front of him stopped. *Is it correct to call him a man? Is it a he?* Turning to face Jude, the beautiful face was smiling, one side of his mouth cocked up higher than the other. He took one step to Jude, reached up, raking his fingers through Jude's hair, and grasped the back of his head, then, bending, kissed Jude, deeply and passionately.

The shock of the kiss made Jude's mouth drop open just enough for the demon's tongue to slip in, and that tongue ... it did things that made Jude's toes curl. It felt like there were suckers on the tongue, but they provided pleasure, pulsating through is body. Feeling a fire in his gut, and a hardening start lower, he reached for the demon's shoulders as he felt weak in his knees. He closed his eyes as a moan escaped him, and he leaned into the demon.

Just as quickly as it began, it ended. The demon stepped back with a smile. "Oh, slave, you'll be fun, won't you? I'll be able to feed off you for years. Vampires are *so* long-lived. Some say immortal even."

Jude's hands began to shake. "Feed from?"

Licking his lips and spreading his hands, the violet-hair beauty bowed his head a bit. "Why, Jude, you didn't know you summoned the demon prince himself? I did name myself thusly at least once. Or were you ignoring that, hoping it wasn't true? Well, my slave, I'm a succubus. My slaves tend to live long lives, but my punishments always involve a feeding. Usually, they involve less clothing and a bed, but it *is* your first day here."

Clasping his hands behind his back, he stared up at his new master. "Punishment?"

The demon continued walking. "Follow. You'll learn your way around the palace. You'll learn the language of the demons so that you can read the marking on the slave's skirts. You'll learn when you should be in my rooms and when you can't, when to eat, and when to have food brought to the room, which slaves you can fuck, and when to be ready for me, and most importantly, that not even your thoughts are yours anymore."

Jude almost tripped at that last one. "You ... you can read my thoughts?"

A laugh. "Let's just say, if you think about killing me, it will more likely befall you, vampire. You know, you're the first vampire I've ever taken as a slave."

Jude stretched his legs to keep up. "Why's that?"

"Let's just say, their origin is near and dear to my heart and loins. Taking a vampire feels a bit like fucking in the family ... but I am a demon ... why not?"

Jude's heart almost stopped. "The stories, the origin stories about vampires, they're true?"

More laughter, as if the question were ridiculous. "I don't sit around listening to your origin stories."

Jogging to get closer to the demon who walked so fast, Jude tried to make sense of what he was hearing. "But you know who the first vampire was? You knew him ... or her?"

The demon stopped and stared at him. "As do you."

Chapter 38

The warehouse cleared out quickly. The werehawks agreed to stay in contact with Casey before heading out. After a final meeting to gather their thoughts, each of the vampire leaders returned to their home. The witches returned, hugging Casey—even Zen, who had been close enough to watch her go toe-to-toe with a demon on their behalf. Her two weeks was close enough to being done that they agreed that, baring quick drop ins, they'd see her in a couple of weeks.

Everyone was tired, and no one wanted to think about working.

Casey knew she had to find Lucas in the next few days and confirm her suspicions, but she'd give him a few days; a lot had happened. It felt like hours, but her watch said it was only eleven forty-seven. Not even an hour had passed. Battle time was weird.

She sat next to Rowan as he drove her home. Sydney, Cyran, and Jaxon were in the back. Despite the questions in her head, the ride was quiet. Everyone seemed like they needed to process everything that had happened.

Personally, Casey wanted to shower and brush her teeth. She'd had a demon tongue in her mouth. Just the thought of it gave her the willies. *Gross!*

Parking in the garage, they slowly made their way into the house. Climbing up the stairs, she saw a weird burn mark on the carpet outside Riley's door leading to the door of her old bedroom. Wanting to check in with Kam, she stretched up on tip toes to kiss Rowan's cheek, then split off from him.

She hadn't made it two steps before she realized he followed her ... of course. They made it to Kam's room. Knocking twice out of respect, she pushed open the door to see Riley sitting on the floor with Kam. They were playing Chutes and Ladders.

Flying above them was a set of silver animals Casey's mom had gotten Kam, not knowing silver wasn't the best metal to get a witch or vampire child. The set included a lion, a tiger, a bear, a monkey, a dragon, a griffin, a unicorn, and a hawk. The set also had a few trees and shrubs for a nature area diorama.

They had put up a shelf across from Kam's bed for the display. She loved looking at the animals, and so far, the silver hadn't bothered her when she played with the figurines.

The set was not made to fly, there were no strings attached. That said, the dragon, griffin, unicorn, and hawk were flying above Riley and Kam's heads. The other animals were prowling and fighting in the trees and bushes. More than that, the dragon was shooting random bursts of fire from its mouth.

Watching the scene, Casey forgot how to breathe for a few seconds. Finally gasping in air, she managed to say, "How?"

Kam smiled up at her. "Daddy! My friends are playing with me! I even got the dragon to make fire, grrr!" Her hands went up into little claws and she jumped up into a fighting stance.

Smiling gently, Casey knelt. "Kam, love, are you doing this?"

Her smile grew. "I am, Daddy. I'm making all my friends play with me!"

Kissing Kam's forehead, she gave her a quick hug. "Wow, sweetie, you are a clever witch, aren't you? Such a good girl."

Kam frowned. "Not a girl, I'm a boy, see!" She held out her pants waistband and jutted her hips out to Casey to show her. "Today I'm a boy!"

Biting her lip to not laugh, Casey nodded. "You are *such* a good boy!"

Kam smiled and bounced. "I am! I'm a good witch and a good girl and a good boy!"

Standing, Casey shifted her gaze to Riley. "When did all this happen?"

Riley shrugged. "You know kids, never can keep up with them, just have to go with the flow."

Thank you for reading Child of Three Halves!

Please Leave a review for this book so others know how much you enjoyed reading it.

Find more information on my [books on my website](website)

Acknowledgements

As always, it takes a village to write a book. This series was kicked into shape by Elizabeth Daly, Angela Grimes, Weslee Imrisek, and Fiona Foster. They are a powerful team to have in your corner, and I'm not sure how I got to be so lucky.

When I started writing, this was the second series I wrote. I've published a bunch of other books between writing this story and getting it presentable for public consumption. At one point I imagined finding a traditional publisher, but in the intervening time realized the indie route seems to work better for me.

There are more books coming out in this world. The books are written, but none of them have been through the ringer of my team. One day they'll be available, and I hope when you get a chance to read them, you'll love them. And yes, they do talk about that pesky demon and angel ... how could they not?

About the Author

Harlowe Frost has been a teacher at both the high school and college level. Her parents instilled a love of reading from a young age. She grew up in the queer community. Her favorite genre growing up was fantasy and science fiction, that is, until she discovered urban fantasy and paranormal romance. What she never found in those books was the diversity in background, gender identity, and sexuality she saw in the people around her. She decided if she couldn't find that in what she read, then she would write it herself. This started her writing paranormal romance with a LGBTQ+ background.